# The Paris Muse

# The Paris Muse

## LOUISA TREGER

BLOOMSBURY PUBLISHING

LONDON • OXFORD • NEW YORK • NEW DELHI • SYDNEY

BLOOMSBURY PUBLISHING
Bloomsbury Publishing Plc
50 Bedford Square, London, WC1B 3DP, UK
29 Earlsfort Terrace, Dublin 2, Ireland

BLOOMSBURY, BLOOMSBURY PUBLISHING and the Diana logo
are trademarks of Bloomsbury Publishing Plc

First published in Great Britain 2024

A catalogue record for this book is available from the British Library

ISBN: HB: 978-1-5266-3929-5; TPB: 978-1-5266-3927-1;
eBook: 978-1-5266-3925-7; ePDF:978-1-5266-3931-8

2 4 6 8 10 9 7 5 3 1

Typeset by by Integra Software Services Pvt. Ltd.
Printed and bound in Great Britain by CPI Group (UK) Ltd, Croydon CR0 4YY

To find out more about our authors and books visit www.bloomsbury.com
and sign up for our newsletters

For A.I. and A, with so much love.

# Prologue

## 1975

**B**UT WHY SHOULD ONE always begin at the beginning? No, I am going to tell you about the end. This afternoon the telephone rang, the sound of it shrill and unaccustomed in my still apartment. A smooth voice said, 'Is that Dora Maar?'

'Yes,' I said, curious.

'I hope you don't mind me calling out of the blue,' he said. 'I got your number from Marcel Fleiss. You see, I would very much like to buy a painting.'

I knew what he wanted but said innocently, 'I've been working on a new landscape series. Or perhaps you'd like to see my photographs?'

Silence. I waited and the man on the other end of the line waited too. To keep the quietness interesting I looked at the gifts Picasso had given me: his paintings and sculptures; the menagerie of animals and birds made of tin, plaster, paper or wood; the random splashes of paint on the wall he transformed into spiders and beetles with a few scratches of his pencil – so lifelike that visitors thought they were real. He did not know how to stop making things. He died two years ago, and I still can't take it in. I prefer to think that he has gone on a trip, that he is simply elsewhere.

At last, the man spoke. He said, 'I'm afraid you misunderstood. I want a Picasso, not a Dora Maar. One of the "Weeping Woman" series.' He cleared his throat. 'Aren't you his "Weeping Woman"? You inspired the best work of his life.'

Anger flared through me and I resolved he would not get a painting. But the fact was that from time to time I had to sell a Picasso to survive, and funds were running low. And so I made a compromise with myself.

'I don't have a painting to sell,' I said, 'but I can offer you a sketchbook with drawings of me as a bird and a portrait in coloured crayon. Very striking and unique.'

An intake of breath. 'Are you sure that's all you have? It's not what I had in mind.'

'I'm sure,' I said firmly. We went back and forth but I didn't budge, and eventually he agreed to come to my apartment to look at the sketchbook.

After we hung up, I sat for a long time thinking. Pablo's last rotten trick had been to curse me with the name 'Weeping Woman', but I was an artist, not a muse. The light faded into pink-and-ashen evening, the objects in the room grew indistinct, my grey striped cat padded disdainfully across the floor and allowed me to pet her briefly. And it came to me that I had to tell my own story before I ran out of time.

1913–1936

# One

I WAS BORN HENRIETTE THEODORA Markovitch. I grew up in a colonial-style villa in Buenos Aires; whitewashed walls, parquet floors, heavy mahogany furniture, everything flooded with sunlight. One of my earliest memories – I must have been about seven – was of lying in bed, looking at the white net curtains over my bedroom door stirring in the breeze. Behind the curtains, windows were set in the door so at any time my parents could look in to see what I was doing. At night they could hear my even breathing and fall asleep in peace. They were in their thirties when I was born. They had lost hope of ever having a child, and it made them overprotective.

On the other side of the door, I could just make out the shape of my parents' bed. I don't think it ever occurred to them that I might be watching them as they watched over me, but I could hardly help it. They were arguing again. Maman's voice was thin with distress.

'I can't stand living in Buenos Aires. It's so primitive, there's dirt and dust everywhere. Rough men staring at me every time I step out of the house, jabbering in Spanish. Such a crude, dirty language.' The only reason Maman had agreed to leave Paris was my father's job as an architect and the promise it would make them rich.

'You'll have to stand it till we can afford to go back to France.' Papito's voice was soft but threatening. I stiffened, sensing how badly he wanted to yell at her, but knowing he couldn't because of me. My father was a big, handsome man with dark eyes and thick, dark-brown hair, but he had a temper.

He was speaking to Maman in her language, French, which we spoke at home, but I also understood his language, Croatian. To me, it sounded gentle and affectionate. He called me *Tatina curica*, Daddy's

3

girl, and *moja slatka Dorita*, my sweet little Dora. I always felt torn between my parents, between Maman's French and Papito's Croatian. And now there was a new language, Spanish, that I was trying to learn, but that Maman insisted was dirty. I felt like I was made up of old and new, clean and grubby parts. Theodora, Dora, Dorita.

The next morning, Maman took me to the park at the end of our street, walking down lush, tree-lined paths that wound around rose beds to the small playground. The roundabout and slide gleamed red and yellow in the sunlight, but I headed straight for the swings and was soon swooping through the sticky air, feeling it turn into a fresh breeze around me. Everything else fell away and I was free. When I slowed down, I noticed a girl on the next swing giving me a measuring look. She had creamy skin, dark eyes and long, dark hair woven into braids.

'I'm Rosita. What's your name?' she asked in Spanish.

'I'm Dora,' I said shyly, putting out a foot to halt the swing.

She smiled, letting forth a stream of Spanish, which I hardly understood, but it didn't matter. We began to swing ourselves higher and higher, perfectly synchronised like acrobats or dancers, until Maman cried out in alarm for us to stop.

Rosita was at the swings the next day and the day after that. Until now I had been isolated from other children by the language barrier, by the starched frocks Maman liked to dress me in, and by her aloofness – I had often heard the words 'stuck up' muttered as we passed. Rosita was the first friend I'd made, and our affinity, cemented by a shared love of swings, felt immensely sweet. But after a week of watching us play Maman said, under her breath, 'I don't like hearing you speak Spanish.'

'What do you mean, Maman?'

She pressed her lips tightly together. 'It's the language of maids, sailors and cattle breeders.'

I tossed my head and said, 'I don't know what you're talking about,' but her words gave me a sinking feeling.

The next time Rosita ran up to us, my mother glared at her and wouldn't greet her. Rosita's face fell and she gave me a puzzled look, but I was turned to stone, unable to respond. My mother froze her out the next day too, and by the third day, Rosita didn't even glance our way. I stood and watched her play, aflame with helpless anger and a deep sense of loss.

Back at home, Maman sent me to wash off the dust, and I scrubbed at my hands and arms till the skin was pink and raw. The bathroom was shot with sunlight, and water gushed from the taps in sequins of light. I looked out at the garden, at the clouds of sweet alyssum, the shadows of trees dancing on the grass, then dried my hands and closed the blind. The garden disappeared and the water in the taps looked completely different – it was plain old water again. I opened and shut the blind several times, distracted from my turmoil by the transformation wrought by light.

I went to fetch Maman.

'I'm a magician! I can turn one thing into another. Here, look!' I said, showing her how easily I could turn water into spangles using nothing but sunlight.

'You silly goose,' said Maman. 'I don't see anything special.'

I realised that she didn't understand the magic of light or my love of make-believe. It didn't upset me, though, because at last I had something of my own, a private sweetness.

That night, noises came from my parents' room, noises that made me press my hands over my ears. Maman sounded like she was in pain and, when it was over, she sobbed. A terrible feeling rose in me – a sense of entrapment and a quiet horror. But as the minutes crept by, I made a discovery. If I concentrated hard enough, I could seal off my parents behind a screen in my head, while turning the rest of my mind to the play of light and its power to transform. It was another world, a safer one, and I disappeared right into it.

The years passed without any sign of Papito's promised fortune, and my mother's agitation grew. My parents' night-time arguments became more virulent, and the smothered sounds of their lovemaking stopped. As I got older, I felt the lack of privacy more and more keenly. In the end, I would dress in the bathroom, the only place I could be alone. Then Maman started coming in to confide in me after their fights, expecting me to take her side.

'I can't cope any more. I don't know what to do. I have to get back to Paris,' she would say, her long nose reddening, tears seeping from her heavy-lidded eyes that were so like mine. I felt sorry for her, but also inadequate. Whatever it was she wanted from me, I couldn't give her.

After Maman had gone I would lie on my bed, feeling her unhappiness enter me – a dark splinter lodged deep inside my chest. I longed to grow up and escape, but my coming of age was still years away. And then, on my fourteenth birthday, my father bought me a camera.

'I know you'll put it to good use. You're artistic, like me,' he said, kissing me on the forehead.

The moment I held it in my hands, I knew that it was my perfect shield against him and Maman, as no one looks at the person behind the camera. I felt a surge of gratitude towards Papito for knowing me better than I'd realised.

Maman touched my arm and said, 'Why don't you try it?'

'I'll take a picture of you both,' I said, and we went into the garden. They posed in front of the still-blooming roses, autumn sunlight slanting through the trees.

I lifted the camera and, for many moments, simply stared at my parents through the lens. I was captivated. Their images were remarkably precise and yet completely altered; they seemed smaller and separate from me, divested of their power. It was otherworldly, like *Alice in Wonderland* – reality and a deeper reality that most people knew nothing of, running alongside each other. Only I set the rules, I chose the subject, I was in control. And then Maman said, 'Hurry up, we're getting cold.'

In the days that followed, I would sometimes set up the camera just to watch the world this way. Of course I took photographs too, and Papito showed me how to develop the film. We set up a make-shift darkroom in the airing cupboard, gazing silently at the paper in its clear solution under the safelight. Gradually, an image of Papito emerged on it, as though it had been hiding in the depths of the grain, and I had drawn it out. Black and white made Papito's features stronger, and I saw that when colour was stripped away, all that was left were shapes, lines and textures. At that moment I experienced a joy that was unlike anything I'd felt before – the joy of creating something that relied on no one else, and I knew I would spend the rest of my life seeking it.

He said, 'You're a natural. Look, you've captured something in me that most people miss – a kind of wistfulness,' and I saw he was right. I realised that I knew all about Maman's dreams, but nothing of his, and I wondered what they might be.

The years flowed by. Argentina was a neutral country during the Great War, and Buenos Aires was full of traumatised Europeans. There were protests and parades, and horrifying news bulletins from the trenches. Even Maman conceded that we were lucky not to live in France. When peace came, work began to pick up for Papito, and he obtained several commissions, including for the embassy of Austria–Hungary. This brought a tranquillity I'd never seen in him before, and I understood that his dream was to become a great architect. It also earned him enough money that by 1926 we were able to return to Paris.

The boat journey was interminable. Maman was seasick and spent most of it in her cabin, while Papito and I went up on deck whenever we could, so that I could capture the sea in all its different guises – sparkling in sunlight or seething and swelling like a pan of water coming to the boil. I had carried on taking photographs for all these years, my passion for it increasing as I'd honed my skills by snapping the girls at school and life on the streets of Buenos Aires. Being behind the camera made me feel quick and definite, in control of my decisions and of myself. And I liked how people responded to my work, with respect and surprise.

Maman disapproved of me wandering around unchaperoned. She wanted a more conventional path for me, and feared that my behaviour would put off suitors, but Papito always supported my talent. On that long voyage, we discussed whether I could make a career out of photography or art.

Finally I found myself standing on French soil, gulls shrieking overhead, and the ground still rocking beneath my feet. Maman was laughing through her tears, and Papito embraced her. I patted my hair. To my parents' horror, I had recently cut it short, *à la garçonne*, in order to start life in Paris looking as chic as possible, which was how I intended to continue.

# Two

## 1927

I WALKED TO THE DINGO, soaking up the way the light fell, the silhouettes of buildings outlined against the sky, the bridges whose beauty brought tears to my eyes. Paris could make an artist out of anyone.

Jacqueline Lamba was leaning against the wall of the Dingo in a short jacket and flowing skirt, a cigarette in her mouth as usual. Her older sister, Huguette, was with her. They looked similar, with milky skin and brown hair, except Huguette was taller and her face angular.

We hugged and then I said to Huguette, 'How's the music?'

'Fine. Got an early masterclass tomorrow. I'm playing Liszt,' she said. She was a piano student at the Conservatoire and was part of Jacqui's group of friends. Jacqui and I had met at the *Ecole des Arts Décoratifs*, where we were taking painting classes. I had decided to make art my career, and Papito had encouraged me to explore all its forms, before deciding which one I wanted to pursue.

'Are you nervous?' I asked Huguette.

She waved a hand in the air. 'A little.'

'Let's go in. I'll buy you a drink to cure it,' I said.

'I can't. I just came to say hello to you.'

'For the love of God,' said Jacqui. 'Come and have one drink with us.'

Huguette shook her head. 'I'd better go home and practise.'

I smiled at her and said, 'Next time I'd love to see you for longer,' and she said, 'Me too.' She turned and started walking away, and Jacqui and I went into the café.

It was a shabby place, the walls decorated with paintings by neighbourhood artists. The proprietor would often accept a drawing from artists who couldn't pay their bill, holding it until that person was in funds again. We found a table and ordered a bottle of wine, absorbing the glorious chaos around us. The air was thick with cigarette smoke and people moved through it restlessly. From time to time, the door opened to let in a new arrival, and everybody turned to look.

'Let's have tarte Tatin. I'm starving,' Jacqui said, as the waiter put two large glasses of wine on the table in front of us. A few dark-red drops splashed onto her hand and she shook them off impatiently.

'I shouldn't, but I will.' My figure had always been ample and I was constantly watching my weight.

Jacqui raised her eyebrows, making her green eyes appear all the larger. 'Life's short. You might as well enjoy it,' she said and placed the order for two slices. The waiter was smiling at her foolishly, clearly smitten by her beauty.

When the tarte came the waiter lingered, checking we had everything we needed. He left, finally, and we began to eat, savouring the dense, buttery base and golden caramel, perfectly offset by sharp, juicy apples.

'How's painting?' I asked, and Jacqui shook her head, making the shell pendants in her ears dance.

'I don't like what I'm doing. I need to find a new style,' she said with her mouth full. 'I look at artists who used to inspire me and they seem so flat. I mean, even Matisse falls short. What does he do except combine lovely colours?'

'Here's the thing,' I said, leaning forwards. 'Impressionism is dead.'

Jacqui nodded vigorously. 'Cubism too. They're both incomplete.'

'It's up to us to find a new way,' I said, and we clinked glasses and drank to that.

'How are you getting on with our Monsieur Lhote?' Jacqui asked after a pause, stabbing the final piece of crust from her plate. André Lhote was our painting teacher, a gifted artist, and a fiery lecturer and critic.

'He's tough,' I said. 'But when he gives praise, it really means something.'

'Oh, I agree.' Jacqui signalled to the waiter for more wine. 'The other day he said, "An artist must experience life in order to have something to say. She must face up to life's turbulence and sublimate it if she can."'

'He's right, as usual.' I forked a stray apple slice into my mouth and pushed the plate away. 'I wonder what turbulence is in store for us that will feed into our work.'

I took my cigarette holder out of my bag – a slender tube with a black Bakelite mouthpiece and a flaring bell – inserted a cigarette, and offered one to Jacqui. She lit them and blew out the match.

'Never mind about turbulence. Here we are, at art school in Paris. It's a goddam dream,' she said. 'We're young, we're gorgeous, and we're going to enjoy ourselves.'

'Let's always share everything and never accept compromise!' I said, taking a deep drag and blowing out a perfect smoke ring. I felt audacious, intoxicated, giddy. But Jacqui was looking around restlessly.

'There's no one interesting here,' she complained. 'Where do the real artists hang out? Where are those famous surrealists?'

I told her about Café Cyrano, where the surrealists gathered every night for poetry-reading and conversation sessions, fuelled by mandarin curaçao cocktails.

'Let's go there soon,' said Jacqui.

We never made it to the Cyrano. The following week, Jacqui turned up at the apartment I shared with my parents on the place de Champerret, crying so hard she couldn't talk.

I held her while Maman made a cup of strong, sweet coffee and the three of us sat down at the heavy wooden table my parents had shipped from Buenos Aires. Jacqui sipped at her coffee, the tears running down her face. She picked up Maman's dog, Sophie, a little white Bichon Frise, and buried her face in her soft fur. Slowly, her sobs ebbed away. When she could speak again, my mother touched her arm. 'Tell us. Come on, my dear. What is it?'

Jacqui closed her eyes briefly. 'Maman's dead,' she said.

'Oh, Jacqui. Oh, you poor thing.' I put my arms around her.

We were quiet for a long time. Then my mother said, 'I'm so sorry for your loss,' and at the same time I said, 'I didn't know she was ill.'

Jacqui gave a tiny shrug. 'She had a massive brain haemorrhage. Happened out of the blue.'

'What a terrible shock for you,' said Maman.

Jacqui nodded. 'Papa died in a car crash when I was three. Maman was everything to me and Huguette.' Fresh tears soaked her cheeks. She wiped her eyes furiously with her handkerchief and added, 'Huguette's not coping. I'm scared.'

'What do you mean?'

Jacqui sighed and sat back. 'She's paralysed by depression.' She looked out of the window as if into the far distance, then turned to face us. 'There isn't enough money to carry on studying. We've lost everything.'

Her eyes filled again but she blew her nose and straightened her back. 'Cousins of Maman have offered to take Huguette in,' she said.

'Thank God. Will you go too?' I said.

'No, I can't. I mean, they're good people, but God are they stuffy! I'll find a room in a boarding house and get a job so I can finish art school.' A small glint appeared in her eyes. 'Nothing's going to stop me becoming a painter.'

Jacqui worked a series of odd jobs to survive: French teacher, window dresser at Aux Trois Quartiers department store, even a naked nymph in a pool as part of an aquatic ballet at the Coliseum on rue Rochechouart. She was so busy, I wondered if she had time to grieve. Huguette was still in a depressed, almost comatose state. She had dropped out of the Conservatoire, unable to play the piano any more, and her family were desperately worried.

Jacqui and I graduated and she never faltered in her determination to become a painter. So what if she had to swim naked in an aquarium, ogled by creepy men? She wasn't one to let obstacles stand in the way of her goals. But I wavered between painting and photography. I knew painting was considered a more serious art form and I enjoyed the layering of textures, the smell of fresh turpentine, the sensation of the brush carrying wet paint across the grain of canvas. But painting never spoke to me in the way photography did. It didn't invite me to step into an enticing parallel world.

My mother was happier in Paris. She'd found work as a dressmaker, and she was more accepting of my career. Papito encouraged me to become a photographer. 'It's easier to make a living. You can do advertisement work and so many other things,' he said, patting the sofa next to him for me to sit. 'And another thing. The line between the artistic and the commercial is blurred in photography. It means you have a better chance of establishing yourself in the creative world.'

I took my place beside him, knowing he was right. André Lhote treated his male and female students equally, but he was unusual. In the outside world, the odds were stacked against women artists. Men were taken seriously because they were men.

I took a breath and said, 'All right, I choose photography.'

'Good girl. I feel better now,' Papito said and gave a rare smile. He had failed to establish himself as an architect in Paris, he worked instead at PUTNIK, the Yugoslavian tourism agency. But architecture was his passion and I felt his grief at having had to let go of it.

I put my head on his shoulder and he briefly touched my cheek. And oh, I was happy! I had lightened my father's spirits and found my life's vocation.

# Three

## 1932

I CHANGED MY NAME TO Dora Maar to celebrate opening my first professional photographic studio. It was catchier, more chic than Theodora Markovitch, and it sat well with my artistic reinvention.

Maar is a German name that means 'molten crater', the result of a volcanic explosion. There's a relationship with fire, with fusion. It's an unsettled word – I chose it for a reason. My whole life I never stopped searching for myself, but at least I found the right name.

I went into partnership with Pierre Kéfer, who had previously worked as a set designer. He was a faunlike, fragile man, with brown eyes that glowed with intelligence. We shared a similar aesthetic and sense of humour, and I was happy.

We worked mostly on advertising and fashion campaigns. There was a large pool in the middle of the studio that could be filled with water or sand, and we let our imaginations roam, conjuring up the sea, the desert, a lake of women and – why not – of men too. One of my favourite images, an advert for hair oil, showed a bottle on its side, ripples of long blonde hair pouring out like the ocean. Another depicted a pearl nestling in a velvet holder, looking for all the world like a clitoris.

'Do you think the editors will notice?' Pierre asked me.

'Of course not. They're men. Most don't even know what a clitoris is.' We started to laugh and couldn't stop.

Our fashion clients included most of the big names of the day: Coco Chanel, Jacques Heim, Elsa Schiaparelli, who gave me some of her glorious hats. Our most exacting client was Jeanne Lanvin and she was also my favourite.

'No Dora, that won't do, that's not how I see it,' she would say, waggling her forefinger at me as everyone sweated under the hot lights in her sumptuous salon, full of mirrors and brocade curtains. Yet she was marvellously gifted – a visionary, really, with a knack for extracting our best work. Pierre and I began to use dramatic lighting and shadows to create a wide, dark area from which a lit body, or a part of a body, emerged. I was fascinated by liminal spaces because they allowed me to explore the line between fantasy and reality.

'You portray woman as untouchable, free and sometimes dangerous. *C'est magnifique!*' said Jeanne, rubbing her hands together. 'Of course, we know it's a fiction. Most women are tied to the home, shop or factory.' She picked an invisible speck of lint off her black jacket and added, 'Dora.'

'What?'

'You actually have that freedom. You live a free life and express it in your art.'

She held her arms out and I hugged her with affection for her understanding of the world and her understanding of me.

My partnership with Pierre lasted for three years, until my father dug deep into his savings and bought me a small studio at 29 rue d'Astorg, in the 8th arrondissement. As much as Pierre and I liked each other, we both felt it was time to strike out on our own, and so we parted on good terms. We had become well known in fashion and advertising, and I hoped my reputation would stand me in good stead for the next phase of my career. I wanted a more personal, less commercial direction, and the artistic freedom to explore unconventionality to the full. When Papito handed me the keys, I put my arms around him and hugged him tightly.

'I love you,' I said, my eyes filling with tears of gratitude, and he hugged me back, saying, 'You're going to make me proud.'

I still lived at home, but began to sleep at the studio whenever I was working late, which happened more and more often, until I realised I had moved in there, almost without noticing. But since I spent most weekends with my parents, they accepted the situation with good grace. Although their marriage was more harmonious now that Maman had achieved her dream of moving back to Paris, I found living with them claustrophobic, and it was a relief to have my own space.

A frightening tide of fascism was sweeping through France, and riots began to break out all over the country. I could see where this might end – a fascist coup d'état, the destruction of everything I stood for – and I felt a powerful need to do something. I started attending leftist meetings, signing petitions and going on marches, sometimes with Pierre, with whom I had stayed friends. One night he took me to a gathering of a discussion group called Masses at the home of the writer and philosopher Georges Bataille. We arrived late to find about twenty people seated in rows in a candlelit living room, and Georges in the middle of a political speech.

'The politics of atmosphere has swept away reasoned debate,' he was saying, clenching his fist. 'The current atmosphere is stormy. It's a contagious emotion that runs from house to house, from suburb to suburb. It turns hesitant men into frenzied beings and that's where the danger begins.'

He was a nice-looking man – tall and thin with a sensual mouth and heavy-lidded blue eyes that lingered over me as I slipped into a chair. I felt myself flush. At the end, he got out his collection of pornographic images and showed it to us without embarrassment.

'Look, they're works of art,' he said, holding up two photographs: a scantily clad prostitute in high heels standing in a sewer, and a naked girl with her head on a guillotine, the blade centimetres from her neck.

'Why are you so fond of the guillotine?' asked a man with long, dark hair and a scar on his forehead.

'It removes the meddling head from the body,' Georges said with a slow, inscrutable smile. 'Imagine if we could do that and go on living?'

Nervous laughter rippled around the room. The atmosphere was one of unease and furtive excitement, and it repelled me a little, but I was drawn to Georges.

'Dora Maar, I am happy to meet you,' he said afterwards, taking both my hands in his. He had the gift of making me feel like I was the only woman in the room. 'I've seen some of your work and can I say it's brilliant? My favourite is the hand emerging from a conch shell, so sensual and violent!'

By now, a few of my photographs had been exhibited, and I was used to a degree of recognition. I thanked him and he said, 'But I didn't know what a sweet voice you have. It's a little sad but reminds me of birdsong. Or what lovely hands.' He raised one of them and we both looked at it. I was proud of my hands – they were long and graceful, with slender fingers and deep blue nails. I painted them in different colours according to my mood.

The man who had asked the question about the guillotine came up to speak to Georges, so I went off to find Pierre. We moved slowly around the room, greeting people we knew, and looking at the paintings and books.

'Our host seems quite taken with you,' said Pierre. 'Be careful.'

'What do you mean?'

He frowned and gestured at a complete set of the Marquis de Sade's works on the shelf. I felt a pulse of excitement, but before I could reply, Georges joined us.

'There you are, Dora. Let's talk where we can't be interrupted.' He turned to Pierre, saying, 'Please excuse us,' and taking my elbow, led me to his study, a high-ceilinged room with book-lined walls. Sitting on a deep sofa in front of a fire, we spoke about everything and nothing, our conversation made luminous by a shared bottle of wine.

Then Georges said, 'I feel like I've known you forever. I can say anything to you.' He gave a smile so warm that my body went soft. 'Tell me something you've never told anyone before.'

I thought for a few moments. 'Actually, I grew up hating my parents. My mother was depressed. My father couldn't deal with her. They fought all the time.' The strangeness of speaking about feelings that had been locked inside me for years made my throat hurt, but there was relief too. Georges' eyes never left my face. He listened to me in a way I hadn't known before, a way that made me feel *seen*.

'My mother was a depressive,' he said, leaning towards me. 'My father caught syphilis when I was young and it destroyed his mind.'

I was shocked, but it explained a great deal about him. I put my hand on his and felt that sweet, warm sensation again.

'I wanted to kill my father,' he said. 'He used to shout with pain because of his illness and oh, it was a terrible sound. He'd get himself into such a state of dirt and stench, and it was my job to clean him up.' He shuddered. 'I truly wanted to kill him.'

'I understand,' I said.

'I wanted to kill my mother too.'

And I said, 'I understand.'

Before we said goodnight, Georges took my phone number, and within just a few weeks we were going to meetings and marching together.

It was early on that we sat in a café on the place du Trocadéro, Ferdinand Foch on his horse and the Eiffel Tower silhouetted against the sunset. Georges reached for my hand and said, 'Dora, I'm so very attracted to you. But there are things about me you should know.'

I felt a prick of fear and sat up straighter. 'Like what?' I asked.

'I'm not like other people. You know that I seek darkness. I'm fascinated by the void.'

At that, a thrill went through me, but I only said, 'Oh, it's all right, I'm different too.'

Georges gave me a look so grateful and tender, my breath went. I felt confident that I could deal with his dark side.

In bed he did exquisite and terrible things to me, things that I had to bury deep during the day. He often had nightmares afterwards, and would wake breathless and sweating. At first, he could only stare at me, as though he didn't know where he was. After some moments, recognition would come back.

'It's you,' he would say. 'It's you. Oh Dora, I'm happy you're here.'

He never told me what his dreams were about and I never asked, despite my curiosity. But he did talk about the guilt that came from his twisted desires. 'I've behaved disgracefully with everyone I've loved,' he said after one of these nightmares.

'You've always been good to me,' I said, stroking his damp forehead.

He pulled away from me. 'You don't understand. I disgust myself. I really do.'

Lying between two graves in the Saint-Vincent Cemetery, I was grateful for the softness of grass beneath my aching body. A full moon hung in the sky, bathing the headstones with a quiet, milky light. Some of them were so old, I couldn't make out the inscriptions. The night air was cool; the only heat came from Georges and me, and from the wine we'd drunk. He had fucked me while I leaned up against a headstone. He'd torn my mouth and I had bitten him back; we were all over the place, high on a blend of violence, horror and ecstasy.

Now he took a mouthful of wine from the bottle and said, 'I've been thinking about your photos.'

'Oh?' I touched a rising lump on my cheek. My mind was far from work. The headiness of what we'd just done was seeping away, and a feeling from my childhood rose up to take its place: a sense of claustrophobia, a muted horror, and another impression that's hard to describe. It was as if I'd been set apart from everyone else but it wasn't immediately visible, as if I gave off an unpleasant smell. And it came to me that Georges was set apart too.

'Your work is brilliant,' he was saying. '"The Years Lie in Wait for You" is so compelling and strange.' I had photographed the beautiful, pensive face of Nusch Éluard with a spider's web superimposed on it, the spider set directly between her eyes. I'd met Nusch and her poet husband, Paul, at another left-wing gathering called Groupe Octobre.

'Thank you,' I said, 'but I sense a "but".'

In the moonlight, I saw Georges smile. 'But why don't you push your limits to the full?'

'What do you mean?' I pulled myself into a sitting position. He had my attention now.

'Like just now,' he said, his eyes gleaming. 'The dangerous, transgressive side of your nature is breathtaking. Why not explore it in your photographs?'

18

'Don't I do that already?'

'Yes, but take it further. Let yourself go.'

I looked down and saw that my arms were smeared with earth. I rubbed them clean. I was thinking hard. My art was transgressive to a point, cheeky, but not truly disturbing. And yet there were images that had always drifted through my head, images I had always pushed away. I felt an insect crawl up my leg and slapped at it, then got to my feet, pulling on my clothes. 'Let's go. I've had enough of this place,' I said.

The streets were quiet on the walk back to rue d'Astorg, and the few people we passed wouldn't look at us. It was as though they sensed what we'd just done, as if it created a wall separating us from everyone else. But I didn't have time to worry about that now because many ideas were running through my head.

We passed a couple embracing in a doorway. I knew that Georges and I were not in love, but I craved the affirmation he gave me, what he brought out of me, how he saw me. In a way I was using him to tap into my dark side, to push my art to the next level, and a shiver of excitement ran through me at the thought.

In the days that followed I let my mind go, entering a strange state of being that accompanied my best photography. I left my body behind and worked in a trance, my hands going about their business of their own accord. The results were somewhere between anguish, absurdity and dream. I twisted reality to the point of rendering it mad. I played with shadows. I inflated mouths until they became grotesque, reversed the direction of things, and created my strangest image yet: an armadillo foetus, which I named *Père Ubu*. Scaly and clawed, it had a distended head, a long snout and hooded eyes that looked at the viewer with indifference and menace. It was also a secret portrait of my psyche: half-armoured yet vulnerable, interesting yet indefinably monstrous. Generally, I was dissatisfied by my work because it rarely matched the ideal image I carried in my head. But I was as pleased with *Ubu* as I'd ever been with a photograph, and wondered how and where it might be exhibited. My dream was to have my own show – in fact, to see Dora Maars hung on the most famous walls in the world – but I wasn't established enough yet. Instead, I resolved to write to all the gallerists I knew, asking them to include *Ubu* as part of a wider exhibition, featuring several artists. From here I shifted into eroticism, and ideas came easily.

'The problem is that my ideas are taboo. No model will pose for them,' I said gloomily to Georges. 'But I don't want to compromise.'

'Of course you mustn't.' We were sitting in my studio, surrounded by my photos, and he pointed at *Ubu*. 'Your work is magnificent. You're at the top of your game. I know you will find a solution.' I gave his hand a squeeze, filled with gratitude for his belief in me. Then he sat upright. 'Why not use one of those experimental techniques you're so fond of?'

'Good idea!' He refilled my wine glass and I sipped at it, thinking hard. At last I said, 'I've got it! I'll use photomontage.'

'What's that?'

'It's where you make a composite image out of several photographs.' My head was filling with ideas; my fingertips tingled in anticipation. 'You've helped me so much. I think I'll start now, if you don't mind.'

'Not at all. I would love to watch you work.'

I shook my head. 'I can't have you distracting me. Please go. I promise I'll make it up to you,' and I gave him a melting look.

His face fell into mock tragic lines. 'You're a hard woman, Dora,' he grumbled, but did as I asked. As soon as the door closed behind him, I selected the photographs I was going to use. I felt strong and sure of myself, in control of my relationship and my art. I sat down at the kitchen table and began to cut, arrange and overlap the photos, moving and rearranging the pieces until I had what I wanted. At the centre was an old shot of a boy mesmerised by a game of dice on a Buenos Aires pavement. When I was satisfied, I glued everything together and took photographs from different angles, so that the result would appear as a seamless physical print. My pulse raced with the excitement of leaving the world and entering another I had created, and with the dark enticement of transgression.

I developed the prints as the dawn chorus started up, and hung them in the bathroom to dry. The sky was pink and grey, with a few streaks of gold radiating out from the rising sun. I made coffee, lit a cigarette, and went back to survey the work. It depicted the boy from Buenos Aires sitting under a desk in a formal, old-fashioned room, spellbound as he looks at a half-naked woman with the face of an old matron riding a man bent over in his suit. The back of my neck tingled with pleasure because it was as strange and shocking as I'd hoped.

I called it *Forbidden Games,* and it was published the following month in *Pages Folles,* a specialised journal that Georges had introduced me to. The copies sold out immediately and the magazine commissioned more work. I never told my parents. Papito loved the strangeness of images like the hand shell, but Maman found it excessive, and I knew that my erotic photos would be too much for either of them.

Before starting the new commission, I made a photomontage for Georges – a boy urinating on an old woman in a grand but empty apartment, the scene reflected in muddy pools of water on the floor. I called it *Le Pisseur.* I was certain that it would excite Georges, and anticipation created flickers of electricity in my belly as I worked. There had been no word from him for a week, and I wondered if I had treated him too harshly. But I didn't give it much thought because I was pouring all my energy into *Le Pisseur.* It took four days to complete, and on the fourth night he turned up at my studio, unannounced.

'Wait till you see what I've been working on,' I said, moving to embrace him. Before my arms made contact, I saw lipstick on his collar. I took a troubled breath and smelled a sweet, cloying perfume on him. He was swaying slightly and his eyes were glassy, unfocused. He didn't notice my agitation.

'Where have you been?' I asked. He didn't answer and my voice rose. 'How dare you arrive in this state?' Inside, I felt myself disintegrate and, for a moment, my vision blurred.

'Oh, Dora. Don't confuse fucking with fidelity,' he said, slurring a little. He tried to catch hold of my arm but I twisted away. 'Listen, it meant nothing. It hasn't put me away from you, but just the opposite.'

I turned so he couldn't see my expression. So many of his games had involved testing me, seeing how far I could go, and I'd been

21

willing, even eager. But I couldn't take this, and the strength of my reaction surprised me. It was my first betrayal in love, and I felt like that wounded child in Buenos Aires again. Sobs rose in my throat. I wept with desperation and Georges made no attempt to comfort me.

At last he said, 'Stop it, Dora. Damn it, just stop. Don't be possessive. It's suffocating.' There was disgust in his voice.

I faced him and he looked straight into my eyes, waiting for me to say something. My lips opened and closed, I could not answer. After many moments, he shrugged and walked out.

I looked around. I felt like a stranger in my studio, and I knew this to be a bad sign. I tidied away my work materials. I looked at *Le Pisseur*, seeing afresh how powerful and disturbing it was, and this made me feel slightly better. If Georges didn't want it, *Pages Folles* or a similar publication would snap it up. I wasn't just his lover, I was an artist with something to say. So instead of moping, I called Jacqui and asked her to meet me at the Dingo the following Tuesday.

As soon as our drinks arrived, Jacqui touched my hand and said, 'Are you all right? You look exhausted.'

I swallowed some wine, too proud to tell her about Georges's infidelity, and that I hadn't heard from him since he'd left my apartment. 'I haven't seen you for weeks,' I said.

'Well, I could tell you I've been busy.' She gave me a hard, serious look. 'But the truth is, I'm uncomfortable around Georges. His conversation, his obsessions are frankly disturbing.'

I flinched. 'Georges is a good man. He's good to me,' I lied. 'It's just that he's in pain.'

Jacqui held up a finger to stop me. 'We're all in pain.'

I felt a flare of indignation.

'Are you in love with him?' she asked.

'Heavens, no. I was just using him for my art,' I said airily.

'Thank God.' She paused, seeming to weigh something up, then blurted out, 'I saw him with Colette Peignot at the Café de Flore.'

I began to shake. First my hands, then my legs, then my teeth. What I felt was unbearable, but at least I understood what had happened. Colette was a writer and poet, known for being brilliant, passionate and volatile.

Jacqui touched my arm. 'Sorry I hurt you. I thought it better you knew,' she said quietly.

'What's she like?' I said.

'Not especially pretty, but I must say, there's something about her. She has a lovely figure. They seemed, uh … quite keen on each other.'

Anger rose in me. 'Good for him!' I snapped.

Jacqui put up her hands and said, 'Steady. My fault for raising it, I guess.'

I shrugged. 'Forget it. Let's talk about something else.'

A look of relief crossed her face. 'Yes, let's.'

'What have you been up to?' I asked.

'Oh, working mostly. And guess what? I finally made it to the Café Cyrano.'

'Ah. What do you think of the famous surrealists?'

'They talk too much and take themselves far too seriously. André Breton is cute, though, with that curly mane of hair falling down his neck. He's like a more masculine Oscar Wilde.'

I smiled. It was impossible to stay cross with Jacqui. 'Have you spoken to him?'

She rolled her eyes. 'He's too busy holding forth to his friends. It's like I'm invisible.'

'I know him a little. Shall I introduce you?' He and I had spoken a few times – there were similarities between our politics and our work.

'Ah, Dora. Thank you, sweetheart. But I prefer to do it on my own,' she said.

I walked home afterwards, my mind in turmoil. I knew it was no good trying to win Georges back because nothing would change, he would be unfaithful again and again. And then, to my surprise, a vast relief moved through me and everything seemed to fall into place. There was a cool breeze coming from the river, and I quickened my steps. I had to get away from Georges, right away. I felt that Paris wasn't big enough for both of us. I wanted to leave the city, to go as far away as I could.

# Four

## 1934

I TRAVELLED TO LONDON AND Barcelona, seeking new avenues in my work and in my personal life. I had moved away from erotic images, associating them with Georges, and had decided to immerse myself in photographing everyday life. Maman was worried about me making the trip alone but Papito overruled her. Perhaps I was fulfilling a dream he couldn't indulge.

The early mornings were my favourite time – the smell of freshly baked bread coming from the cafés and the pavements being washed down. I had breakfast at seven and was out by eight in my long white coat, my Rolleiflex in its brown leather case dangling from my arm, faster and lighter than any other camera. I stalked the streets like a huntress searching for a kill.

Ever since my Argentinian childhood, I'd been painfully aware of the poverty-stricken, those living on the margins of society. I wanted to draw the world's attention to them, and so I concentrated on outlying neighbourhoods, border zones, shacks. The unpredictability of the street provided me with infinite quirky juxtapositions. I photographed hawkers, beggars, old men asleep in the street – since the stock market crash, there were more of them than ever. My favourite subjects were children. They were fascinated by the camera and crowded around it. Adults were often reluctant to have their photograph taken, or else they wanted something in return.

In Barcelona, I photographed a boy walking on his hands, spindly legs in the air, espadrilles laced around his ankles. He was thrilled and asked me to take the pictures out of the camera, so he could look at them. I explained that they had to be printed first.

He thought about it, then gave a gap-toothed smile. 'Want some?' he asked, holding out a sausage that seemed to be made of breadcrumbs.

'Thank you, but I want you to eat it all,' I said, pressing a couple of pesetas into his hand. My last sight of him was a pair of skinny legs pounding down the street, on his way to give the coins to his mother.

I liked that boy and it shows in the picture. As I was photographing him, I could see myself developing the prints, playing with light and shadows, putting my stamp on the scene. It didn't matter how rough the area was. That was what I wanted. Rough, unsettling work – images that made people see the world differently.

When I returned from Spain my photographs were published in the magazines *Le Spectateur* and *Arts et Métiers*, and they were well received.

Jacqui came to see me a few days after I got home. I had been gone for five weeks and she had changed more dramatically than I, at least in appearance. Her hair was bleached white-blonde, her skin was dewy and her eyes shone. She had always been beautiful but now she was dazzling. I made coffee and we sat in the kitchen.

'Tell me what's making you glow like that. I want to bottle it and bathe in it,' I said.

'Well, I do have some news. I finally caught André Breton's eye!'

'Fantastic! But how?'

'I devised a strategy. I sat by myself in the Cyrano night after night, writing, till he noticed me. He said later that he thought I was writing to him.'

I laughed and said, 'Poets are so self-absorbed. So naive.'

Jacqui smiled wryly and said, 'I was only pretending to write to get his attention.' She sat up straighter, putting her hands on the table. 'Actually, I succeeded beyond my wildest hopes. We spent last night together, walking through Paris. We went through night markets and church squares, all the way to the Tour Saint-Jacques.' She took my hand. 'Guess what, Dora? He proposed to me underneath it! We're getting married in August.'

'Congratulations!' I said, embracing her so she wouldn't see my shocked expression. 'That's only three months away!'

'Yes, but once you know, you know. What's the point in waiting?'

I was happy for her but I felt an ache, an emptiness. I wanted what she had: a lover who would also be my mentor. I craved excitement and risk; *un amour fou.*

I opened a bottle of champagne and we toasted her new life as Madame Breton.

'Any news of Georges?' I said. Jacqui knew all about our break-up by now, and she was the only person I trusted enough to ask.

She bit her lip. 'Are you sure you want to hear?'

I nodded and she said, 'He's in Tossa de Mar with Colette Peignot.' I felt a sharp pain, but almost at once it gave way to relief. I felt like I could breathe again and I knew my travels had done their job.

In the weeks that followed, Jacqui was so absorbed by André, I hardly saw her. At least my work was going well. The Museum of Modern Art in New York wrote to say they wanted to exhibit my *Père Ubu* and it filled me with elation. Finally, I was making a name for myself on my own terms. And I understood that Georges had nudged my art in a fertile direction, and this was his gift to me.

I was asked to be a set photographer for one of Jean Renoir's films, *The Crime of Monsieur Lange,* a low-budget movie about a publishing collective in which the workers triumph against a tyrannical boss. Renoir gave his actors a lot of freedom to improvise, which was just as well, as its star, Jules Berry, found it impossible to remember his lines. Along with some wildly erratic camera movements and rough-and-ready editing, the film already had spontaneity and a wistful charm that I loved.

Two weeks in, there was great excitement because Pablo Picasso came to see the set. He was in his fifties and already very famous. He wore a saggy old suit, a Basque beret, and a long moss-coloured scarf knotted at the throat. There was a line of us waiting to be introduced, and as he came closer, I noticed a kind of electricity emanating from him, a vibration, something that set him apart from other people. When it was my turn he took my hand, murmuring

'*Enchanté*,' and turned to the next person, quickly forgetting me. But I was mesmerised by his intense black gaze that seemed to look right into me. I wanted to see him again.

'I need to ask you something,' I said to Jacqui that evening. I looked in the big mirror on the wall of the Dingo and touched my hair. 'How do I meet Picasso? I mean, I met him on set today. But how do I make him notice me?'

Jacqui took a sip of wine and said, 'You go to his café. You put yourself in his path. That's how it's done.'

I shook my head. 'It's not enough.'

She narrowed her eyes. 'Why not? It worked for me.'

'It needs to be more daring. Picasso likes living on the edge,' I said.

Jacqui frowned. 'He has a terrible reputation.'

I nodded. It was common knowledge that he had discarded his wife and embarked on a string of affairs, going from one woman to another as quickly and avidly as he finished his paintings. He was a titan of the art world and he was scandalous.

'Careful,' said Jacqui, putting her hand on my arm. 'Be careful. You've just been hurt by a complicated man. Do you really want another one?'

I shifted away. 'I know it's risky but I learned a lot from Georges. I think I can play the game and stay in control.'

Jacqui looked straight ahead, as though she was pondering something. Then she shook her head and looked at me again. 'He's too old for you,' she said.

'He's ageless,' I said, shrugging.

'Hmm. Maybe,' she said, waving a hand. 'Well, I can see the thrill of seducing such a great artist, even if he is disgraceful.' She grinned. 'Or maybe *because* he's disgraceful.'

I gave her a stern look. 'Don't even think of trying it.'

She laughed. 'Oh, I won't.' And then, with a hint of smugness, 'I'm taken.'

Of course, Jacqui was right about the thrill – and the danger. But I had no idea how meeting Picasso would change the course of my life forever.

# Five

## 1935

I SAT AT A CORNER table at the Deux Magots, sipping absinthe, gathering the nerve to play a game I had heard about from Georges. It was a dark game and it was also art. Picasso stood nearby, talking to a man with a pointed nose, thin lips and white hair the texture of cotton candy. At last his gaze met mine.

I took a breath and slipped off my gloves, giving him a chance to admire my hands. Taking a knife from my bag, I began to drive it into the table between my splayed fingers, the reflection of the blade flashing in the polished tabletop as my arm plunged down from greater and greater heights, seeing how close I could come to my flesh without cutting it. I could feel his eyes devouring me and a bolt of desire that was carnal, almost savage, went through me. Sometimes the knife missed and before I stopped playing, my hand was covered in blood, though I felt no pain.

Then, without cleaning my hand, without glancing up, I pulled my gloves back on. The show was over.

'Magnificent,' he said in Spanish to his companion. 'She is like a beautiful, banderilla-throwing torero.'

I met his eyes. 'A torero with a taste for transgression,' I said in fluent Spanish, enjoying his surprise. Picasso left the man and joined me at my table. 'I'm Pablo,' he said. His voice was dense and throaty, and every word he spoke was charged.

'I know who you are,' I said, gazing calmly at him.

'What's your name?' he asked, seeming not to remember that we had already met.

'Dora Maar,' I said, taking my cigarettes and holder out of my bag. He fumbled to offer his lighter and, as I leaned towards him to catch his flame, I saw that his hand was shaking.

'Where did you learn to speak Spanish?' he said, snapping the lighter shut.

I inhaled, holding smoke in my lungs before blowing it towards the ceiling. 'In Argentina. My father is an architect; we went there in search of his fortune. We never found it but that's another story. I grew up in Buenos Aires.'

'Perhaps that's why you seem exotic,' he said. 'Did you know, there's a lovely alternation of light and shade passing over your face? I would like to paint you.'

The way he was looking at me made my breath catch, but I couldn't let my feelings show. I had to make him realise the difficulty of keeping me. Soon afterwards, I rose to leave.

Pablo got to his feet too. 'This might sound odd,' he said, and I waited for him to continue, eyebrows lifted in encouragement. 'Can I have your glove?'

'What for?'

'To put in my cabinet for special mementos,' he said, and I wondered what else was in it.

'Actually, you can have my hand,' I said, making my voice linger on the last syllable, full of promise. And slowly, very slowly, I peeled off the bloodstained garment and gave it to him. Our fingers brushed and a shiver ran through me.

Emboldened by the success of my little blood game, I decided to turn the tables on Pablo. I wrote to him, inviting him to pose for a series of portraits. I understood that the surrender of one's likeness suggests a willingness to be possessed, just as the capture of a likeness is as good as a stolen kiss.

He accepted by return and my confidence melted away immediately, like syrup in warm water. I had captured his attention once, but what made me think I could keep it? No other woman had succeeded. And what if he didn't turn up? He was a famous man, he must have far more important demands on his time. I had achieved a measure of poise and professional success, but underneath it I still felt like that child in Buenos Aires, not belonging anywhere.

Our session took place on a chilly Tuesday afternoon, ten days after the knife game. There was a smart rap on the door at three o'clock prompt, as we'd arranged. After checking my hair one last time in the mirror, I hurried to open it and my stomach fell away at the sight of him. But it was imperative to carry on playing the game without letting my feelings show.

'Well, here I am,' he said, making a gesture towards himself, demonstrating the obvious.

'Come in,' I said brightly, and took the first photograph then and there. I knew my power to hold his interest lay in being unpredictable. He was still in his overcoat and scarf, smiling at me, surprised. The look of surprise remained as his eyes sparked over my studio, which I had transformed into a temporary theatre, with perilous stacks of books, tripods, developing agent and huge tilted mirrors.

'What's this for?' he asked, pointing to a dark, convex looking-glass.

'It's my witch's mirror, my seer's eye. The curve deforms, but it also creates the fullest vision.'

He grinned. 'I suspected you were a sorceress, Dora. Now I know it.' It seemed to amuse him to pronounce my name with a guttural roll of the r. 'Dorrra.'

He was sturdy and broad-chested – a fine specimen. But I also sensed something hurt and lost in him, and I wanted to get that too. I began to walk around him, checking for unsightly shadows, trying to work out which gestures looked the most natural, searching for the telling detail that would capture his essence. I was never very interested in the technical side of photography. What gripped me was the intensity of the image, the chosen moment, the relationship between light and shadow. I was trying to reach that magical point of fusion where my model and my idea for the photograph were the same.

When I finally had what I wanted, I began to take shots of him. Close-up, whole body, seated, standing. I directed and he obeyed, taking off his coat, his jacket; soon he was down to his shirtsleeves, wreathed in smoke from his cigarette. As he shed his clothes, I could feel him relaxing, submitting to the gaze of my camera.

'Now I see why some cultures believe that taking your photograph is stealing your soul,' he said. He was leaning against a wall, smoking. 'You're operating by witchcraft. I feel tamed. Appropriated. It's a new sensation.'

I hid myself behind my black curtain and focused my lens. 'What are you working on?' I asked when the shot was done.

Pablo's eyes softened with emotion. 'Caricatures of myself,' he said. 'They're nothing but doodles, really. I'm a dwarf, a monkey, a man with a mask. It's a travesty.' He tapped his ash, frowning. 'Do you know this is the first time I haven't been able to paint? I haven't painted or sculpted anything for eight months. When I wake in the morning, I say to myself, "You can't be Picasso."'

'Awful for you. What do you think caused the block?'

'Turmoil in my personal life. But I hope that's at an end now.' He looked at me meaningfully and my heart gave a small, thrilling jolt.

I held his gaze. 'Since you can't paint or sculpt, what do you do with your days?'

'I write poetry. Writing is my only dependable companion.'

'Oh? I write poetry too.'

A swift, secret amusement shone from his face, as if some private hope or suspicion had been confirmed. 'Will you show it to me?'

'I will, but not today. If you like, I will show you my photographs.'

He looked at everything, praised its dreamlike, poetic quality, its heightened sense of the peculiar, the macabre edge to my humour. He was looking at a self-portrait of me smiling into the face of a skull. The inscription read: 'There you are again, my love.'

I showed him everything I had. We were both surprised by how much work I had done. It was over five years' worth and would easily fill a gallery.

'You're a surrealist,' he said, sweeping back the lock of greying hair that had drifted over his forehead.

I shrugged. 'My photos are tinged with surrealism, but I'm not an official member of the group. I don't like belonging to anything.'

'Actually, they remind me of De Chirico's early paintings. You should have your own show.' He smiled.

31

Of course I was thrilled. A show was my goal, the mark of making it as an artist, and Picasso thought it was within my reach. He left shortly afterwards. At the door, he said, 'I want you to send me a photograph of you. It's only fair.' For a moment, he put his hand on my arm, his fingers resting on the fleshy part between shoulder and elbow. It was a light touch, yet it burned through my shirt, a tingling bracelet of heat.

In the days that followed, Pablo filled my thoughts – he was more exciting, more alive than anyone I'd ever met. I sent him the photo he had asked for: a studio shot of me in three-quarter profile gazing into the distance, my hair scraped back, Spanish style. On the back, I drew an inky self-portrait showing me holding my camera, and I wrote my phone number beside it.

He rang the next day: 'I'd like you to come and see my studio.' This wasn't expressed as a hint or an invitation, but as a statement of fact, as if the future was shaped by his whim. Of course, I agreed.

The following Wednesday saw me walking down rue La Boétie, a busy thoroughfare lined with shops selling carpets and expensive, semi-antique furniture. Pablo's apartment, at number 23, was sandwiched between two art galleries. I took the lift to the sixth floor and he opened his door at once, as if he had been waiting beside it.

'Come in, come in!' he cried, taking my hands and drawing me into the hall, which had a grand fireplace surmounted by a mirror but was otherwise bare of furniture. He was wearing a worn pair of trousers that hung loosely from his hips and a striped sailor's jersey.

'You look well,' I said.

He scowled slightly. 'If you could see me how I see myself, it would break your heart.'

An Afghan hound came trotting up to greet me. He had a long, rich, silky coat, and his whole appearance was dignified and graceful. 'Meet Elft,' said Pablo, and I rubbed his muzzle and let him sniff my hands. Pablo grinned and said, 'Ah, he likes you! He's a great judge of character. If Elft approves, I know you're all right.'

We went to his studio, a large, airy room. Three south-facing windows looked out over a forest of red and black chimneys, with the silhouette of the Eiffel Tower in the distance. It was filled with a wild disorder of paintings of all sizes, colours and states of completion. They were placed on several easels, leaning against furniture or propped up with stacks of books. The floor, tables and chairs were strewn with African masks, ceramics, plaster casts and peculiar hats. Piles of papers rose up like stalagmites. There was hardly space to move.

'This is where I do my painting,' he said, waving his hand at a pile of canvases set out beside a window. I went over to examine them, and saw a large blonde nude in ochre tones and several mothers with outsized children. I couldn't take my eyes off them, entranced by the blend of realism and poetic magic. I was familiar with Pablo's work, but seeing it so intimately was like the revelation of a new universe. He was watching me closely.

'My paintings are my children. Whether good or bad, they go out and lead lives of their own,' he said. 'And now I can't make new ones and it's killing me.' He let out a breath.

'You have to trust that it will come back,' I said, turning to him.

'Do you think so?'

'Yes, I do. Your work is astonishing. It has such power and assurance, you have so much to say. You're not going to be blocked for long.'

He gave a marvellous smile. 'Ah, Dora, it does me good to see you. You give me strength to keep going.'

When I had finished looking at everything, we went through to the kitchen, Elft's claws clicking on the wooden floor as he followed us. The first thing I noticed was the cages of canaries, pigeons and lovebirds. The birds smelled awful. The canaries sang, the pigeons cooed, but the lovebirds really laughed. Pablo made coffee and we sat side by side at the kitchen table to drink it. He lit cigarettes for us both, took a deep drag of his and exhaled. The kitchen was painted white, and apart from the birds' feathers, the only colour in the room came from three Spanish plates on the wall.

'How pretty,' I said, pointing at them.

'My mother sent them from Barcelona,' he said, and a shadow passed over his face. 'A group of extremists tried to shoot each other near her house yesterday. Things are very bad in Spain. I worry for my family.'

'Terrible for you,' I said, laying my hand on his arm.

He nodded glumly and said, 'It gives me nightmares.'

'Tell me?'

He thought for a few moments, looking straight ahead. Then he licked his lips and said, 'It's a dream I've been having since child-hood. It makes me very anxious. My limbs grow to a monstrous size and then shrink down again. All around me, other people are going through the same changes, getting huge or very small.'

I wanted to put my hand on his. Instead I said, 'I'm sorry, but do you know something?'

He shook his head. 'What?'

'Now I understand the paintings you showed me – the huge nude and gigantic children. Hideous as it is, that dream feeds your art.'

His lips curved into a faint smile. 'You're right. Do you dream, Dora? Tell me about *your* dreams.'

I sipped at my coffee – Pablo had made it strong, just as I liked it. 'I don't dream much while I'm working. All my imagination goes into the photos, and there's hardly anything left over.'

'What about when you're not working?'

I waited, not sure how much to reveal. Then I said, 'Well, I often dream about the house I grew up in.'

'In Buenos Aires?' he shot back. 'Tell me more, I want to imagine you there.'

And so, in bits and pieces, I found myself telling him everything: my parents' unhappiness, the glass door between our bedrooms, the feeling of living in a fishbowl.

He listened, tilting his head thoughtfully, then he said, 'Glass exposes. It doesn't protect. I know the feeling of not being able to breathe.'

I felt *seen* by him, in ways I'd never been seen before, and oh God, the freedom that came with it! 'How come?' I asked.

He hesitated. 'I had a sister. Conchita.'

'Yes?' I prompted gently.

'She … she died of diphtheria when she was eight. That's when I started having nightmares.'

'I am sorry,' I said, covering my eyes for a moment with my hand. 'My God, I'm so sorry.'

There was such pain on his face. 'She was brave but we knew how she suffered. My parents tried to keep things going, celebrating Christmas and birthdays as if everything was normal. At the time I was confused but now I think they didn't want her to know she was dying.' He mashed his cigarette out savagely. 'She knew it anyway.'

I couldn't stop tears welling up. I took his hand and held it between both of mine. He let it rest there.

'My parents were never the same again,' he said. 'My father hardly left the house. He used to sit with his forehead pressed against the window, watching the rain. We lived in Corunna then, and it was all fog, rain and gales.' A sigh – caught and held. 'Papito's depression frightened me. It spread through the house. I was scared of catching it.'

'I'm so very sorry.'

He raised a hand. 'There's one more thing. My father was an artist, but he worked less and less. A few months after Conchita died, he gave me his paints and brushes, and said, "Your talent is mature now. In fact, it's already bigger than mine." He never painted again.'

'God,' I said. 'My *God*. How did you feel? Was it a burden?'

He shook his head. 'It was like being trusted with a sacred mission. I swore I'd become a great painter, and from then on, painting took over my life.'

'You amaze me. What you went through might have broken a lesser man, but you've come through it so well.'

A gleam appeared in his eye. 'Do you think so? It took years, but time and painting have helped. And since we met, I am happier than I've been for a long time.'

My cigarette had gone out without me noticing, and a small stream of ash fell onto my chest. Pablo brushed it away tenderly, spreading sensations that were like pinpricks of light. He said, 'The more I see you, the more I want your company.'

'I feel the same.' I brought my eyes up to meet his and leaned closer, half-shutting my eyes. His lips met mine; light spread all through me. The lovebirds had been all attention while we were speaking but seconds after we started kissing, they began to laugh. We drew back, the mood ruined.

'They are really birds for a philosopher,' he said ruefully. 'All human behaviour has its ridiculous side, and I have the lovebirds to make sure I don't forget it.' He shook his head.

I was reeling from the emotions we'd shared and dying for him to kiss me again, but before we could build up to it, the lovebirds began to mate, their feathers rustling sharply.

'They always do this,' Pablo said. 'I'd like to know what goes on in their heads. And the odd thing is they're both male.' He turned his palms up, his eyes twinkling. 'Do you think they could be perverts?'

I smiled at him. 'I know an old lady who does embroidery for the great couturiers,' I said. 'She has a male lovebird too. One day I saw the bird sitting on a china egg. The woman told me that male lovebirds get broody, and when the mood takes him, he sits on that false egg for days.'

Pablo chuckled. 'I'm glad mine aren't alone in their strangeness.'

I left soon afterwards, as I was booked to do a fashion shoot for Jeanne Lanvin. 'Give her my regards,' said Pablo, touching his fingers to his lips and pressing them lightly against mine.

Once I was outside, I looked back up at the windows of the studio. I could see him behind the glass, watching me. Then I saw the light of a burning match which turned into the red tip of his cigarette. I walked to Jeanne's salon beneath a cloud-streaked sky, the ache of missing him already sharp enough to take my breath away.

# Six

## 1936

'YOU WERE RIGHT!' I said triumphantly. 'Going to Pablo's café worked.'

'I'm so glad!' said Jacqui and, like a child, clapped her hands. 'Are you happy, darling?'

I smiled at her. 'Never been happier.'

We were sitting in her small dining room, which was filled with belle-époque furniture, ornate and beautiful. Art by Braque and Magritte hung on the walls, but the wallpaper in between was faded and peeling. She and André were married now. She had worn black for the small ceremony and had refused to invite any family except Huguette. Jacqui had fallen pregnant soon afterwards, throwing herself into the project as passionately as she entered into all the other adventures of her life. Today, she was wearing a flowing Mexican dress inspired by Frida Kahlo, her idol, and she'd just shown me the baby clothes she was sewing, trimmed with antique lace. I was happy for her, but wasn't yet ready to tread the same path.

'Have a piece of lemon cake,' she said, cutting sturdy wedges and handing me one on a Delft china plate. Like me, she wore her fingernails long, and hers were painted crimson.

For several moments we ate in silence. Then she said, 'Since I've been pregnant, my past life seems so far away. Do you remember how we used to walk through Paris, talking about art?'

'I'll never forget it,' I said dreamily.

Jacqui held up a finger and said, 'But school was never the same after Maman died. I've been thinking about her a lot, now that I'm going to be a mother myself.' I touched her arm.

'How are your parents?' she asked.

I loaded my fork with cake and said, 'The same as ever. Maman is as content as her nature allows. Papa is still sad. But let's not talk about them. I've missed you, I want to see more of you.'

'The baby is taking all my energy. I feel like my body doesn't belong to me,' she said, flipping back her curtain of blonde hair. 'And things are difficult because André wants me to be a muse and housekeeper, but I want to paint.' She was speaking quickly now. 'It's always been difficult because I'm a woman, and now things are even worse. I am trapped by domestic chores. They suck up so much time! Oh, Dora, sometimes I'm scared that becoming a mother will stop me painting completely.'

'Sweetheart,' I said, reaching for her hand. 'It won't stop you if you don't let it.'

Jacqui gave my hand a tiny squeeze and said, 'Tell me about *your* work. At least one of us is doing great things.'

I started talking about the shoot I'd just done for Jeanne Lanvin but the doorbell rang.

'It's Huguette,' Jacqui said, getting to her feet. 'I asked her to come. You don't mind, do you?' And she went to open the door without waiting for an answer.

Huguette came in and we kissed on each cheek. I hadn't seen her since Jacqui's wedding and she was thinner than ever. Her expression had changed: there was a blankness behind her eyes. For a moment I wondered what it was like to have a younger sister who was better looking, tougher, more interesting. Jacqui poured Huguette coffee and cut her a slice of cake.

'It's been a long time. Far too long. How are you?' I said to Huguette.

'I'm all right, thank you. I'm doing all right.' She gave a tiny shrug.

'Are you playing the piano?' Jacqui asked. 'You said you wanted to try again.'

Huguette looked past her sister towards the window, and her mouth worked. 'I did try. But it's not the same since Maman ...'

'I'm sorry,' said Jacqui, laying a hand on her arm. 'I think your music will come back in its own time.'

38

Huguette let out a long sigh. 'I wish I was more like you.'

'Don't, darling. I'm a mess. I don't do anything properly.' Jacqui ran her fingers through her hair. 'Why don't you aspire to be like Dora? She just did a shoot for Jeanne Lanvin.'

'Amazing! I'm so pleased for you,' said Huguette.

'What's more, she's in love!' Jacqui turned to me. 'Tell Huguette.'

I shook my head. The attraction between me and Pablo was so new and fragile, I feared it might evaporate if exposed to the scrutiny of others.

When I got back to my apartment, I could hear the phone ringing from outside the front door. I fumbled for my key in my bag, scared it would stop before I reached it, but it was still ringing when I got there.

'Hello?' I said.

'Hola!' said Pablo's voice. 'Guess what? I can finally draw again.'

'Oh, I'm so pleased!'

'I made two lithographs of the lovebirds mating,' he said happily. 'The first is in purplish red, the second is yellow. I've superimposed one on top of the other to show the fluttering and shuddering that goes on while they're in action.' His voice dropped, grew intimate. 'I couldn't have done it without you. You've inspired me.'

I felt a rush of surprise and exaltation. 'That makes me happier than you know.'

'Come and visit me at my château,' he said, after a short pause. 'Let's photograph each other there.'

We made a date for the following week and said goodbye, my pulse racing with excitement.

Boisgeloup was an eighteenth-century château set in a park, an hour's drive north-west of Paris. Pablo was waiting at the entrance as I pulled up in a taxi.

'Here you are! You made it!' he exclaimed, once I had paid the driver. He clasped my shoulders and kissed me on both cheeks. 'I hope your journey was easy. I'll show you around.'

It was a handsome property built around a square courtyard, with a rose arbour, an old, ivy-covered chapel, and a crumbling pigeon house coated in droppings. The grey stone château had a beautifully proportioned slate roof and windows, and was backed by enormous trees. Most of the rooms were unfurnished, except for a hippopotamus skull on a plinth in the hall, and a few large Picassos on the walls. It was an exceptionally mild day for February and the light was changing, growing yellower, a whisper of promise. But the rooms were chilly and bleak, without heating or even electricity. 'Just because I bought it doesn't mean I have to modernise it,' he said, as if reading my thoughts.

His studio, in one of the outbuildings, had all the life the house lacked. It was large and high-ceilinged, almost as cluttered as his Paris studio. A big stepladder stood in the centre, hung with all sorts of bizarre objects: a red-and-yellow feather duster, a rabbit's foot, and a number of out-of-circulation bank notes. I was struck by how closely the layout of the room resembled his paintings. We were at the centre of a world created by him.

He lit a stove in the corner and said, 'I've managed to do some more work since we met. Would you like to see it?'

'I would love to.'

Smiling, he selected a large album of sketches from one of the tables. We sat on a wide green couch to look at them, close but not quite touching, and again I felt a tug of desire, a hypnotic pull towards him. He turned over some pages, pausing at a sketch of a blonde girl, nude but for a necklace made of seashells. Opposite her stood another girl with dark hair and eyes, partly clothed. 'That's you,' he said, pointing to the dark girl. 'You see the resemblance, don't you?'

Pablo turned over several more pages filled with men, minotaurs, satyrs and a lot of women. Most of them were naked, and they seemed to have stepped from the pages of a Greek myth. I studied them, wondering who the blonde could be. Evidently she haunted his imagination as powerfully as I did, and a shiver of foreboding ran through me.

'All this takes place on a mountainous island, like Crete,' he said. 'The minotaurs live there, by the coast. They're bad and dangerous, but full of life. As the sun sets, there are parties, and they dance with beautiful women. Everyone feasts on oysters and champagne, until it turns into an orgy.'

Pablo lowered his voice. 'A minotaur knows he's a monster, but he also has a human side.' He turned to another drawing, of a minotaur looking at a woman asleep in bed and said, 'He's wondering if she loves him *because* he's a monster.' Pablo shot me a quick glance. 'Women are strange that way, you know. It's impossible to tell if he wants to kiss her or strangle her.' His voice dropped to a thread. 'Of course, I am the minotaur.'

At that, another chill went through me, but I was in too deep to draw back. He turned over a few more pages and we were at the end of the book. I told him how extraordinary his drawings were, and he thanked me and said, 'Let's get to work!'

At first, I photographed him surrounded by his paintings. Then he took my camera – my beloved Rolleiflex that no one else was allowed to touch – and shot his own portraits of me: full-frontal, three-quarter profile and profile. It was a riposte to our first photo session, only this time it was his turn to possess me. In the profile shot, I turned away to read a newspaper, feigning indifference, though my body was warm and jittery with desire.

'You have the most erotic hands I've ever seen,' he said. For a moment, I thought of Georges, but what I felt for Pablo was so much deeper. He picked them up, examining their shape, the deep red nails. He began running his fingers lightly over my skin, looking into my eyes, while I scarcely breathed. 'I love that we can speak Spanish,' he continued. 'Even more, we both have Spanish souls.'

He pushed back a strand of hair that had fallen over my face and then he kissed me. He was tender and gentle, running his hands over me like a sculptor checking his work. He found textures in me that weren't there before; under his fingers my body unfurled like a flower in the sun.

Spring arrived in Paris. Day after day the skies were blue, and the fountains were full of rainbow spray. Daffodils opened, and then tulips and irises. The parks turned feathery green, like a Fragonard painting. Pablo fell into the habit of calling whenever he decided to have lunch at the Catalan, his favourite Spanish restaurant. He would say, 'Hello. Is that you? It's me. I'm leaving now, come down.'

Once I was known for my pride, my *froideur*. But at Pablo's signal, I would grab my bag, hurry down my two flights of stairs, and meet him at the corner of the rue des Grands-Augustins. Often I waited, my skin prickling with anticipation. If by any chance I was late, he never waited, but would head straight for the restaurant.

The Catalan had red-and-white-checked cloths, heavy brass candlesticks on the tables, and wine vaults packed with casks lining the walls. The air was perfumed with olive oil and garlic. The owner, M. Arnau, a thickset, Spanish-speaking Marseillais, greeted us at the door. By now he was used to seeing me on Pablo's arm.

'Señor Picasso, Señorita Maar! Always an honour to have you here.' He shook us both by the hand. 'I have a corner table for you, nice and private. I trust that will be satisfactory?'

Once we were seated, Pablo took a paper napkin, folding and tearing it, and when he unfolded it, I saw that it had been turned into a magical frieze of dancers and dogs. I slipped it into my handbag to display in my apartment later. We were so comfortable together, it felt perfectly natural to do this. 'I feel so free with you,' I said.

'Me too!' he said, taking my hand. 'When I was young, I struggled to find anyone compatible. It was desperately lonely, and I retreated into art. As I got older, I met a few people I could talk to.' He shook his head wonderingly. 'But with you I can be completely myself. I can say anything, I don't have to wear a mask. We speak the same language.'

The waiter brought wine and a basket of bread. Pablo buttered a roll and slid it into my mouth. I savoured the cold, creamy butter, the warm dough melting on my tongue. He fed it to me bite by bite, and I ate it down to the golden, crusty point.

After lunch, he invited me back to his studio. We didn't talk much on the short walk there. As usual, Pablo looked at everyone and everything. A boy in shorts making chalk drawings on the pavement, window boxes flaring with colour, a poster fixed to a tree. Nothing escaped his attention. At the entrance to his building, he fished out his keys and opened the door with a flourish.

The contrast between the empty hallway and the chaos of his studio was a perpetual shock. I had realised that he was a hoarder, like me, except he took it to new levels. He kept everything he was given – eau de cologne, chocolate, cigarettes, and even their empty packets. He believed that anything that came into his hands contained a portion of him, and to throw it away was equivalent to hacking off a pound of flesh.

A man appeared in the doorway. I recognised him from the café on the night Pablo and I met. He was dressed entirely in black, down to his black beret and black-rimmed glasses, thick as portholes. He peered distrustfully at me.

'Dora, this is Sabartés, my secretary and front man,' said Pablo, snatching my hand and holding it out to him. 'Look at her, Jaime, isn't she lovely?'

'Yes, yes. I remember her,' said Sabartés, dropping my hand. He blinked a few times and tutted. 'This doesn't look good, Pablo. The thing is, I know you. What's more, she is far too young.'

Their eyes met unpleasantly. 'Mind your own business,' Pablo snapped. 'I'm not interested in your miserable thoughts. Keep them to yourself and go find some work to do.'

Sabartés left the room, shaking his head. Pablo exhaled roughly and led me into the bedroom, an austere space with a red-tiled floor and a huge brass bedstead. Behind the bed were drawings attached by clothes pegs to long nails driven into the wall. There were papers, envelopes and newspaper clippings scattered over the sheets. Pablo pushed them aside and drew me onto the bed, Sabartés forgotten.


'There's something I want you to know. I'm, uh … I'm seeing Pablo Picasso. I'm in love with him,' I said to my parents over coffee in their apartment. I watched the shock on their faces and a knot of anxiety formed in my stomach. But I couldn't hide Pablo from them, as I had Georges, because this relationship was too important.

There was silence for many moments. It was a blustery, overcast afternoon in April, and the light coming through the windows was grey and muted. Sophie was lying with her nose pointed towards the uneaten cake, too well behaved to beg. Outside, bits of rubbish skittered across the place de Champerret and people walked with their heads bowed against the gusts.

At last my mother said, 'You're dazzled by his fame. But every-one knows he's a degenerate.' She pushed her cup away, her lips tightening. 'You're going to be the gossip of Paris.'

'Who cares?' I said, sitting back.

Sophie watched us through her long fringe, uncertain who to go to. And I marvelled at the sweet nature of dogs, and how much they absorb from us.

'With a talent like yours, to go off with Picasso!' fumed my father, shaking his head.

Maman let out a sigh. 'It's not what we want for you, that's all. Life with him can only bring suffering and uncertainty.'

I wondered if my parents had ever tasted the passion that drove someone to risk losing everything – just because they couldn't stay away from the blaze that eclipsed all else.

'You don't know what you're getting into,' said Maman. 'I don't think any woman could be happy with him.' She sat back, her face exhausted.

'I'm an adult and it's my life to live as I choose,' I retorted coolly. 'All I ask for is the space to do that.'

But Maman couldn't or wouldn't give me space. In the days that followed, we had the most appalling rows. Deep down I wanted her to approve of Pablo, to ask about my life with him. A week after my visit, we were on the phone and the urge to talk about him was so strong that I blurted out, 'Pablo's awfully good to me. I wish you could see him the way I do.'

There was silence. 'Maman?'

Still she said nothing, and I realised my mistake. Finally she let out a great sigh and said, 'You're headed for heartache.'

'Maybe you're right,' I said, 'but I have no intention of avoiding it.' And I hung up on her.

I was too angry to work. Fresh air was what I needed; it would clear my head. I had always loved walking; the solid feel of my footfalls on the pavement, the frisson of rubbing shoulders with strangers as I took in the endless quirky life of the streets. I went to the front door, but stopped when I saw a letter from Pablo on the mat. I picked it up and opened it. Pablo's handwriting was like his painting – confident and free.

Beloved Dora,

I love you more than the taste of your lips
more than your cheeks
more than your hands
more than your warm thighs
I love you every moment a little bit more
and I sign

Pablo

In some ways a letter was even better than being with him because I could savour it in my own time, whilst experiencing his presence as a burning inside. But a few days later, he suddenly went silent on me.

He stopped returning my phone calls. He didn't appear at the Catalan, though I went there regularly to look for him. I even swallowed my pride and knocked on the door of his studio. Sabartés opened it just a crack.

'Pablo is away on a trip,' he said. 'He needed a change of air, and to find himself. But somewhere else because he couldn't do it here.' His thin, triumphant smile made my pride surge up, almost choking me. He closed the door with a firm click.

I was devastated. My mind kept returning to the blonde girl in Pablo's album, and I took to spending most of my time in bed, staring at my ceiling and crying. I suppose I should have written him off in my heart right then, but my feelings were stronger than the warning signals. Nothing was as good as the elation I felt in his company, the vibrancy, the aching sweetness of his touch. So I waited and hoped, with the strange sense that I deserved this treatment. It was as if I'd done something wrong, something heinous, years ago, and Pablo had found me out and was punishing me for it.

# Seven

PABLO APPEARED AGAIN AT the beginning of June. He wrote letter after letter pleading for another chance, and I ignored every one of them. After three weeks of this, Paul Éluard telephoned and invited me to Mougins for the summer.

'We've found a gem of a hotel, the Vaste Horizon. Do come, Dora, it will be fun. A few others are joining us.'

I'd been on friendly terms with Paul and his wife since I had photographed Nusch with a spider's web on her face. But I also knew that they were close to Pablo and I smelled a plot. 'Who are the others?' I asked innocently.

'Roland and Valentine Penrose.' He hesitated. 'Oh, and Pablo Picasso.'

Now it was my turn to hesitate, looking at my fingernails which were bare of polish and gnawed to the quick. I wanted to accept the invitation as badly as I'd wanted to answer Pablo's letters, but knew that I must hold firm for my own preservation. What's more, I didn't want to renege on the holiday plans I had already made. So I said breezily, 'I am sorry, I can't. I'm going to the Cap des Salins to stay with Lise Deharme.'

'Well, that's not far from Mougins!' said Paul quickly. 'We'll come and pick you up there.'

A moment's stunned silence, then Paul carried on talking: Nusch was longing to see me, I would find the Penroses interesting, Mougins was a dream. We went back and forth, and I began to waver. What was the point of resisting? My work had suffered without Pablo. Moreover, I was a grown woman, walking into this with my eyes open. Surely I could handle the consequences?

'I'll tell you what,' I said. 'I'll spend the first week with Lise. After that, she has more guests coming. You can collect me then.'

'I am glad, Dora.' There was relief in his voice.

We fixed a date, and after hanging up, I sat in my studio in front of the witch's mirror. I had been wretched for so long that happiness didn't come at once. I could feel it percolate through me as I thought about the sun-soaked weeks ahead with Pablo. But there was trepidation too. He had hurt me once, he could do it again. I raised my eyes to my reflection in the convex glass and it stared back at me, distorted and diminished.

Lise was dark and slight, not beautiful but chic, with shining eyes and a low, throaty voice. 'You've brought perfect weather!' she exclaimed when I arrived on her doorstep. 'It rained all last week. I nearly went mad.' She held me at arm's length to examine me. 'Hmm, you look tired and thin, my dear. But a week of sea air and good food will put you right.'

She led me into her rambling villa, which was filled with surrealist sculpture by Salvador Dalí and Man Ray, and old rococo furniture. It felt like coming into a safe harbour after being lost at sea. In the days that followed, she made sure that I ate, swam and lay in the sun till my body was a rich brown. And she listened to me talk.

'I can't live without Pablo, but the thought of a future together is terrifying,' I said on the second night. We were sitting on the veranda, watching the moon rise in a sky sprinkled with stars. 'I don't know him. I mean, the way he disappeared … He isn't the person I thought he was.'

'You're grieving for that person,' Lise said.

'I knew you'd understand,' I said.

'Well, I do know a thing or two about grief …' She had lost her husband two years before.

'I'm sorry,' I said, laying my hand on her arm. 'The two of you had a rare connection.'

'Yes, and I don't expect to have anything like it again.' She let out a long sigh. 'Oh, I haven't given up on life, don't worry.

I'm still writing, still entertaining. I know it's what he would want me to do. But he was my home and that's gone now.' It was too dark to see her face, but I could hear her voice thicken with tears.

We fell silent, the tips of our cigarettes glowing orange and dimming and flaring up again. The breeze from the garden was warm and scented, and the moonlight was like a spell.

'Look, it's nearly full,' Lise said, gesturing towards the moon. 'Sitting out here, well, it's nourishment for a hurt soul, isn't it?'

'Yes,' I said, suddenly overcome by the strange sense that Pablo and I were moving on pre-ordained lines towards our inevitable destiny of being together.

On the last day, Lise and I left the seclusion of the Cap des Salins for the restaurants and beach clubs of Saint-Tropez, where we enjoyed langoustines and crisp white wine, and watched the thin, achingly stylish women in their Chanel hats and swimsuits. Feathery clouds drifted across a deep blue sky and the sun warmed our skin. Lise was wearing a white sleeveless dress and a magnificent cabochon ruby ring set in agate and gold.

'What a glorious piece!' I said, taking her hand to admire the stone dancing and dazzling in the light.

Lise smiled. 'Thank you! I treated myself to it when my first book was published.' She forked a stray morsel of langoustine into her mouth and pushed the plate away. 'I must say, my dear, you look like a different person to the one who arrived on my doorstep a week ago.'

'It's been such a wonderful holiday,' I said. 'I can't thank you enough.' I took off my sunglasses so that Lise could see my eyes. 'Will you forgive me leaving early?'

She looked at me, her head on one side. Finally she said, 'This passion – I can see it's stronger than you. Follow it, darling. It's the only true gift life gives us.' She leaned over and kissed me on the forehead.

The next day was bright and windy. Pablo and the Éluards arrived at the villa in the late afternoon, in Pablo's Hispano, driven by Marcel, his chauffeur. The car seated eight or nine, and I couldn't help thinking that it was like the automobiles used by star matadors for their grand entrances. As they got out and walked towards us,

Pablo carried himself with the assurance of a torero at the head of a procession.

Amidst the flurry of greetings, my eyes met his in silence, like an indrawn breath, and suddenly he didn't seem so assured. He looked tired and older than I remembered. For an instant I examined him with detachment, as if he were a stranger; then my feelings for him came crowding back. Lise ushered us into the villa and made Aperol spritzes for everyone. We drank them on the veranda, looking at the trees in the garden whipping in the wind and the waves foaming beyond, everything bathed in crystal-clear sunlight. Lise began to ask Nusch about her life before she met Paul.

'My father was a circus artist in a travelling show,' she said, in a guttural Alsatian accent that hardly matched her fragile appearance.

Lise clapped her hands. 'Wonderful, so different! Were you part of his act?' Nusch nodded and Lise said, 'What did you do?'

Nusch gave a smile of great sweetness. 'My father chained me up,' she said, watching Lise's eyes widen. 'He would invite members of the audience to come onstage and help him, so they could see I was tightly bound. Then I'd thrash about, struggling to free myself. Finally, I would throw off my chains and do a dance of freedom.' Raising her arms above her head, she shut her eyes and swayed in time to imaginary music.

'You're extraordinary!' said Lise.

'Isn't she?' agreed Paul. 'But look at her – she's still untamed.'

Nusch stopped dancing and they exchanged an amused glance. Paul was tall, with clear, almost liquid blue eyes, a high forehead and a sensitive face. He looked like a photograph of Baudelaire as a young man. Nusch was slender, with brown, rebellious hair, and her face was full of light.

'How did you meet?' Lise asked them.

Paul said, 'I was out walking one day, when I saw a lovely, ethereal girl practising cartwheels on the pavement. I was captivated.' He laid a hand on Nusch's thigh. 'We got married soon afterwards.'

'Shall we go for a stroll?' Pablo whispered to me. I nodded, and we rose and slipped away, without comment from the others. At first, we walked among pines and vineyards, and then on the wild beach with its white sand, piles of driftwood, and the sea moving hungrily beside us.

'You're probably wondering why I disappeared,' Pablo began. 'I am sorry if I upset—'

'Of course I'm upset!' I said coldly. 'You seem to think you can come back whenever you feel like it and I'll fall into your arms.'

'Dora, don't. Let me explain,' he beseeched me, touching my shoulder. I shook him off. 'There's no nice way to say this,' he said, letting out a sigh. 'I am involved with two other women.'

My stomach tightened. My heart was pounding in my throat. And yet I wasn't surprised. I had known it ever since he went silent on me. He began to talk about his wife, Olga, who had been a dancer with the Ballets Russes. They had met when he designed sets and costumes for the ballet *Parade*. I hadn't realised that he was still married to her, and I had to clamp my lips together in order to stay calm and let him speak.

'She wasn't one of the better dancers,' he said. 'But she was pretty and fresh-looking. The morals of the company were pretty lax, you see. The contrast between this innocent girl and the rest of them excited me.' His eyes narrowed. 'But we couldn't get along. Olga didn't really care for ballet. She knew nothing about painting. She only liked *le high-life* – coffee, cakes and caviar.'

'And you don't?' I tried to keep my voice steady.

He grinned. 'Me? I like Catalan sausage and beans.' His smile faded. 'I just mean to say that we were too different and I should have known sooner.' He paused, then spoke with suddenness. 'You may have heard, we have a son.' I nodded – it was public knowledge – and he went on, 'It should have brought us closer but the strain of a new baby made things unbearable. She screamed at me all day long. We separated last year but I can't divorce her.'

'Why not?'

He rubbed the side of his mouth, frowning. 'We married in community of property. She would get half of everything I own, including my work.'

'I see,' I said slowly. Evidently, Pablo liked to hold on to his assets and his women. But before I'd had time to digest the story of his marriage, he launched into telling me about his mistress and muse, Marie-Thérèse Walter.

'She was seventeen when we met, practically a child.' His eyes had been hard while he was talking about Olga but now they grew very gentle. 'I saw her through the window of the Galeries Lafayette. I waited till she came out, then said, "Mademoiselle, you have an interesting face. I would like to paint you."'

I realised that Marie-Thérèse was the blonde in his album and my jaw clenched so hard it hurt.

He said, 'We were happy together till she gave birth to our daughter. The baby is adorable, but caring for her takes a lot out of Marie-Thérèse. She is always tired, there's not much left for anyone else.' He frowned.

'You have a new baby? How can you do this?' I asked, stunned. I tried to say more, but words deserted me. I tried again: 'Pablo …' To my dismay, tears rose instead of speech.

'Dora,' he said, putting his arms around me. 'Oh Dora, I'm sorry. It's just the way I'm made.'

I was crying openly now, all the confusion and misery of the past weeks coming out. Pablo dried my tears with his fingertips, sweet and contrite. For a few moments I leaned my head against his chest, enjoying being comforted by him, then forced myself to pull away. 'Who were you with when you vanished?' I asked.

Pablo sucked air between his teeth. 'Marie-Thérèse. I took her and Maya to Juan-les-Pins. She needed a break.'

Waves of pain were rolling through me. 'Why did you come here, telling me this? I'm not asking you for anything.'

'I'm telling you because I hope you'll become a permanent part of my life,' he said, looking into my eyes. 'But of course there's the condition – that you let me keep the other women.'

A gust of wind buffeted me, blowing strands of hair across my face. My eyes started watering again, whether from the wind or from weeping I didn't know. I stopped walking and looked blindly out to sea, trying to think. Pablo stood a little way off.

Little by little, my head cleared, and my hurt ebbed slightly. At least he was being honest with me, and he had clearly fallen out of love with Olga. I was less sure of his feelings for Marie-Thérèse, but he never brought her among his friends, so how could she be a serious rival? Perhaps it was only the child keeping them together. It was obvious that he cared for me and had suffered without me. A conviction was strengthening in me – that whatever happened between us, however magical or painful, would be hugely important; probably, the most important event of my life. And it was this, more than anything else, that made me decide I was strong enough to take the risk. Strong enough to cope with Marie-Thérèse and with Olga too.

'I accept your terms,' I shouted into the wind, watching relief spark in his eyes. I went over to him and wound my arms around his neck. He wiped away my tears and we kissed slowly, lingeringly. His lips were warm and soft, and shivers ran all the way down my spine. I traced the contours of his cheek with my fingertips, the shape of his chin, his mouth – as though his face was a map of some place I was trying to get to.

When we got back to the villa, I packed my bags, kissed Lise goodbye, and climbed into the Hispano with the Éluards and Pablo. I would have gone with him to the ends of the earth.

# Eight

**M**OUGINS WAS A MEDIEVAL hilltop village above Cannes, set among pines, olives and cypress groves. The Vaste Horizon was a hotel of beautiful simplicity, overlooking a courtyard and vineyards, while far below, we could see the rooftops of Cannes and the Mediterranean in the distance. Pablo and I had a big bedroom and balcony with a wonderful view of the bay, everything bathed in the honeyed light of the south.

We spent our first morning swimming and sunbathing at la Garoupe, a secluded beach near Antibes, hugged by pine trees. The sun, the sea and the air sent exhilaration rushing through me. Pablo wasn't tall, but his body was well-set and compact, and he quickly turned bronze in the sun. He enjoyed lying on the sand and doing nothing all morning, but I couldn't sit still for long and broke up my sunbathing with swimming.

On the second day, I swam with Valentine Penrose, a strikingly beautiful poet. The water was perfect: calm and clear, with glimmering sand on the bottom and tiny fish below us. Valentine sliced through the waves with clean, confident strokes, as at home in the sea as I was.

'You are like a mermaid, Valentine,' I said. 'Have you always been this wild and free?'

We paused to rest, treading water. 'Hardly!' she laughed, flipping over onto her back, and staring into the sky. 'Believe it or not I have a staunch military background. I went to la Légion d'Honneur, the school for officers' daughters.' She narrowed her eyes, adding, 'I couldn't take it. I cut my hair, wore breeches, and generally did the opposite of what was expected of me.'

'But you're so feminine!' I exclaimed.

She smiled. 'That may be but I was hell-bent on rebelling against every convention of family life. My parents were furious; we fought for years. It wasn't till I went off to study at an ashram in Calcutta that they finally realised they'd lost the battle.' She closed her eyes. 'Have you ever been to India?'

'No, but I would love to.'

'You should,' she said dreamily. 'It was the best experience of my life. The food, the clothes, the mixture of sensuality and spirituality. I married Roland in a sari. I wish the wedding could have been in India.' She stretched her arms above her head, looking wistful. 'Shall we turn back?'

On our way, we met Pablo bouncing in the waves like some mythical creature. Valentine waved at him and carried on swimming, while he and I floated together in the warm swell. He drew me close, murmuring, 'I've been dreaming about the lush shapes of your body, your Madonna face. I think you've cast a spell on me.' He kissed me deeply, sending jolts of intense physical feeling through me. When we finally broke for breath, he said, 'Actually, you remind me of an ancient deity of the deeps.'

'That's funny,' I smiled. 'I was thinking the same about you.'

We paddled back, bantering about which one of us had greater mythical powers. He towelled me dry and we lay close together, the sun saturating our skins, our hair drying around our faces.

Later, Pablo made inspired doodles in the wet sand by the shoreline. Nusch and I sat together, watching him sketch a water nymph with a few quick movements of his forefinger.

'You're good for him,' Nusch said quietly.

'Oh, do you think so?'

'Definitely. He's calmer and happier than I've ever seen him.'

Ripples of joy spread through me. 'Really?' I said.

'Yes, and he doesn't stop talking about you. "Dora said this, Dora read that …"'

'Oh, I hope it doesn't drive you crazy.'

'Not at all! We are relieved he's chosen someone we like,' she said, smiling.

Just then, a large, fair-haired woman approached Pablo. She had a damp, pink face and wore a red bathing suit, the fabric straining across her ample stomach and hips.

'I'm Maude. This is Henry,' she said in American English, pointing to the lean, grey-haired man in a checked shirt and shorts standing behind her. Henry raised a hand in greeting. 'We're awful pleased to meet you,' he said.

Pablo gave a slight bow. 'Pablo Picasso.'

'We know who you are,' said Maude, simpering. 'We're visiting from Baltimore, and we just love your beautiful country.' She cleared her throat. 'We're great admirers of your work ... I don't suppose you would give us an autograph? We'd be delighted.'

Pablo turned his palms outwards, smiling. 'I would be happy to, but I have nothing to write on,' he said in heavily accented English.

'Gee, neither do I! But perhaps you can sign my beach bag?' Maude thrust a striped red-and-silver carryall at him. 'Give him your pen, Henry.' Henry extracted a pen from his wallet, a light flush rising on his cheeks. At the same moment, a wave broke, washing away Pablo's doodle.

'Oh, your precious drawing! What a waste!' Maude gasped.

'It's only the sea following its nature. We can't change it,' said Pablo amiably, writing his name in large letters across the bag.

'I can't thank you enough! I'll treasure this forever,' exclaimed Maude, and they said goodbye and walked off.

I was impressed by the unassuming courtesy with which he had dealt with them, as they had nothing in common. Luckily, few people came to la Garoupe, but the encounter made me realise for the first time that Pablo was public property. It shocked me a little. I had always known that he was a famous figure, but I'd felt that this was a surface he wore lightly, and that beneath it, he was a private man, unavailable to the world at large. Seeing him on the beach made me recognise that, on the contrary, the whole world felt entitled to a piece of him. I wondered how many people had seen his pictures, and what that level of fame felt like. And I hoped that one day I would find out.

When the beach grew so hot that the sand scorched our feet, we returned to the hotel for a simple lunch of cold cuts, salads and fresh bread, washed down with plenty of chilled white wine. We ate on a grapevine-sheltered pergola, edged with terracotta pots full of red and white geraniums.

'We must make this a celebratory lunch for Roland,' said Valentine of her husband – an English painter, who was also blessed with a collector's eye and the money to indulge it. With Paul's help, he had just organised the London International Surrealist Exhibition, bringing together many of the finest artists of the twentieth century, including René Magritte, Max Ernst, Alexander Calder, Alberto Giacometti, Paul Klee, Joan Miró, Henry Moore, Salvador Dalí and, of course, Pablo Picasso. My *Père Ubu* was there too, with one of Jacqui's paintings, and it made me feel joyful and optimistic because my goals seemed attainable.

'Well done!' said Paul, raising his glass to Roland. 'You set the Thames on fire.'

'I couldn't have done it without your help,' said Roland, running his hand through the shock of dark hair that swept over a narrow, astute face.

We lifted our glasses and drank to their health. Sunlight splashed gold through the canes above our heads, and the shadows lay dense and sharp, decorating everyone with ribbons of light and shade. The air was filled with the dry, peppery smell of geraniums and the elusive scent of grapevine flowers.

'Sounds like a triumph,' I said.

'That's what everyone said,' agreed Valentine, deftly pulling her hair into a chignon. 'By the way your *Ubu* got a lot of attention. What a powerful and unsettling piece it is!'

'Thank you,' I said, and a lovely glow filled me. 'Did you see Jacqui's *Les Heures*?' Jacqui's painting depicted the profile of a woman-shell lying dormant on its back, alone at the bottom of a dark ocean. I thought it referred to her pregnancy and to her role as André's muse.

'Yes, it was hanging near *Ubu*,' said Valentine.

'I'm glad. Her work doesn't get enough recognition,' I said.

'I agree,' said Valentine, 'and I don't know why because it's quirky and wonderful. People really loved *Les Heures*.' She flung up her hands. 'Actually, I think the whole exhibition was loved because it's quirky. You know how eccentric the English are.'

'How do you define quirkiness, Valentine?' asked Pablo carefully.

Before Valentine could answer, Nusch leaned towards him and said, 'I'll tell you. The show opened on a boiling-hot day, but Sheila Legge arrived with a pork chop. It went off immediately.' She cut a thick piece of dry-cured sausage and bit into it. 'Have you tried this? It's divine.' She cut another slice and held it out to Pablo.

Nusch was so artlessly seductive, so comfortably herself, that I couldn't help loving her. But the way Pablo smiled at her as he took the sausage sent a jab of pain through me. 'Sheila is a great performance artist,' he said.

'This was one of her best acts,' said Paul, covering Nusch's hand with his. 'She wore a white satin gown. Her head was hidden by a bunch of roses with ladybirds crawling all over it.'

'She had to throw the pork chop away – the smell was making people ill,' Nusch said, turning to me. 'So she waved an artificial leg around instead.'

Laughter rippled around the table.

'What else?' I asked, popping a scroll of the tenderest Parma ham into my mouth, and feeling it melt on my tongue, salty and nutty.

'Dylan Thomas handed out coffee cups, asking people if they liked it weak or strong,' said Paul.

'The *pièce de résistance* was Dalí's,' said Roland.

'Why?' said Pablo, and his eyes went small.

'Well, he wanted to give his lecture in a full diving suit, to illustrate his dive into the subconscious,' Roland said. 'But he hadn't realised there was no air supply in the helmet. We watched him suffocate inside it, thrashing about and flailing his arms. By the time we prised it off, he was nearly unconscious.'

'My God!' I said. 'What did the audience do? Was there a stampede?'

'Quite the opposite – the audience roared with laughter. They thought it was part of his act,' said Paul. He drained his glass, tilting it high to catch the last drops of wine. 'Afterwards, I said to Dalí, "You really went too far this time." And he said, "It's the only place I ever wanted to go."'

Everyone smiled except Pablo. 'The man's nothing but an attention-seeker,' he grumbled.

'That may be,' said Paul affably. 'But you can't help admiring his dedication. He recovered and went on to finish his presentation with a slide show. The slides were upside down, of course.'

Pablo gave a short, surprised laugh. Paul was better than anyone else at putting him in a good mood.

'It was funny,' Roland said. 'But the exhibition had a serious point too.'

'You were making fun of civilisation to try and cure its rotten-ness,' said Valentine, biting into a slice of melon.

'Yes,' said Roland, watching the juice run down her chin. His eyes followed her wherever she went. 'But if that was too ambitious I hope we at least made people reappraise what art is—'

'Look at this!' Pablo interrupted, emptying his matchbox onto the table and beginning to break the matches into small bits. We fell silent, watching as he rebuilt them into a perfect replica of the vineyards below us, with Cannes in the distance. Maybe he didn't like not being the centre of attention and maybe he was showing off, but he was also demonstrating what could be done with the slightest means. 'Didn't Goya paint with a spoon when he had no brushes?' he asked, without looking up. 'And what about Titian claiming he could recreate Venus's flesh from mud?'

Glancing around the table, I saw that Pablo had the same effect on the others as he had on me: he charged our emotional batteries to the full. He was like a wizard, always astonishing, always find-ing new possibilities in everyday objects. While he was making his model, I had been quietly weaving a flaming crown of geraniums. Once he had finished, I stood up and laid the flowers gently on his head as the others applauded, and he gave me a look that made my heart turn over.

After lunch we retired to our room for a siesta, tearing off our clothes before we even reached the bed, the sun seeping through the shutters, striping our bodies. Pablo was wholly mine again and the extraordinary pleasure of our lovemaking made me realise that I'd never been truly alive until I met him.

Afterwards, I watched him sleep. I liked the tan of his limbs against the white sheets, the way he fell into sleep greedily, his face smoothed out. I looked at him for a long time and then I took his photo, surreptitiously, like a thief.

That evening, he and I sat on the terrace, drinking wine and watching the early evening sunshine deepen over the roofs of Cannes, staining them gold.

'See how the light is tactile – almost liquefied,' Pablo said, putting his hand on my thigh. 'I love this landscape like a person. There's no better place to paint.'

He had made a full return to his art, working late into the night while I slept. It was as if a deep current were breaking through to the surface, and I could feel the joy and energy coursing through him. As for me, I was hardly working, apart from photographing Pablo. My affair with him was its own work of art, absorbing all my energies. It was strange because I'd never felt like this before, but for now, it was the only creative act I needed. Suddenly, he took my chin in his hand, lifted my head, and turned it to the side.

'That's it! Don't move,' he said. He got up, fetched a pad and pencil, and returned to the table.

I didn't move, but watched him from the corner of my eye. He looked at me intently for a moment, and then drew very fast with one continuous line, the pencil rasping across the paper. Submitting to his gaze was exciting and I wanted it to go on, but he only glanced at me once or twice more – the sketch was finished in a few minutes.

'Here it is,' he said, handing me the pad. 'Do you like it?'

I nodded, too entranced to speak. Where there had been nothing, suddenly, there was the essence of me, and it was exquisite. Pablo had given me a life beyond life.

From then on, he couldn't stop drawing and painting me. To him, I was in constant metamorphosis: a water nymph, a mermaid peering from the sea, a woman with features made of flowers. At other times, he depicted me as various mythological creatures, taloned because of my fingernails which had grown long again. I was a sphinx, a siren, a minotauresse.

He would look at me meditatively and say, 'I can see another, better way of painting you now. You're anything I want you to be. That's a great advantage when falling in love.'

It was intoxicating, like being a guest at a sumptuous banquet, where the menu was constantly being improvised while it was underway. Marie-Thérèse and Olga receded in my mind to the point where I felt that I was Pablo's only love. I began to dare to believe in happiness. He said, 'Our relationship brings light into both our lives,' and I agreed. He was light and oxygen to me. There were times when it seemed I could not breathe outside his presence.

# Nine

O N THE TENTH DAY of the holiday, we came to breakfast to find Paul and Nusch already at table. There was no sign of the Penroses.

'Hola! How did you sleep?' Pablo asked them.

'Like a baby. I'm still drowsy,' said Nusch, and we sat in comfortable silence, soaking up the colours and scents of the garden.

A pretty, red-headed maid brought a tray loaded with peaches, croissants, coffee and a folded newspaper. We thanked her and she smiled shyly. As she laid everything on the table I saw the headline, SPANISH REVOLUTION. Pablo grabbed the paper and started scanning the article. We had been expecting this news, but he looked frantic with shock even so.

'What does it say?' asked Paul, and Pablo began to read aloud:

Yesterday, July 17th, a serious revolt broke out among the armed forces in garrison towns throughout Spain. It was aimed at the overthrow of the left-wing Republican Government and at the establishment of a right-wing dictatorship in its place. We fear that if not immediately extinguished, this struggle between democracy and fascism could signal the beginning of a Civil War.

His voice broke and he put down the paper. There was no sound but the continuous high-pitched whine of the cicadas, which seemed to accentuate the tension.

'I think civil war is inevitable,' said Paul, shaking his head. 'What a mess Europe's in.' In March, Hitler's troops had advanced into the Rhineland without resistance, and Nazi Germany was continuing to re-arm. The whole of France was on edge.

61

Pablo rubbed his face. 'Franco's no leader, he's a corridor tactician. But he is dangerous because he cloaks himself in mystery, and underneath it, he's ferocious.' A look of fear passed over him. 'Do you think I should go to Barcelona to fetch Mamá and the others?'

'I don't know.' Paul shrugged slightly. 'There's so much uncertainty right now. It's hard to know how things might develop.'

'That's true,' said Pablo. 'Perhaps I'm better off not doing anything. For all I know, the journey to France will put them in more danger. I don't even know if Mamá is strong enough to travel.' He turned away to look at the sea being whipped into peaks by the wind.

He spent the rest of day struggling with the dilemma – we discussed all the reasons for going or for staying put. That night, a telegram came from his mother, saying she was too old to move anywhere. It solved the problem, but he couldn't stop worrying about her.

'Surely your fame gives your family some protection?' I asked when we were in bed.

'Well it might, except I haven't taken up a position with a convincing political declaration,' he said, pressing his hands to the sides of his head.

'Why don't you, then?'

'Because I don't know what I am,' he said angrily, and I realised that the conflict brought him face to face with social and political problems he had always avoided.

'You're Spanish to the core,' I said, putting my arms around him. 'No wonder you feel awful.'

Over the next few days, we received news that the initial military coup had failed to win control of the country and civil war was erupting. Reports appeared in the papers of executions, murders and assassinations on both sides; bloody battles, bodies thrown into shallow burial pits like animals. Pablo was filled with grief and anxiety, and his dream about his limbs growing and shrinking repulsively came back. When things were really bad, he would nudge me and say, 'Are you awake?'

'I am now,' I'd say sleepily, wanting to comfort him.

'Talk to me. Please talk, about anything you like,' he would beg. And I would tell stories about my life before him, about opening the studios and my days as a street photographer. I never mentioned Georges.

He often struggled to get back to sleep afterwards, and we began to take late-night walks around the village. Once, we drove to the beach. The moon was like a polished coin, lighting our way, casting its silver reflection on the sea.

'We're on the same wavelength, in bed and everywhere else. I've never had that before,' he said. He drew me to him and kissed me, and I felt warmth spread all through me.

We began to walk, our shadows shifting and lengthening. 'I've managed to work out a few things,' he said.

'Oh? Tell me.'

'Well, ever since I started to paint, I've struggled against everything reactionary. It makes me realise that I belong to the revolutionary camp, as I've always identified my life with my work.'

'That's the answer to your political dilemma! Your position has to be against the military uprising and in favour of the republican government,' I said.

Moonlight danced in his eyes as he turned to look at me. '*Dorrra*, you're right!'

For days afterwards, he seemed relieved. But as the holiday neared its end and the chilling news bulletins kept rolling in, a terrible darkness and pain descended on him. I felt the horror too; it matched my previous feelings about fascism, but I was more worried about Pablo than myself. Nothing could shift his mood, and so he turned to the outlet that rarely failed him. Abandoning everything he'd been working on, he began a new painting. He refused to show it to anyone and would only say that he had called it *Dora and the Minotaur*.

Pablo presented me with the painting on the last full day of the holiday. I saw, with discomfort, that he had portrayed himself as the Minotaur, raping me in a harsh landscape beneath flaming skies. Though he looked a little sad, he was venting his impulse to dominate, while I was half submitting, half being violated.

'What do you think?' he asked expectantly. I hesitated. 'Well?' he said.

I stared at the picture again. 'It's disturbing.'

'I am sorry you don't like it,' he said, his face darkening.

I braced myself for an argument but to my relief, the clock struck one. 'We'd better go to lunch,' I said.

Pablo scowled and breathed out loudly, but thankfully said no more. He was sullen at lunch, impervious to Paul's jokes, Nusch's charm and the Penroses' attempts to engage him in conversation. Eventually they gave up and left him alone. I think they understood that to be Pablo's friend, one also had to be his acolyte, sensitive to his needs and moods. I was paralysed by misery. I knew that his bad humour was not my fault, yet didn't know what I could have done to prevent it, and I was shaken by his portrayal of me in *Dora and the Minotaur*.

That night, in our room, he said, 'I need to tell you something.'

'What is it?' I was sitting at the dressing table, dabbing cold cream on my face.

'The secret of my childhood,' he said quietly.

I turned to face him, and the look in his eyes made me go to him on the bed. 'Tell me,' I said.

'It's about Conchita.' He paused and cleared his throat; he seemed to have difficulty in knowing how to begin. 'I was desperate while she was dying,' he finally said.

'It must have been frightful.'

He nodded. 'I made a pact with God. I would sacrifice my gift to Him and never paint again, if He would make her better.'

My skin prickled with foreboding. 'Go on.'

'I felt so torn. Obviously, I loved Conchita and willed her to get better. But I couldn't help wanting her to die, so my talent would be saved.' He made fists with his hands. 'I can't stay away from painting. It's my life.'

'Of course it is,' I said.

'She died anyway.' He turned his head away, as if he were inside that moment, reliving it. I gathered him in my arms and he laid his cheek on my breasts. 'From then on, I was sure God was evil,' he continued, his stubble scraping my skin. 'But I also thought that my uncertainty had let him kill Conchita.'

'Dear Lord!' I said, tightening my arms around him. 'You were a child. You couldn't possibly have influenced the world around you, much less God.'

'But I thought I could. In fact, I still think it.' He hesitated, then said in a rush, 'I was sure her death had released me to be a painter and to use my gifts – whatever the consequences.'

I was quiet for a while, letting the enormity of his words sink in. Tears gleamed on his cheeks.

'Stay with me, Dora. Don't ever leave,' he begged. 'I need you.'

'I'm not going anywhere,' I said softly.

He broke down and I held him while he sobbed. I knew he was weeping for Conchita and for himself – for what had broken in him forever when she died – and for the war in Spain too. Then it dawned on me why he identified with the Minotaur, to whom women had to be sacrificed, and a terrible dread crept through me.

We didn't talk much after that. The room was hot and sticky. A ceiling fan stirred the air without cooling it, and I could hear the whine and drone of a mosquito close by. I felt it bite and slapped at it but missed, and it danced away. I fell asleep at last, slipping in and out of dreams and nightmares that left me exhausted. In them, I climbed flights of stairs that crumbled underfoot, sending me hurtling to the ground. I did a fashion shoot for Jeanne Lanvin, and when I opened the camera afterwards, it was empty of film.

In the morning, my eyes were dry, and my chest was tight and scratchy. Pablo was in a buoyant mood, as if nothing had happened. 'How did you sleep?' he asked, throwing open the shutters so that sunlight shrieked across the room.

'Not too well,' I said, wincing.

'Oh darling, I'm sorry.' He smoothed my hair away from my face. 'Let's get you coffee and something to eat.'

I pulled on a sleeveless white dress, a large hat and sunglasses, and we went to have breakfast with the others. They greeted us cautiously, brightening when they saw Pablo smile. We sat down and helped ourselves to bread and croissants fresh from the oven, washed down with strong black coffee. The sky was huge and flawless and, on either side of us, a line of mountains faded into a bluish haze. Cannes glittered far below, with boats bobbing on the white-flecked waves. The sun soaked into my flesh, Pablo's hand lay in mine, and my distress began to lift. An enormous hornet arrived to inspect our meal, and I decided that Pablo must really love and need me to have confided in me like that.

'It's been the most wonderful holiday,' said Paul.

'I'll never forget it,' said Nusch.

'Me neither. We should do this every year,' said Pablo, and everyone agreed.

Valentine bit into a croissant and the hornet began circling around her. She batted it away, but it flew back to the table and stayed there, buzzing ferociously. The other women and I shrank into ourselves. Pablo stood up, and with one stroke of the bread knife, sliced the hornet in two.

'You have such style. Thank you,' breathed Valentine, and Pablo bowed, smiling.

After breakfast, we returned to our rooms to pack. The Hispano arrived shortly afterwards, with Marcel at the wheel. He had thick, grizzled hair and handsome features, and as he got out and greeted us, I saw that he looked sunburned and slightly heavier. He loaded the canvases, paints, brushes and sketchbooks expertly onto the back seat, ignoring Pablo's cries of, 'No, not that way! Careful! Can't you see you'll damage them?'

We said affectionate goodbyes to the others, promising to meet again in Paris at the earliest opportunity. Then Pablo and I climbed into the car and sat on the folding seats opposite the paintings, uncomfortable but happy, as we watched over our precious cargo.

# Ten

ACK IN PARIS, THE leaves were starting to turn red and gold, and the mornings carried a breath of cool, diluting the sensuality of summer. I felt refreshed, invigorated. Pablo and I were spending most nights together, either at my place or his. I preferred being at mine because, as I continued to turn up regularly at rue La Boétie, Sabartés became more and more hostile. Any time I entered a room he was in, he would walk out of it, mournful and sullen. I was hurt and puzzled by his behaviour. He was always there – I decided he must live with Pablo – and it gave me the uneasy feeling that Pablo and I were never quite alone.

'Have you seen how he looks at me?' I asked Pablo. 'It's the Spanish Inquisition.'

'He's so short-sighted, he looks at everyone like that. Don't take it personally. Actually, it makes him an excellent gatekeeper.'

I wasn't at all satisfied by Pablo's answer but I could see that Sabartés's manner was an asset in dealing with the many visitors who turned up at Pablo's studio. Friends, dealers, collectors and supplicants dropped in every morning, and it was his job to remove the ones Pablo didn't want to see. The mere sight of Sabartés's gloomy face was enough to get rid of the faint-hearted ones.

'Don't all these people distract you from your work?' I asked Pablo, after one of these sessions.

'Quite the opposite!' he said. 'If there were no visitors, I'd have nothing to work on. Visitors recharge my battery, they brighten my whole day.' The vulnerability on his face made me realise how much he needed to be with people who believed in him and his work, and could be relied on to follow him into the future.

Our days fell into a pattern. Pablo went to bed late and rose late. In the mornings we took a stroll and stopped off at a café, before dealing with the visitors and settling down to work. A few weeks after our return to Paris, I left an unexposed photographic plate lying on a table. I was getting back into the rhythm of work and it made me feel like myself again. Pablo picked up the plate, sniffed it, and turned it over in his hands. Then, unable to resist decorating a surface so smooth and shiny, he took an etching needle and began to engrave a woman's profile on it. At the end, he held it out, and I saw that the woman was me. A warm glow filled me.

'Can I take it away and pull a first proof of it?' I asked.

'No, I have a better idea. How about blending photography and printmaking? The results might be interesting.' He looked at me, opening his eyes very wide so that light reflected off his irises, making them glitter.

Thus began a series of experiments in my studio. First, Pablo painted outline portraits of me onto sheets of glass, then turned them into negatives by spreading a thick layer of oil paint over the glass and engraving lines in the paint with a knife blade. The ideas for our experiments were mostly his, but he depended on my skill in the darkroom. I loved collaborating with him; it was a different kind of closeness.

'I'm having fun with this. It's turned me into a living camera,' he said, two days in. He held up a plate in which he'd created a scarf for me by putting a fragment of lace between the glass and photographic paper. 'What do you think? Can we make it work?'

'Yes, I can light it so the lace stands out.'

'Excellent,' he said, laying his hand on the back of my neck, underneath my hair. 'I've been thinking about adding crystals to make you a pair of earrings. I could even use your jewellery.'

I opened my mouth to speak, but he had already turned back to the plate, fully absorbed. Nothing else existed for him while he was working. He soon moved from playing with textures to playing with light, altering or halting its passage.

'Look!' he said, holding a negative at arm's length to see it better. 'See how the "real" is reduced to its shadows, transparencies and structure?'

I tucked my arm into his and said, 'Amazing! It's like an object that's been eaten by fire but the ashes have stayed intact.'

'You get it!' he said approvingly. But after ten days, he began to tire of our experiments, like a game that has served its purpose.

'Photographers and dentists are the two professions who are never satisfied with what they do,' he said, looking up from the finished pile of pictures he was signing *Picamar*, a fusion of our names. 'Every dentist would like to be a doctor. In every photographer there's a painter longing to get out.'

'What nonsense!' I said, shaken by his scorn.

'You should try painting. You have a gold mine and you're mining for salt.'

'Oh, no,' I said, 'photography *is* gold. I photograph like you paint. I transform my subjects just as freely.' Pablo said nothing, so I plunged ahead. 'Photography does things you can't do with a paintbrush. It reveals what the eye can't see. Who knows, maybe in the future photography will replace art!'

His face was blank and I saw that it was useless to try and convince him. Photography was of little consequence to him; all that mattered was painting. He left the studio and I began to tidy up.

I was stacking our pictures into neat piles when I spotted a drawing of a corpse. Her limp, nude body was carried by two naked women, one of whom had my dark, wavy hair. The corpse was Marie-Thérèse.

I felt a crackle of alarm. Then I wondered if Pablo had left the drawing out on purpose – a message to make it clear that I was the one who mattered. It seemed that the heat and dazzle of our affair had destroyed the ties that bound him to Marie-Thérèse, and happiness bubbled up inside me. I decided not to mention the drawing and neither did he.

We made love that night with an appetite that was more ravenous and profound than ever, vying for possession of each other. Instead of being tired afterwards, it left us in a state of excitement. Pablo calmed himself by writing poetry, sprawled naked across the bed, while I painted my nails purple, enjoying the symmetry of being artist and canvas at the same time. The only sounds in the room were his pen scratching over paper and a fly buzzing drowsily against the windowpane. When the poem was finished, he kissed me goodnight and fell asleep.

My mind was too full for sleep, and as soon as my nails were dry, I began to transcribe his scrawl into something more legible, using my favourite red ink. Pablo had developed a process of 'semi-automatic' writing similar to the work of the surrealists: a kaleidoscopic flow of visual images that lacked punctuation and often made no sense, but held the mysterious power of his art.

> outsized flood of doves released drunk on
> the cutting festoons of prisms fixed to the bells decomposing
> with its thousand
> lit candles the green flocks of wool illuminated by the gentle
> acrobatics of
> the lanterns hanging from each arc string and the definitive
> dawn

Drowsiness began creeping over me as I worked. Pablo stretched in his sleep and murmured something inaudible, sunk fathoms deep in a dream. Just then, a line of poetry jumped out:

> Narcissus looking at himself in the broth of the pot au feu at
> two-thirty in the morning.

Pablo was Narcissus, I decided, setting the poem aside and lying down beside him. To some extent I was an echo, an extension of his unquiet nature. But I was more than an echo, or a muse. I was a collaborator, in poetry and in art – on a different level to his other women. We shared an intensity of creativity that was unique to us, and that left its trace on everything we did. I yawned and my body began to shape itself into the curve I would sleep in. My last coherent thought before drifting off was that the occasional heartache of being his lover was worth it tenfold for this.

I woke the next morning to find Pablo already up and lathering his face for shaving. I went to the toilet in my nightgown and bumped straight into Sabartés.

'Good morning,' I said, feeling my cheeks grow hot.

He didn't answer, but gave me a look that said exactly what he thought of young women wandering around in their nightclothes. When I returned, Pablo came to lie with me on the bed. I thought of telling him about Sabartés, but decided not to. It wouldn't change anything.

'I want to know about Georges Bataille,' Pablo said, out of the blue.

'Why are you so interested? I never ask about *your* old loves,' I said.

'Your affair with him makes me even more curious about you.'

'Why?'

He offered me a cigarette. I shook my head. He lit one for himself and drew deeply on it. 'It makes me wonder what forbidden games you are capable of,' he said, exhaling smoke through his nostrils. Georges' erotic obsessions were well known.

I sat up. 'If you really want to know I'll tell you. But maybe I'll have that cigarette, after all.'

He handed me his own and I savoured that first, delicious breath of smoke. And slowly, haltingly, I began to tell him about Georges' difficult background. I spoke about his desire to transgress and his remorse for his sins.

Pablo raised a hand to cut me off. 'I don't give a damn about his psyche. I want to know how he fucked you.' My eyes widened and he added, 'Though you were hardly an innocent trapped in his world.'

'That may be,' I said. 'But it was a master–pupil relationship, and I learned a lot from it.'

'Show me.' He had grown hard and was pressing himself against me.

I took his thumb and placed it inside me.

'Was this how you did it with him?' he asked hoarsely.

'Yes. This too.' I placed the cigarette between his thumb and forefinger, pulling his hand towards my breasts.

'Like this?' He brought the burning tip of the cigarette closer. His hand was shaking.

'Yes. Georges used to say, "A person who plays finds in the game the force to overcome what the game contains of horror."'

71

Pablo's thumb moved inside me. 'Was that true of you?' he asked. I hesitated. 'Yes, at times.'

He brought the cigarette closer and closer, until it trembled just above my skin. I braced myself for pain, yet there was excitement too, my heart pounding. Finally, he groaned and mashed out the cigarette. 'I can't do it. I just can't,' he said. He took me right away. It was brutal and ecstatic.

This was the start of a period of many weeks in which Pablo did delicious and unspeakable things to me. One of his penchants was to deny me an orgasm for as long as possible. Thus he could love and torment me at the same time. Once while he was doing this, I scratched him with my fingernails and blood welled up from the cuts. I pressed my lips to his shoulder, savouring the salty, iron taste. When I'd had my fill, I scooped up the last drops with my fingernails and transferred them to a small, empty bottle.

I treasured that vial of dried blood among my souvenirs, just as Pablo still kept my bloodied glove in his cabinet.

# Eleven

PABLO'S SON, PAULO, WAS a tall, skinny teenager. He resembled his father, except he had blue eyes and red hair that looked like a fiery halo in the sunlight streaming through the windows at rue La Boétie. He had come for breakfast before school; it was our first meeting, and my stomach twinged with nerves.

Pablo clapped him on the back, saying, 'Good to see you. This is my friend, Dora.' Paulo shook my hand.

'It's a pleasure,' I said.

'Likewise.' His voice was low and hesitant.

Pablo led the way to the kitchen. Paulo greeted each of the birds by name, opened the cages and put birdseed on his shoulders, so that the birds came to him to feed and flew around the kitchen, swooping and fluttering, alighting on the surfaces or wheeling back to pick up the seed once more. Paulo was grinning, his eyes fixed on Pablo's, and I saw that his antics were an expression of affection for his father. Pablo watched him benignly. When it was over, I set coffee and croissants on the table, and we sat down. Paulo broke off a piece of croissant with his thin fingers and pushed it into his mouth. 'Delicious,' he said to me.

Pablo said, 'How's that mother of yours?' and his foot bounced up and down.

'Not good, I'm afraid.' Paulo glanced at me and said, 'Can I talk in front of Dora?'

'I'm fine with it if you are,' I said, suddenly on edge, but also curious to learn about my rival. Pablo nodded.

Paulo took a breath, lining up his thoughts. 'She's been making horrible scenes. I watch her cry and swear, and I don't know what to do for her.' He began to tear the croissant into small pieces. 'She wasn't like this when I was younger. She's turned into someone I don't know. And I miss you, Papa.' His mouth trembled.

Pablo's face hardened. 'You're too old to miss me,' he said brusquely. He waited, and then said, 'I am sorry about your mother, but there's nothing I can do. I have my own problems.'

I felt a flare of anger. Paulo blinked a few times as though he'd been struck.

'How is school?' I asked, and Pablo looked at me, sensing the lack of complicity.

Paulo said, 'It's good, thanks. I got full marks in the last maths test. It's my favourite subject.' He looked at his father for approval.

Pablo crossed his arms. 'There's no point in being good at school. It serves no purpose.' Paulo's face went red, and he stared at his hands balled up in his lap. His father added, 'At San Rafael in Malaga, where my parents put me out of desperation, I failed in every subject. That hasn't stopped me from excelling.'

I could feel my anger building, but worked to contain it. 'What do you want to do when you leave school?' I asked Paulo.

He gave me a smile that lit his whole face. 'It's my dream to become a motorcycle racing driver.'

Pablo blew out a breath and glared at him. 'Please, give up this stupidity.'

'But it's my passion,' said Paulo. 'You're always telling me to find my passion in life and follow it.'

'That's enough. I don't want to hear about it,' said Pablo, clamping his lips together. 'Find something else to be good at.'

'I'm good at riding a motorcycle.' Paulo looked his father in the eye, his lips twitching, and I saw that he lacked neither courage nor a sense of humour.

'Try to do something else – but I know it won't amount to anything. How could it with a mother like yours?'

'Stop it, Pablo. Just stop. How can you speak to him like that?' I said coldly.

Paulo looked down. 'It doesn't matter. Really,' he said, and I gave his shoulder a squeeze. He leaned towards me, and I kept my hand there for an extra moment. But Pablo said, 'Don't coddle the boy. You'll make milksop of him.'

74

What I felt seemed intolerable. I wanted to get up and pace around the room. That poor boy! He had never got the things he needed from either parent. Suddenly, I understood why I felt such grief and affection for him. I, too, had needed things from my parents, and in the early days of their unhappiness, they hadn't been there for me.

Pablo was scowling at us both. It was a side to him I hadn't seen before, and I couldn't understand why he kept knocking Paulo down like a ninepin. Was it because he hated Olga? What about his child with Marie-Thérèse, did he treat her as harshly? Then I thought, *What if he behaves like that towards me?* and I felt very scared. But the next moment he gave me a warm look – there was no doubt that he loved me. I pushed my trepidation away and asked Paulo what he was learning in maths.

That afternoon, Jacqui walked into the Catalan, dazzling in an eighteenth-century dress she'd bought at a theatrical establishment – almost floor-length, with a narrow waist and full around the hips. Her long fingernails were painted the same shade of green as her eyes and I wondered how she managed them with the baby, whom they had named Aube, after the dawn. André was a few paces behind. They made a striking couple.

We rose to greet them. Pablo and André already knew each other, and I introduced Jacqui to Pablo. He took her hand and gave her an intoxicating look. 'Madame Breton! *Charmé.*'

I felt a twinge of jealousy and glanced at André. His face was grave, almost severe as he said, 'Please don't flirt with my wife, Pablo. I know you.'

Pablo held up both hands, smiling. 'I'll behave, I promise,' he said, and we sat down. But the exchange reminded me of his old ways, and I realised that I had settled into a state of comfortable ignorance. My mind went to Marie-Thérèse; it was the second time I had thought about her in one day. But there was something else bothering me, and after a few moments, I realised what it was. Pablo no longer stood at his window, watching, when I left his apartment. And then I felt truly uneasy.

Pablo was saying to Jacqui, 'So, you and Dora have known each other a long time?'

'Yes, since art school. She's my oldest friend,' said Jacqui, flipping her hair back.

'Jacqui was only sixteen when we met,' I said. 'She was a cheeky thing. For the first few weeks, she insisted that I called her Jacques.'

Jacqui shrugged. 'My birth was a great disappointment to my parents. They wanted a boy, not a girl, and so they called me "Jacques" instead of "Jacqueline". I clung to the name for years, even though it made me angry.'

'Speaking of your family, how's Huguette?' I asked.

'Still sad and displaced. I despair of her ever getting better.'

'You're a great support to her. She's lucky to have you,' said André, giving her a fond look.

Jacqui frowned. 'I try my best, but I'm too selfish to be as good as you say I am.'

A waiter came over with wine and bread rolls and took our order. 'How is Aube?' I asked when he'd gone.

'She's blooming,' said Jacqui, buttering a roll. 'But no one ever told me how boring motherhood is.'

André's brow lowered. 'How can you say that?'

Their eyes locked and Jacqui said, 'It's an endless cycle of feeding and laundry, and the worst of it is that I don't have time to paint.' She spoke in a rush, as though she'd been suppressing these thoughts for some time.

Pablo was looking from one to the other, his eyes gleaming. He was enjoying himself, and I saw that no help would come from him. So I said to André, 'What are you working on at the moment?'

He brightened. 'I'm planning to open an art gallery,' he said, and turned to Pablo. 'I'd be honoured if you would make a drawing as its emblem.'

'I'll think about it,' Pablo said pleasantly. 'What are you going to call it?'

'Gradiva,' said André. 'Each letter stands for a surrealist muse or artist, like Gisèle Prassinos and Alice Rahon. "D" is for Dora.'

'What an honour! Thank you!' I said, feeling my face grow warm with pleasure.

But Jacqui was glaring at André. 'It seems you have more admiration for Dora's photos than for my paintings,' she said, and my heart fell. 'In fact, you think less of me all round since Aube was born.'

André said, 'You're wrong—'

Jacqui put her hand up to silence him. 'After women give birth, their husbands only see them as mothers. A man forgets that the woman he fell in love with has other identities.' She kept her voice calm, though I knew she was churning with rage.

'That's not true,' said André quickly. 'Since Aube, I worship you even more.'

'That's exactly my point,' said Jacqui, and at the same time, Pablo said, 'Motherhood is a woman's highest calling.'

'Motherhood is beautiful, but we're so much more than that,' I said, angry with both men. The food arrived, creating a diversion, and from then on we stuck to safe topics: exhibitions, Pablo's work and art gossip.

After lunch, he returned to his studio to paint, and I walked part of the way home along the banks of the Seine. The sun made everything sparkle: the tugboats, the barges and the water, as though handfuls of tiny sequins had been scattered all over. I thought about Jacqui. She was like a creature hurling herself against bars, and I wished there was more I could do for her. Presently, I became aware of an uncomfortable pricking sensation at my back, as though someone's eyes were on me. I glanced behind me, but the street was empty.

I carried on my way, watching two old women walking slowly towards me pushing hand carts with tortoises in them. The uneasy feeling was still there. I looked back again and saw a short woman in a fur hat and coat, too warmly dressed for the weather, and the respectable figure of a man in a suit. There was no cause for concern. Yet I was not comfortable; the sense of being watched wouldn't leave me. Perhaps my imagination was getting the better of me? My thoughts flew helplessly to being stabbed or worse. This was the seedy underbelly of Paris coming to meet me. The hairs on my arms rose, and fear quickened my steps. At last, I saw a bus that stopped near my apartment, and boarded it with relief.

I felt unsettled for the rest of the day, too restless to develop the set of prints that was waiting in my darkroom. Pablo was coming for supper, and I made paella to please him, but burned it.

'Don't worry about it,' he said when I set the dish in front of him, apologising for its scorched appearance. I watched him delicately pick out the blackened bits.

'You can blame the cooker,' I said, and he laughed. It was a private joke – my cooker was usually given credit for any good dishes I made.

After that the meal passed off pleasantly, though Pablo was unusually abstracted, drumming his fingers on the table, and not seeming to hear when I spoke about my fear of being followed. At the end, I stood and wound my arms around his neck, saying throatily, 'What would you like to do tonight?' I was wearing stockings and suspenders, but no panties, and I put his hand up my skirt to show him.

'Very nice,' he said politely, removing his hand. He cleared his throat. '*Dorrra*, I can't stay. I have another engagement.' He got to his feet.

'Really? With whom?' I said, stunned. He always stayed over.

He was walking towards the front door, hat in hand. 'I have to see a dealer about a commission,' he said, half-turning back to me. There was something in his eyes I'd never seen before, a terrible, closed look, and I knew that he was lying.

'Do you take me for a fool?' I burst out. 'Where are you really going?'

He turned around fully and said, 'To see Marie-Thérèse.' I bit into my cigarette holder so hard that it shot upwards. He added, 'We talked about this at Lise's. You agreed, remember? And anyhow, I want to spend more time with my daughter.' His features were set, and his voice had an edge I'd never heard before.

'Does … does this mean Marie-Thérèse will always be part of our lives?' My voice was a mere thread.

'Yes, and the child too. Motherhood is beautiful. You said so yourself.'

He left, shutting the door loudly behind him.

The floor under me seemed to be falling and I sat down heavily on the sofa. *This can't be happening*, I thought. *This can't be happening*. The pain was so raw and shocking, I could hardly breathe. I clenched and unclenched my fists to try and calm myself, and my heart hammered against my ribcage. One of my legs began to tremble so badly that I rose from the sofa and walked to the window. In the darkness, the well-known shapes of rooftops and chimney pots were just visible, and lights were on in different apartments. I listened to the rumble of traffic, to the bells of the buses ringing out, and I tried to absorb the peace of my familiar, beloved surroundings, the embodiment of my creative life. But I couldn't stop my thoughts.

I knew I should leave Pablo now, to end my suffering. But cutting him out of my life would be like disembowelling myself; just as damaging as staying with him. A wave of terror passed through me – what would become of me? It seemed to release a deep and terrible darkness inside me. I tried to comfort myself with the thought that Marie-Thérèse was simply an old habit of Pablo's, that in time he would see I was his life's mate, not her. And his feelings towards Maya might sour, as with Paulo, so that she would cease to be another rival for his attention. But the pain was so intense, I couldn't stand it.

Pablo came home at midnight. I was nowhere near composed enough to face him and I had my pride. So I pretended to be asleep, my body turned away from him, my cheek cupped in my hand. I had no idea whether my performance was convincing or not, but he didn't try to rouse me. He undressed by the bed, letting his clothes fall in a heap on the floor. Then he climbed in beside me and, before long, his breathing fell into the deep, regular rhythm of sleep. I moved closer to him. I could feel the warmth of his body, yet he wasn't mine, and it was a whole new level of pain. I wept, stuffing the sheet in my mouth so I wouldn't disturb him. I wept until my hair was drenched with tears. Eventually, I sank into a terrible sleep, in which things started coming apart. Repulsive, dark, amorphous things that I had to pin down, but couldn't.

The next morning, I rose early and splashed cold water on my face. I put on a black Balenciaga suit and an Elsa Schiaparelli cloche hat – my work uniform – and made up my face. I drank two cups of black coffee and was out of the house before Pablo was awake, on my way to photograph Marie-Laure de Noailles. She and her husband, Charles, were art patrons who had long been at the centre of the Parisian avant-garde.

It was a glorious morning, cool and crisp, with deep, clear skies. The leaves were a welter of colours. Paris was at its most beautiful and here was I with this ugly turmoil going on inside me, in no fit state to work. I was fairly sure that I had landed the commission because I was Pablo's *maîtresse en titre*, or official mistress, and the de Noailles were curious about me. But it was also a chance to show what I could do and I didn't want to ruin it. Walking with the sun on my skin and a fresh breeze flowing around me was restorative, and by the time I reached their palatial townhouse at place des États-Unis, something inside me had strengthened and sharpened.

I entered beneath a vaulted porte cochère, and a pair of glass doors opened onto a grand entrance hall. A butler greeted me courteously and ushered me up a marble staircase lined with Goyas and Titians to the vicomtesse's comfortable, crowded quarters, which were filled with votive offerings, photographs of bullfighters, fetishes and mementos. Marie-Laure swept in and greeted me, her arms outstretched, eyes shining. 'Dora Maar! I've been looking forward to meeting you!' she exclaimed.

I returned her embrace, sensing that the key to gaining her respect was not to be intimidated by her, or by the splendour of her house.

She was a striking woman, with a long, narrow face framed by waves of wild black hair. She looked like Marie Antoinette, though she soon told me that she was half-Jewish, a millionaire banker's daughter, and a direct descendant of the Marquis de Sade.

'My maternal grandmother was the Marquis's great-grand-daughter,' she explained. 'She was the first French society woman to say the word "*merde*" in public.' Marie-Laure's eyes sparkled. Evidently, she had inherited her grandmother's pleasure in shocking people. But I was amused and liked her forthrightness.

I began to set up my apparatus and check the lighting, and we soon settled down to work. Marie-Laure was a fidget, a difficult subject. After half an hour, she wanted a break, and so we sat in armchairs in front of the fire. The butler brought coffee in a silver pot and a plate of small biscuits, lightly dusted with sugar. We sipped at our drinks in silence.

'I'm not much good at small talk. It bores me,' Marie-Laure said, at last. She took a biscuit and bit into it, brushing sugar from her lips. 'So, tell me. How old were you when you became yourself?'

I suspected this was a game, and something of a test, but there was no mistaking the warmth of her curiosity. 'I'd like a minute to think about it, if that's all right,' I said. 'In the meantime, please tell me how old you were?'

A pause, the hint of a frown. Then she looked me in the eye and said, 'I was twenty-seven. It was 1929. I walked into my husband's room and found him in bed with our gym teacher.'

I gasped, shocked by how fast she had divulged something so personal. Yet I knew what that pain felt like.

'You know, it's not amusing for a young wife to walk into her husband's room and find him in bed with another man,' she said, looking out of the window at the tree-filled square below. 'I was deeply in love with him.'

'I'm sorry,' I said.

'Ah, well. It was a bad time,' she said, turning back to me. 'But I discovered consolations, eventually.'

'Do you mind me asking what they were?'

'Not at all,' she said, smiling. 'For one thing, the revelation gave me a new sense of power. Until then, I was rather reticent. But afterwards, I began to talk and I haven't stopped since.' She took another mouthful of coffee. 'And all was not lost between Charles and me. We're still perfectly compatible – everywhere but in the bedroom.'

I wondered if I would ever be able to face Pablo's infidelity with such equanimity. I didn't think so, but perhaps I could learn from Marie-Laure. She was watching me so closely that I wondered if she knew about Marie-Thérèse.

'It's your turn to answer my question,' she said.

I was tempted to tell her that I became myself when I met Pablo, but held back because she was so indiscreet. 'I became myself when I changed my name,' I said, thinking about how much I had gained and lost since then. 'I was born Henriette Theodora Markovitch.'

'Dora Maar is the right name. Chic and revolutionary, just like you,' she said, setting her cup on the table. 'Shall we try a few last photographs?'

I took the shots knowing they would be the best of all, because now I understood her essence, the combination of toughness and vulnerability. And I wondered if I would become like her if I stayed with Pablo.

# Twelve

After the assignment, I went back to my apartment. I longed for Pablo, but he had gone to Marie-Thérèse. The waiting started again. I was heartsick and lethargic. I knew that I should develop Marie-Laure's prints, that work was my only outlet for this pain, but the effort was too much. Then David LaGrange rang and asked me to have dinner with him. He was a painter, a nice enough man.

I chewed at my fingernails and said, 'I can't say yes or no until dinner time. You see, if I make a date and then Pablo calls to say he is taking me to dinner, he'll be furious to learn I have other plans.'

Moments passed. Then David said quietly, 'I understand, Dora. Goodbye then.' He put the receiver down and did not phone again.

Hours later, I gathered the strength to go to my darkroom – oh, it was daunting! I got out the stop bath and began to mix chemicals; my hands were clumsy, as if I were wearing gloves. But I persisted and it gave a sense of normality to my life. I could feel the gravitational pull into that other world and, by the time the latent images swam up on paper, I was fully inside it, alive to its magic.

The prints were better than I'd hoped – and to think I had created them with nothing but light! It was a moment of grace, a realisation that even while I was falling apart, my work mattered after all. But a few hours later, feelings of sadness and utter loss dropped through me. I couldn't work any more, couldn't stop thinking about Marie-Thérèse. My mind began to conjure images of her making love to Pablo, poured over him like cream. What was she *like*? I wanted to know everything.

That evening, while Pablo was out, I searched his apartment for her letters but couldn't find any, though I knew they must exist. Frustrated, I looked through the stacks of paintings in his studio and found portrait after portrait of Marie-Thérèse. I had seen some of them before, but hadn't grasped their sheer number. He was obsessed and it made me sick. My stomach burned, and there was a sour taste in my mouth. He portrayed her as a voluptuous being, all curves and inviting arms. A painting of her sleeping caught my eye – it was so tender and dreamlike. Day seemed to dissolve into night, and mellow shadows folded themselves around her body. Then I heard a man clear his throat and Sabartés's voice said, 'Isn't she beautiful?'

I whipped around to face him, my cheeks flaming. I hadn't heard him come in. But despite the state I was in, I couldn't help asking, 'What's she like?'

'Marie-Thérèse?' he said, eyes gleaming. 'Oh, she's lovely. She inspires Pablo like no one else. He says the light falls just right on her.'

Needles of jealousy burrowed into my flesh and my shame burned deeper. 'Tell me more,' I said in a small voice, knowing I wouldn't like the answer.

Sabartés pushed his glasses up his nose and said, 'She has a wonderful laugh, she's very natural. Crazy about sport too, especially swimming and cycling. Pablo finds her refreshing.'

He went on singing her praises, each word a barb, designed to hurt as much as possible. But he also seemed genuinely fond of Marie-Thérèse, and I wondered if this was the reason he had no time for me.

Writing poetry gave me a little relief. Most of my efforts were incoherent but a few came close to expressing my feelings.

Let patience and silence
offer me their hand.
Let jealousy
Dangle its proud claws
And absence get its needles ready
to reach me at the first heartbeat of day.

I stuck the nib of my pen into the soft skin of my inner arm, over and over again. I did it out of curiosity, and also I wanted to desensitise myself to pain. By the time I had finished, there were several punctures, more dirty black than red because of the ink.

Pablo came home at eleven thirty, and I made no effort to hide them from him. His eyes turned sharp with disgust, but the next moment he grew loving and contrite. 'My poor darling, why get yourself worked up like this? Nothing's changed between us,' he said, kissing each cut, and then my throat and eyelids. Gentle, butterfly brushes that kindled a slow warmth in me. He undressed me like a child and we made love. He looked into my eyes and mouthed 'I love you,' and the sweetness and pain were unbearable. He had a quick orgasm that left me unsatisfied.

Afterwards I lay beside him while he slept and crushing disappointment set in. This relationship was not what I'd hoped it would be. I wondered if I'd ever really had him, if there was ever a time I meant something to him. Marie-Thérèse had cast doubt on every word and touch. I went over my memories, back and forth, fine-combing them, till my eyes watered. When sleep eventually came, it was an uneasy, vertiginous, Pablo-haunted darkness.

The next day, my cuts had crusted over, and Pablo took me to the Catalan for lunch – a peace offering. The air was cool and breezy, twining my dress around my legs. A gust of wind lifted an eddy of dust on the corner and dropped again, spent. Before long, that bristling feeling of being watched returned. I glanced over my shoulder a few times but saw nothing unusual – a beautiful girl hunched deep inside her coat, a bald man walking a poodle. Then a small, middle-aged woman with red hair and thin, tight lips crossed the street and walked up to us. Her face was freckled and crinkly, and she moved with short, stiff steps like a parade horse. She looked oddly familiar.

'Olga,' said Pablo, without surprise. 'What are you doing here?'

So this was Olga, his wife and Paulo's mother. It came to me in a rush that she looked familiar because she was the person who had followed me before. Chills ran through me.

She said, 'I thought it was time I met your girlfriend. Won't you introduce us?' She spoke aggressively, in a harsh Russian accent, and her brown eyes darted everywhere but never met mine.

'You know that's a bad idea,' Pablo said in the same expressionless tone.

Olga tossed her head, her mouth twisting. 'I think it's an *excellent* idea.'

Pablo took me by the elbow and began to steer me away.

'Don't think you'll be happy with him! He only belongs to his art!' Olga shouted at my retreating back. We didn't stop or turn around. 'You haven't seen the last of me!' she shrieked.

My skin broke into goosebumps and my mouth was dry. I was thankful for the firm pressure of Pablo's hand on my elbow, keeping me going. We reached the Catalan and were greeted at the door by M. Arnau.

'Señor Picasso, Señorita Maar! A pleasure to see you!' he exclaimed, shaking our hands. His normality, the bulk of him, was reassuring. He showed us to our table, saying, 'There's beef from Haute-Loire on the menu. Melts in the mouth like butter.'

We sat down and ordered the beef with frites and salad. M. Arnau left. I was so troubled by Olga, I wanted to cry. I couldn't stop wondering why she had followed us. What did she want from us? My eyes met Pablo's and I realised that my trepidation was also due to the coldness – indifference, almost – with which he treated her. I remembered how he had spoken of her to her own son. At times, he seemed like a different person, and it scared me. I squeezed my eyes shut. *Don't think about it now*. A waiter brought a bottle of red wine, and I began to drink steadily. 'Your wife frightens me,' I said.

Pablo took a small sip of wine; he preferred drinking Evian water. 'She's my estranged wife,' he said, sliding back in his chair and crossing his legs, seeming completely at ease.

'Is that all you have to say? Don't you care how I feel? Oh, you really are a heartless man!' I cried.

He stared at the ceiling for a moment, controlling his irritation, then said, 'Don't let Olga get to you. She's crazy but harmless.'

I looked at him, considering this. My fear of Olga stemmed from not being sure what she was capable of. But if Pablo dismissed her as his mad ex-wife, perhaps that's all she was. Perhaps she only wanted to spoil our happiness.

'Let's not spend lunch talking about her,' he said in a tone that closed the subject. We sat in prickly silence until a waiter brought our food. Pablo sliced into his meat and we both watched the juice bleed out onto the plate.

'What *do* you want to talk about?' I asked at last.

'Painting,' he said, forking a cube of beef into his mouth and chewing it vigorously. 'I've been thinking about my goals.'

'Tell me?' Anything was better than silence.

I watched his Adam's apple move as he swallowed. 'I want to wake people up!' he said. 'Shake them, make them aware of the world they live in. But to do that, I have to take them outside of it.'

'What do you mean?' I asked, swirling the wine around in my glass.

'Look, if you move an eye out of its socket and put it somewhere else on the face, it will register in a totally different way. People will be shocked into seeing it freshly.' He balled his hands up into fists. 'I want to turn the way we see things on its head! Force people to grasp that they're living in a world that's not reassuring, not what they think it is.'

'I understand,' I said, 'but be careful. If you go too far down that path, you might get into a chaotic state where nothing is recognisable.' I pushed around the pile of frites on my plate and put one in my mouth.

'I'll rely on you to pull me back,' he said and began to stroke my arm. 'You're the only person I can talk to like this, *mia Dorrra*. The only one who understands.'

It was a crumb of consolation, and I took it.

We went on like this for several weeks. The waiting for Pablo's call, which began as soon as I woke up. Fleeting moments of happiness when we were together, and a constant ache in me, like a churning void. How was I supposed to *live* like this? I thought again about leaving him, but here was the crux of it. He had opened the doors to a reality in which everything was heightened – more vivid, more enchanting – and he'd let me drink deeply. I was in thrall to what he could give me, and I kept hoping it would come back. Oh God,

I craved it like a drug user craves cocaine, and hope kept me by his side. I couldn't return to my previous existence.

A fortnight after meeting Olga, Paulo showed up with no warning at Pablo's apartment. There were dark circles under his eyes and my heart ached for him because now I knew exactly what he endured at home.

'Hello! It's nice to see you,' I said. 'Your father went to visit Paul Rosenberg.'

His face fell but he collected himself at once. 'That's all right. I'm happy to be with you.' I hugged him, feeling the thin bones of his shoulder blades through his shirt.

I had no idea how to entertain teenage boys but I was in the middle of developing some prints, using the bathroom as a temporary darkroom, and I offered to show him how to do it. He was good with his hands, a quick learner. 'This is great! It's halfway between art and science,' he said. Afterwards, over coffee, I asked if he would like to be a photographer.

'Photography is fun but my real love is speed. The wind in my hair, the feel of the curves.' He opened his hands on his lap. 'It's the only thing that makes me happy. I'm going to work with bikes or cars.' I remembered how Pablo had tried to crush this desire out of him, and once again, I felt a surge of grief and affection for the boy.

Paulo looked at me as if he was weighing up something, then said in a rush, 'I've been street racing down the Champs Elysées with my friends. We go late at night. It's so much fun.' I must have looked concerned, as he added, 'Don't tell my father.'

'I won't, but I wish you'd stop. You'll get hurt or hurt someone else.'

He shrugged but did not answer, and I understood that the thrill was addictive. Anxiety tugged at my belly.

As he left, he said, 'I wish I could be with you more. I think I'd be better,' and I put an arm around him.

'Come any time you like,' I said, and meant it. His company did me good too. I thought that one day I would like to have a son like Paulo, and I vowed that my child would not be damaged as he and I had been.

On a rainy evening at the beginning of October, Pablo came to my studio. 'Hola! How are you?' he said, bringing from behind his back a small painting of me, inscribed with the words *made with love*. In it, the blackness of my hair glistened with blues and greens, the contours of my face were rounded and tender, my eyes sparkled.

Tears filled my eyes. 'It's beautiful. How can I thank you?' I said.

'I don't need thanks. I'm just glad you like it,' he said, carrying it into the living room and setting it on the mantelpiece. He stood with his arms hanging by his sides. 'Dora, I'm tired. I want the warm glow of being close to you.'

He lay down on the rug in front of the fire, gesturing for me to join him. He wrapped his arms around me, so that I couldn't tell where he ended and I began; my edges blissfully blurred into his. There was silence, except for the hiss and spit of the flames. I gazed into the landscape of molten craters at their centre, hoping that our old magic had returned.

At last Pablo said, 'I have news. Ambroise Vollard has lent me his house in Le Tremblay-sur-Mauldre.'

'Wonderful!' I said. Vollard was one of Paris's leading art dealers. He had made Cézanne famous and was responsible for the first Van Gogh retrospective, but his boldest move had been to give Pablo his first show at the age of nineteen, beginning a lasting relationship. I held Pablo tighter, adding, 'What fun it will be as a country retreat!'

We had lost Boisgeloup to Olga not long after I'd visited Pablo there, so now I imagined the parties we would throw at Le Tremblay, full of the most talented artists and writers in Paris. And I thought of our rapturous time alone after the guests had left.

'I've moved Marie-Thérèse there with Maya,' Pablo said.

I pushed him away, I couldn't speak. He had created a home for them, a rural idyll, without even telling me until it was a fait accompli. I imagined the plans, the happy discussions he and Marie-Thérèse must have shared.

'I'm going to spend weekends with them,' Pablo said. A log tumbled, sending up a shower of fine sparks. 'Isn't it easier if you're in different places? Paris and the weekdays will be yours.' He kissed me on the cheek and began to list the paintings he would take to Le Tremblay, seeming not to notice my silence.

Afterwards, I sat for a long time gazing into the dying fire, stunned by the damage people do to each other, the heedlessness with which Pablo kept shattering my life. Eventually, numbness crept into my soul. I think it was the blessed anaesthesia the body produces after it has received a deadly wound. I fell into a restless sleep on the sofa and, when I woke, the blunted feeling was still there. It lasted for several days. I welcomed it because it cushioned me, allowing me to go through the motions of being with Pablo without making a scene. But when Marcel drove him to Le Tremblay that Friday afternoon, my insensibility gave way to a fury and pain so deep I thought my heart would explode. I couldn't sleep, couldn't eat, nor sit still. I phoned my parents in tears. We had become distant because they refused to have anything to do with Pablo, and I hadn't wanted them to be right about him, convinced I could handle the relationship. But now I was desperate.

'I am sorry you are suffering,' said Maman. 'Truly I am. But what did you expect getting mixed up with Picasso?' I pictured her pressing her lips together, my father shaking his head. I said goodbye, feeling let down and humiliated. My head was roaring. I dialled Lise's number but the phone rang and rang. Next, I tried Jacqui. She took a long time to answer, and when she did, I could hear a thin wailing in the background.

'Dora!' she said, sounding surprised. We hadn't seen each other for some time because she was as consumed by domesticity as I was by Pablo.

'Why is Aube crying like that?' I asked.

She sighed. 'The poor thing caught a tummy bug. I'm up to my elbows in shit and vomit.'

I thought about our time at art school and how full of promise we had been, and a hole opened up in me.

The baby's crying grew louder, and Jacqui said, 'Look, sweetheart, it's wonderful to hear your voice. But can we talk another time?'

'Yes, of course. I understand.'

I replaced the receiver in its cradle, wondering who else I could turn to. I thought of Nusch, but she was too close to Pablo. There was no one else, and the chill of loneliness crept in.

I spent the weekend walking around aimlessly. There were lots of people on the streets but I hardly noticed them. The impersonal beauty of the city, the lights, made me feel worse than ever.

Pablo came back on Monday morning, happy and sated. He found me with a puffy face and red-rimmed eyes. 'Did you have a nice time?' I asked in a voice blank with distress.

He smiled and said, 'Yes, it was very pleasant,' and I realised that nothing I said or did could break the cycle of him leaving me for her. Just like that, anger broke out, filling my head with red mist. 'Listen to me, Pablo. *Listen* to me.' My voice rose. 'I can't bear this. I don't know what to *do*. You must give her up. I can't bear it, do you hear?'

He put up a hand. 'That's enough. We're playing out one of the oldest scenes in the book, and I'm not interested.'

'Dear God, you never listen. You're destroying me!' I said.

Pablo's eyes looked small. 'Dora, you agreed to this. You knew it was going to happen. Why all this vitriol now?' He turned away and went over to the windows, jingling loose coins in his pocket.

I felt a violent rage. I wanted to hit him again and again. I clenched my fists and yelled, 'You're a monster!' My behaviour alarmed me, my rising hysteria. It alarmed me that I could lose control so easily.

I watched Pablo's back. I heard, or thought I heard, the exasperated intake of his breath. Could this really be love? I was like an addict, always wanting more, no matter how bad he was for me. To get his attention, I grabbed his sculpture, *Head of a Woman*, whose features were based on Marie-Thérèse, and dashed it to the ground. It landed with an ugly crack that made Pablo spin around. He inhaled sharply and I saw that part of the nose had broken off. A chilled, sick feeling gripped me. I braced myself for his fit of rage, or for that other kind of anger – cold, full of wrath – that was more dangerous than his outbursts.

He picked up the sculpture, turning it over and over, assessing the damage. 'Luckily, the break is repairable,' he said, with a calmness that surprised me. But I couldn't get it out of my head that I might have destroyed one of his works of genius, and it shocked me out of my temper like a slap in the face. I cried inconsolably.

'Your expression is marvellous,' Pablo said. He picked up a pencil and began to draw me, tears pouring down my face. 'You look tortured,' he added, with a smile.

'I'm not tortured,' I said, wiping at my eyes. 'I am hurt.'

He gave me a measuring look. 'You were a sorceress when I met you. Now you're a martyr. I hope you know how unattractive it is.'

I stared at him in silence, cut to the quick, then glanced at the sketch. He had drawn me with enormous, tearful eyes, ample breasts, birds' wings, and strong claws perched on a rock. That was how he saw me, a maleficent harpy, the claws representing not only my sharpness, but my moody and jealous nature. It plunged me into new depths of misery.

The next Friday he packed a small bag and left for Le Tremblay again. I went to bed and wept and mulled over the mess my life was in, until I couldn't stand being inside my head any longer. Then I remembered that the de Noailles had invited us to a party that night.

'Well,' I said aloud, and sat upright. I blew my nose. I was still an artist in my own right, I was not just Pablo's counterpart. And so I got out of bed and washed my face. I dabbed Chanel N° 5 onto my pulse points and put on a long, black Chanel dress, red lipstick and an ivory necklace, gloriously engraved by Pablo with cavorting minotaurs and maenads. I left the apartment quickly, before there was time to change my mind.

It was a windy night. A young couple sat on a bench under the chestnut trees with their arms around each other, talking and laughing, while shifting shadows played over them. I hailed a taxi and, as it pulled away, I could have sworn I caught a glimpse of Olga standing on the pavement, like a sad ghost. I felt a moment's exasperation, followed by unease. But once I reached the de Noailles' house, all thought was subsumed by the pounding of my heart. The glass doors opened, and I was shown to a vast ballroom filled with people.

I was aware of Corinthian columns and crystal chandeliers, rococo gilt and huge mirrors, paintings by Rubens, Manet, Delacroix, and a portrait of Marie-Laure by Pablo. Tables glittered with Fabergé eggs and other precious *objets*. I had hoped that Lise would be here but I couldn't see her in the crowd. There were a few familiar faces: Alberto Giacometti, Jean Cocteau with his lover, Marcel Khill, and Ambroise Vollard, whom I had to thank for Pablo's weekend idylls: a hulking figure with a high, domed forehead and a bulldog-like nose. His eyes met mine and immediately slid away. Luckily, Marie-Laure saw me and came over with a beautiful young man on her arm, whom she introduced as Igor Markevitch.

'Igor is a composer and conductor. If you haven't heard his work, you should,' she said. 'He's very gifted.'

They exchanged a charged look, and I wondered if he was one of the consolations she had mentioned to me. She was radiantly happy. But Igor had a certain look, hard to describe, that made me fear he was a man who preferred men. Evidently she had a knack for choosing them, and I felt a pang for her. She called to a waiter for a glass of champagne for me and said, 'What a day I've had!'

'What happened?' I asked.

'I went to Jeanne Paquin's funeral, but it turned into a farce.' She shook her head.

'How so?'

'There was a terrible mix-up. Wreaths that were meant for an old man's coffin ended up on Jeanne's. No one would have noticed if they hadn't said "To our adored uncle".'

'God!' said Igor, his eyes widening. 'My God.'

Marie-Laure stroked his arm. 'The mourners went up to pay their respects, pretending not to notice. It was like something from a play.'

We laughed, Marie-Laure loudest of all. She went off to talk to her other guests, taking Igor with her, and I wandered around, sipping at my champagne and admiring the paintings. I was beginning to enjoy myself. Charles de Noailles stopped me and kissed my hand with exquisite courtesy, saying, 'I love your photographs of my wife. You captured a fragility in her that few people see.'

Before I could answer, I heard a cry of 'Dora, there you are!' and turned around to see Jean Cocteau bearing down on me. Charles slipped away.

Jean had an angular face, and his blue eyes were sparkling yet steely. His hair grew in all directions, but had been brushed into a kind of halo above his forehead. 'How nice to see you!' he exclaimed, kissing me on both cheeks. 'Have you met Marcel?'

Marcel – slender, with beautiful dark eyes – stepped forwards. 'It's a pleasure,' he said, in a low, deep voice.

'How glorious you look!' Jean said to me. 'The epitome of chic.' I thanked him, feeling my cheeks grow warm, and he said, 'I didn't know you knew the de Noailles.'

'I only met Marie-Laure recently. Have you known her long?' I said.

'We were teenage sweethearts,' he said, and a loaded look passed between him and Marcel.

'Really?' I was surprised.

'Yes, really.' He waved a long-fingered hand in the air. 'I love her to pieces, though she can be spoiled and childish.'

I shifted uncomfortably. 'That may be true, but I like her very much. She's brave and open-handed. Think of all the new ideas and work that wouldn't get made without her.'

A waiter came up and refilled our glasses, and Jean began telling us about his recent trip to Rome, during which a group of American ladies had kissed the Pope's hand so fervently that his white gloves turned red from their lipstick.

'And that wasn't the only drama,' he said, rolling his eyes. 'The Pope decided that his dignitaries' trains should be cut short. This annoyed a roguish old cardinal so much that he sewed the bits from the other cardinals' trains onto his own.' And Jean imitated the prelate at his sewing machine, bungling the task so badly that his train wobbled the whole way up the aisle of St Peter's, until Marcel and I were helpless with laughter.

A man came up, tall and long-limbed, with cropped dark hair and brown eyes. He was about the same age as me.

'Jean, Marcel! How good to see you,' he said cordially. 'Won't you introduce me to your friend?'

'Dora Maar, this is Alexandre Laval. Alexandre, meet Dora,' said Jean, his eyes gleaming.

'*Enchanté*,' said Alexandre, raising my hand to his lips. 'I've admired your work for a long time.'

'Are you an artist too?' I asked, as Marcel and Jean drifted away.

'No, I'm not creative enough. I'm just a surgeon with a passion for collecting,' Alexandre said self-deprecatingly. 'Years ago, I tried to buy your portrait of Leonor Fini, but the bidding shot out of control.' I had photographed Leonor with the same defiant stare as Manet's *Olympia*, but with runs in her stockings and a kitten nestled between her thighs. 'It's a striking image. You're like an alchemist,' Alexandre added, and his eyes roamed over my face.

We carried on talking, and I soaked up every bit of praise and attention, realising how parched I had been. I stood up straighter, feeling confident and powerful. And then it came to me that I couldn't go on with such a meagre share of Pablo's attention. I deserved more than the scraps he threw my way. I must confront him and break it off. And I would do it now, while the lovely glow of self-belief lasted.

'I must go. Forgive me,' I said to Alexandre abruptly.

'Was it something I said?' he asked, bemused, and I said, 'No, no, please don't think that. It's just me.'

Outside, the wind was crisp against my face. There was a taxi rank on the other side of the street with a solitary driver dozing on his wheel. I woke him up and asked him to take me to Le Tremblay. There was little traffic. As we sped along the open road, the dim shapes of fields and trees flashed past, and I thought about the showdown I was about to have. I would tell Pablo that I could not carry on, that he must decide between me and Marie-Thérèse once and for all. And even if the worst happened and he chose her, at least I would be free. Adrenalin raced through me and I felt exhilarated. When we arrived, I got out of the car, slamming the door behind me.

Vollard's house was rustic and charming, with stone walls mellowed by age and a big garden. The windows were shuttered, yet behind them I knew that Pablo was sleeping with Marie-Thérèse and the little girl. A picture of them together appeared in my head and reality hit me. My breath went, as though someone had rammed me in the chest, and I steadied myself against the wall.

I began to weep – great tearing sobs that hurt my chest. All I knew was that I could not live without him. I wept from the pain of not being able to see the break-up through, but also because I had lost the last shreds of my dignity. I had become pitiable and it undid me.

I stumbled back to the taxi, and we began the drive to Paris. It must have seemed very strange. A young woman in an evening gown weeping in the back of a taxi, driving through the country-side. It was almost dawn. The trees were fiery; they looked as if they were about to explode into the sunrise.

The driver craned his neck to glance at me and said, 'Please don't cry. It makes me think of when my wife died.' He was quite old, but his eyes were gentle, set in a web of wrinkles. We stopped in Versailles for coffee, and he told me about his wife, Hélène.

'She was always there for me, always ready to listen. Her smile filled my life with the brightest happiness.' He passed a handker-chief over his eyes and got up to buy me an almond croissant. Returning to the table, he said, 'Eat it all. It will make you feel better.' I did and he was right. I wondered if I should be more like his wife, more ready to listen to Pablo and accept his needs.

After that night, I decided to exercise my will and call a truce. My ugly, degrading scenes were doing no one any good; they only drove Pablo further away. If I wanted to keep him, I would have to bear his visits to Marie-Thérèse. In calmer moments, I saw that he was set apart from other men; a genius who bypassed the rules in his human relationships as completely as he did in his art. I reminded myself that supporting his art was the most important thing I could ever do for him. Besides, although he left me, he always came back. For five days out of seven, he was mine.

When Pablo returned from Le Tremblay, I greeted him bathed, perfumed and made up. I was rewarded with a loving smile; he took me in his arms.

'Sorry,' I murmured into his neck. 'I'm sorry. Don't take my scenes seriously. I'll be better. No more whining, no more shouting. That's finished now.'

He drew me onto the bed and said, 'I am happy to hear it, *Dorrra*, especially after the weekend I've had.'

'What happened?'

'Maya had an earache; she wouldn't stop screaming. I couldn't hear myself think, let alone work. It's good to come home to you and peace.'

I sighed with relief and gladness. Pablo began to make love to me, and I felt a rip of jealousy because he'd just been with Marie-Thérèse, but it was quickly superseded by pleasure. My body eased into a comfortable warmth, passion overtaking us both, like night over the city.

Afterwards we lay in each other's arms. Pablo stroked my hair. I felt moved and tender, and an idea began to form in my mind. He might be irritated with Maya now, but he adored her, painting whimsical portraits of her with her toys – a doll, a boat, a little horse. Perhaps I could make him mine again by giving him a baby? If I fell pregnant, he would return to me, more loving, more considerate, more dependent than ever.

# Thirteen

A s Pablo's fame grew, more and more people turned up in the mornings, wanting to see him. Some talked with passion about 'the primitive coming to life' in his pictures, while others simply cried, 'Leonardesque! Leonardesque!'

Pablo still spent weekends at Le Tremblay, but we were close during the week. Even when he was working, he would come out at intervals to smoke a cigarette and talk to me.

'It was a strange session,' he said, on an afternoon of low, grey skies. 'Bristles from my brush got embedded in my painting.'

'Oh!' I said, 'Did you manage to get them out?'

He drew in smoke and exhaled slowly. 'No, but I painted a bird's nest, so it turned out well.' He gave a sigh and added, 'You know, chance plays a very small part in my work. I must think and go on thinking. It's exhausting.'

Meanwhile, unbeknown to Pablo, I was having my own encounters with chance. My monthlies continued to arrive in their usual irregular fashion. I told myself not to lose hope, it was still early days, but each time I saw the tell-tale spots of blood in my underwear, pangs of grief went through me.

One morning in late October, while he was out at a meeting, I decided to have another look at his work. Pale sunlight poured through the windows, falling onto the brushes strewn over the floor, the squeezed and contorted tubes of paint, and a new portrait of Marie-Thérèse on his easel. I drew in my breath. Mentally, I had just about accepted that he would always paint her, but seeing this picture gave me tremendous pain. Moving closer, I realised she was wearing a white silk blouse that belonged to me, a gift from Pablo. Pain sank its hooks deeper.

I wanted to ask him to explain himself but a cold thought stopped me. Perhaps it was better not to draw attention to the portrait? He was contrary enough that my distress might spur him to paint others like it. So I said nothing and found myself plunged into the draining battle of trying not to let my feelings show. But the effort was wasted because, within a week, Pablo had begun a new set of paintings of Marie-Thérèse and me, sometimes in identical poses, often together. And then, days later, I took a cup of coffee to him in the studio and saw he had started a portrait that combined our features in a single form: a black-haired woman with my heavy jaw but with Marie-Thérèse's bland, cheerful expression and her breasts bulging out. It was too much.

'Why do you have to blend us into one being?' I cried.

Pablo was stirring his brushes in turpentine to clean them. His gaze flicked up to meet mine, then returned to his task. 'I'm digging deep into my mind and painting the images I find there,' he said.

I put the coffee on the table, my hands shaking so badly that half of it sloshed into the saucer. 'But you're hurting me.'

He shrugged. 'You should know that everything has its cost. Anything worthwhile – art, inspiration – has an underside of pain.'

'I've often thought you were evil and now I know it!' I said.

He was wiping the bristles against the side of the bowl; his eyes looked small. 'And you're an angel?' he said mockingly. 'Maybe so, but a fallen one.'

I turned away, my eyes filling with tears, and he did not try to comfort me but disappeared from the room. He soon came back, grinning, with a large rectangular box tied with green ribbon. I opened it assuming it was a peace offering. Under layers of tissue paper was a green-and-white striped dress with a rounded collar and puffed sleeves. Not my usual style but it was pretty. 'How lovely!' I exclaimed.

I lifted it from the box, shaking out the folds of fabric, and saw it was much too big for me. Pablo was examining my face, his eyes glinting. My mind flew to all the times he had amalgamated Marie-Thérèse and me in his art, and clarity dawned. His mistake was intentional – the dress was for her, not me. It was another deliberate reminder that I was not the sole recipient of his affections, and an emotion that was like a wail or a shriek filled me.

'Why do you keep doing this?' I cried.

Pablo raised his brows. 'Doing what?'

'Any fool can see the dress is for Marie-Thérèse! Isn't it enough that I tolerate another woman in your life? Must you rub my nose in it?'

He took a deep breath and let it out slowly. 'Don't make this something it's not, Dora. The shop sent the wrong size. I'll phone them tomorrow and put it right.'

I was about to ask if he'd bought the dress for Marie-Thérèse in my size, but the anger suddenly left his face, and he said, 'Let's drop this silliness. We'll have dinner at the Catalan. I have good news for you.'

'I'm too upset.'

He looked at me steadily, his eyebrows raised in reproach. 'I thought you'd stopped getting moody about Marie-Thérèse. Don't start again. It's tedious.' He spoke pleasantly but with a flinty undertone, and I saw that it was useless to argue with him. Sensing my surrender, he held out his arms. I walked into them, exhausted by the rollercoaster of loving him.

We walked the short distance to the Catalan hand in hand. The night was stingingly cold; our breath made globules of steam. Arriving was a relief – a coal stove burned at either end of the room, and enticing smells filled the air. We sat down and I ordered a glass of red wine. It came at once and I drank quickly, feeling its warmth spread through me, holding me up. We spoke little until our salted cod croquettes and patatas bravas arrived.

'I got a letter from my mother,' Pablo said, taking a mouthful of potato.

'Oh?'

He set down his fork. 'Franco's men burned down a convent, yards from her apartment. Her eyes are still running from the smoke, the rooms reek of it. She can't get the nuns' cries out of her head.'

My hand went to my mouth. 'So things are getting worse?'

He grimaced. 'There are terrible street battles, children caught in the crossfire, dead and wounded everywhere.'

100

It seemed that Pablo knew more than the newspapers because of his mother, and I fell silent, trying to digest this new horror. But there was a sense of unreality, as if my mind could not take it in.

'Mamá might be killed. My family might be killed,' he said in a low, appalled voice. 'You know what scares me even more than the fighting?' I shook my head. 'Franco's air force. Just think what will happen if he decides to attack Barcelona from the air.'

I imagined being trapped indoors, listening to the humming, rumbling and pounding of enemy planes coming closer. And this felt real, unbearably so. To distract us both, I said, 'What was the good news you wanted to tell me?'

He gave a faint smile. 'Well, you know I'm selling some of my pictures to support the relief efforts?'

I nodded, thinking about his generosity and his sadism; the staggering contradictions of him.

'The Spanish government found out about my help.'

'And?'

He paused again, drawing out the moment. 'They've appointed me director of the Prado in Madrid!'

I felt a rush of love for him. It absorbed some of my hurt. 'How marvellous!' I said, squeezing his hand. 'It's a huge accolade.'

He took the letter from his pocket and gave it to me to read. 'My father took me there as a child to see the great masters. And now all those artists belong to me,' he said, beaming.

This reminded me of my own dreams, and how I was allowing them to be swallowed up by Pablo. These days, I wanted him more than fame. The loss of my ambitions made me sad, but I pushed the feeling away and ordered champagne. M. Arnau brought it to the table, opening and pouring it without spilling a drop. The light in the room was the same colour as the liquid in our glasses. I raised my glass to Pablo, and the other diners in the restaurant clapped, not knowing what the occasion was, but realising that it was momentous.

Afterwards, we went to meet Paul and Nusch for a celebratory drink at the Café de Flore. It was noisy and crowded, and the air was heavy with smoke. M. Boubal, the proprietor, greeted us with his usual Gauloise between his fingers. Pablo said good evening to the blonde and genial Madame Boubal, sitting inside her glass cashier's booth. The Éluards were already settled at a table by the window, and we went to join them.

'Hola!' said Pablo, taking Nusch by the shoulders and kissing her on both cheeks. 'Look at you. You're a living painting by Degas.' She was wearing a fur-collared coat, from which her neck rose, white and slender, making her look more ethereally beautiful than ever.

'How are *you*, my friend?' Paul asked him. 'You must be on top of the world!' M. Boubal came over with Pablo's Evian and a magnum of Dom Pérignon, and filled our glasses. We thanked him and Paul raised his glass. 'To you!' he said. 'Congratulations on your latest magnificent achievement! You're unstoppable – a force of nature!'

'Congratulations!'

'*La santé!*'

It seemed as though Pablo gently filled as he listened to the adulation. Just then, Sabartés arrived with Paulo and Elft. Paulo hugged me and said, 'I'm happy to see you,' but Sabartés scarcely acknowledged me. Pablo handed them each a glass of champagne and Sabartés raised his, saying: 'Bravo, my friend! I couldn't be prouder of you.' He sat down and spoke little after that. But he never stopped watching Pablo like a mother hen, and his eyes hardened whenever they fell on me.

Paulo drank his champagne down like water and went to join a game of dice being played in the corner. The dog went from table to table, begging for scraps, while steadfastly ignoring his master's reproving glances.

We spoke of the situation in Europe, of the coalition that had just been formed between Italy and Germany – the Rome–Berlin Axis.

'It cements the fascists and the Nazis,' said Pablo, 'and we know how that will end.'

'Terrifying,' I said, and my stomach knotted up.

The others looked tense and gloomy, and I saw what a bad effect the current state of affairs was having on us all. I watched Paulo across the room – his head bent over the dice table, downing glass after glass of beer – and a small shudder went through me. Then Sabartés excused himself to go and greet some Spanish friends who had just come in.

'Tell me about Sabartés. What's his story?' I asked Paul quietly, leaving Pablo and Nusch to talk.

For a moment, Paul hesitated. 'I'm sure you know that when you met Pablo, he was going through the worst crisis of his life,' he said. 'He was devastated by his broken marriage and couldn't paint. So he wrote to Sabartés, his childhood friend, and asked if he would move to Paris to take care of him.'

I was hurt and indignant that Pablo hadn't told me this himself. If he had, it would have reassured me that Sabartés's treatment of me wasn't personal; he was simply protective of his friend. I steadied myself by drinking the rest of my champagne.

'What was Sabartés's life like, that he could drop everything and go?' I asked, dabbing at my lips.

'In his quiet way, Sabartés was as desperate as Pablo,' said Paul. 'He had failed to make it as a writer in South America. He'd just come home to Barcelona with his wife and their handicapped child.' He offered me a cigarette and took one himself. He lit them both, blowing out the match. 'The marriage had always been unhappy. Having the child made him even more desperate for a way out.'

'I see,' I mused. 'So Pablo gave him that chance.'

Paul let smoke stream slowly from his nostrils. 'Yes. From the day Sabartés left, the course of his life has followed Pablo's.'

'But what about Sabartés's family?' I burst out. 'They must have suffered horribly being abandoned like that. How could he have done it? How could Pablo have let him?'

'It was wrong,' said Paul, shaking his head. 'Well, look, Dora. Pablo is Pablo. Sabartés does send them money.'

'It's not the same. That poor child,' I said, grinding out my cigarette. But upset as I was, I finally understood Sabartés's hostility towards me. Pablo was the centre of his existence; Sabartés had nothing else. And it was that, even more than his fondness for Marie-Thérèse, that made him so possessive of Pablo, so jealous of anyone who got close to him.

At the end of the evening, we went to fetch Paulo from his dice game. 'Time to go, mon ami,' said Pablo but Paulo scarcely looked up. Pablo prodded him in the back.

'I don't want to leave,' Paulo mumbled.

The man sitting next to him – much older, stocky, with almost no neck – put an arm around his shoulders. 'It's a pity, kid. You were playing a fine game,' he said. 'But you know where to find us next time.'

Pablo shot him a filthy stare and pulled Paulo to his feet, so that the man's arm fell abruptly from the boy's shoulders. He repeated, 'Time to go. Get your jacket. Sabartés will see you to your mother's.'

'Can't I stay with you?' Paulo asked, and I saw the yearning on his face.

I said, 'Of course you can,' but Pablo cut across me: 'No, not tonight.' His tone of voice did not permit any argument, and so Paulo reluctantly left with Sabartés.

Pablo and I walked home under a star-sprinkled sky. He held me close, saying how much he loved me, but I was worried about his son and tried to talk about it. Pablo held up a hand. 'I don't want to think about him. It disturbs my work.'

I envied Pablo's single-mindedness, but also wished that for once he would put his son first.

For several days afterwards, Pablo was loving and attentive, buoyed up by the directorship, and making amends for the cruelty of the dress. He was enormously generous. He gave me a black Balenciaga suit in exactly the right size, and a small red velvet box. I opened it and saw a familiar-looking ruby ring set in gold and agate. I was confused, but then comprehension dawned, filling me with happiness.

'It's Lise's ring!' I exclaimed. 'I've loved it since I saw her wearing it in San Tropez! How did you know?'

Pablo gave me a mischievous look and said, 'It was your eyes. They lit up like lanterns every time they fell on it.' He took it out of the box and slipped it gently onto the ring finger of my right hand. It fitted perfectly.

'How did you get her to part with it? It's one of her most treasured possessions,' I said, turning my hand this way and that to admire the stone.

'I offered her one of my watercolours for it,' he said, and a shadow passed over his face. But he dismissed it with a marvellous smile, adding, 'It worked like a charm.'

I smiled at him. Gently, he tucked a lock of hair behind my ear. '*Dorrra*, my little love, my heart's desire. It does me good to see you like this.'

A knock on the door. A messenger boy stood on the threshold, with a thick cream envelope addressed to Pablo. It was from Luis Araquistáin, the Spanish ambassador to France, asking him to paint a large mural for the Spanish Pavilion at the Paris World's Fair, which was dedicated to Art and Technology in Modern Life. Pablo read aloud, 'A modern pavilion will show the world that the government, not Franco's nationalists, represent the Spanish people. And who more fitting to create the centrepiece than you?'

'I'm so proud of you!' I said.

'So you think I should accept?' he said, his eyes glowing.

'Of course!'

'I'll make some sketches tonight. I can already see it as an allegorical composition.'

Before bed, I went to his studio to see the drawings. To my disappointment they were flat and uninspired – a group of uniformed soldiers in repose, a raised arm holding a hammer and sickle.

'I can't decide what direction it should take,' he said, frowning.

'It will come,' I reassured him.

But as weeks passed, he procrastinated and worked on other paintings, apparently not having any clearer idea for it. Germany and Italy recognised Franco as head of Spain's government, which made it even harder for him to find focus for the commission. And so the year ended on an ominous note.

1937

# One

PABLO RAN OUT OF space at rue La Boétie and in the new year, I found him a huge, abandoned loft at 7 rue des Grands-Augustins. It was a majestic building made of yellow-beige stone, separated from the street by an arched gateway and a cobbled courtyard. The interior was a perfect blend of grandeur and mystery, with high windows, a hidden staircase, eerie corridors and cosy nooks that offset the strangeness.

He soon filled it with his possessions, setting up a studio for painting and one for sculpture, and installing his own press and engraving equipment. His painting studio was enormous – fourteen metres long and eight metres wide – with beautiful light. His bedroom and bathroom were in the attic, and comfort was basic, but I insisted on hiring builders to install central heating and hot water, and so he had the pleasure of a hot bath every morning. I was still a sorceress, still had my powers.

'Look here,' he would say, switching on a tap and putting his finger under the jet of water until it grew warm. 'Isn't it amazing?' And he would turn to beam at me.

Apart from worry about his family, and his ongoing block about the Spanish government's commission, he seemed content. We spent most weeknights together but he still wouldn't let me go to his apartment without an invitation. I would wait impatiently for his summons or for him to turn up at my place unannounced, while he disappeared into work and the rest of his life. It was galling, but he held firm, and I was forced to submit.

Winter slowly melted into spring so that, one morning in late April, I went out to buy croissants in my shirtsleeves. It was a beautiful day. Cherry trees were exploding into clouds of pink and white blossom, window boxes blazed with colour, the sky was as blue as the ocean. I stopped on the way to pick up a copy of *L'Humanité*, the Communist newspaper.

The headline read: A THOUSAND INCENDIARY BOMBS DROPPED BY HITLER AND MUSSOLINI PLANES! On the front page was a photograph of sobbing Basque soldiers collecting the charred bodies of women and children, amid ruined buildings. My skin pimpled and a sound escaped my lips. I looked at the picture more closely, at the blackened corpses, the soldiers' features distorted by horror and grief, and still my mind struggled to take it in. I began to read the article:

Yesterday, Monday 26 April 1937, the small Basque town of Guernica was bombed by German and Italian air forces at the request of General Francisco Franco.

It happened at four o'clock in the afternoon on a market day, and the people were gathered outside when the church bell rang the alarm for approaching aeroplanes. Five minutes later a single German bomber appeared, circled over the town at low altitude, and then dropped six heavy bombs. It was followed by a second bomber and, a quarter of an hour later, by three more. Houses collapsed until the streets became long heaps of red impenetrable debris. Those who managed to survive were consumed by the flames or asphyxiated by the lack of oxygen. The horrific attack continued until 7.45, levelling the town centre, killing 1,654, and wounding 889.

I crumpled up the newspaper, unable to read any more. I felt each death as a physical pain deep in my chest. An appalling sense of helplessness came over me and I made my way home, sobbing. By the time I walked through the door, my face was a mess of tears and snot.

Pablo was sitting at the kitchen table, sketching, a cigarette in his left hand. The room was shot with grains of sunlight.

'Let's have breakfast,' he said without glancing up. When I didn't answer, he looked at me and asked, 'What's wrong?'

I showed him the article. His face was expressionless as he read it, which upset me even more. He handed back the paper. I waved it under his nose, crying: 'Don't you have anything to say?'

He opened his mouth and breathed out a cloud of smoke, which blurred and vanished, spectral in the bright light. Finally he said, 'It's a terrible crime against humanity, of course it is. But what can we do about it?'

I stared at him in disbelief and said, 'I'm going back to my political groups! We'll sign petitions, we'll march, we'll shout. But *you* have to do something too!' My voice rose. 'Did you know there are rumours that you don't support the republican government?'

Pablo's eyes went small. 'How can that be?'

'You haven't taken a public stand, so they think you're a fascist sympathiser!' I banged my fist on the table and he flinched. 'You *have* to fight Franco with the weapons you possess. It's your duty!'

Pablo was silent for many moments, his cigarette burning itself out unheeded between his fingers. 'Call the Paris International Exhibition,' he said at last. 'Tell them I will deliver a painting and it will be called *Guernica*.'

He ground out his cigarette just in time to stop the glowing end making contact with his skin, and I threw my arms around him.

I had always felt excluded by Pablo's need to work alone, and so I was moved when he asked me to be by his side while he painted *Guernica*.

'Will you stay with me till it's finished, to document its creation?' His eyes searched my face. 'I want you to record the different "states" of it, which normally disappear in the course of work. When I put brush to canvas, I never know what will happen. It's not indecision; it simply changes as I paint.'

A slow joy was rising in me. 'What about Sabartés?' I said. 'Think of the friction it will cause.'

Pablo made a dismissive motion with his hands. 'Don't worry, I've asked him to move out for the duration and take Elft with him. It'll be just us and the birds. What do you say?'

The lovebirds began to laugh. Pablo shot me an electrifying look, and I succumbed to happiness. 'When do we begin?' I said.

'Tomorrow,' he said.

Starting our adventure eased some of the helplessness I felt about Guernica. At least I was helping Pablo draw the world's attention

111

to it. It wasn't enough, but it was something. I soon discovered how challenging conditions for photography were. The canvas was three and a half metres tall, and so we tilted it backwards to fit under the ceiling, and I had to use tricks to correct the distortions in perspective. The light in the studio was too harsh, so I softened it with the help of photomontage, cutting, rearranging, re-photographing the images. The difficulties were intimidating but I solved each one. My creativity came flooding back – fire and wine racing through my bloodstream.

I photographed Pablo painting from all angles; his eyes burning with anger, his face lit with passion for the work. The upper part of the canvas could only be reached with a long brush from the top of a ladder, so I crouched down and took him standing on it, fearless, just his head and brush showing over the top rung. Then I climbed the ladder to get a bird's eye view of him, paintbrush in his right hand, cigarette in his left.

Sometimes I put my camera down and simply watched him paint. It was mesmerising. He stood in front of the canvas for three or four hours at a time, consumed by some internal fire, some vision that ruled him. The brush was seldom lifted from the canvas, and the lines it left behind didn't seem to come from a conscious decision but to appear by themselves, as though predestined. The only sound was the brush travelling across the grain of the canvas; the noise changing as it moved – the liquid squelch of paint giving way to the scritch of two dry surfaces as I watched, tense with anticipation of what he might do next.

Occasionally, he walked to the other side of the studio and studied the canvas, chain-smoking and dropping the butts on the floor, adding to the soft carpet of cigarette ends underfoot. For him, painting didn't mean the formal depiction of objects; it held all kinds of possibilities and solutions, and it was clear that he was pursuing these while he smoked and thought. Afterwards, he went back to painting. At times, he said, 'I can't follow that idea any more,' and started working on a different section. He was often dissatisfied, moving from one to another. He worked like that from early afternoon until eleven in the evening before stopping for dinner. His favourite time for working was at night because the lack of interruption left more room for his imagination. And I think he liked being conscious while the rest of the city slept; it made him feel vibrant and almost invincible, as though he were cheating death.

Gradually the painting took shape: first the horse in agony, the bull, a woman at her window with a lamp in her hand to throw light on the catastrophe into which they'd been plunged. The sun with a bare light bulb filling its centre, like the flashbulb of my camera documenting the scene, an electric eye. Later, the dead child, the house on fire, lacerated bodies, cries of agony – all in black, white and grey. Pablo made a few attempts at colour, pasting in bits of striped or flowered paper for the women's dresses, but I encouraged him to discard colour in favour of the immediacy of a black-and-white photograph. Thus the work mirrored the prints that I developed each night to show him the next day.

He often consulted me. 'I'm thinking of adding a dove, like a streak of light, but I'm not sure where to put it,' he said, a week into the project. 'What do you think?'

I studied the painting. 'I think it should go between the bull and the horse, so you get a tableau of animals.'

'You're right!' he said, a grin flashing across his face, and he began to outline the bird. As I watched, I realised that the ravaged, open-mouthed women who seemed to be crying drops of blood had my features. And I felt proud that my face had been contorted into an emblem of the suffering of wartime.

A few hours later, Pablo held out a paintbrush. 'I need your help,' he said. 'I must work on the women now. Will you finish the horse for me?'

I took it from him, my heart racing with excitement. 'Of course.'

He showed me how to create the short, vertical strokes on the horse's flank and legs, his hand over mine on the brush, guiding me. I could feel his energy flowing through me and it was electrifying. Once I'd got the hang of it, he let go of my hand and we worked side by side. My mind relaxed, letting go of all the things that had hurt me or made me anxious, and it brought a deep sense of release.

We made love that night with a new intensity, clinging together, melting into each other; a spark of warmth and connection in

113

the encroaching darkness. Guernica had ended our experiments in sadism and masochism – we'd lost the taste for it when people were being tortured and suffering in real life. Kinkiness had been replaced by a passionate tenderness. Afterwards Pablo fell asleep quickly, but I lay awake for a long time.

*Guernica* was a cry of agony – a combination of Pablo's personal anguish and a protest against the barbarity of war. But it was also a fusion of his painting and my photography, sparked by our passion and intimacy. I flooded into it. Pablo turned in his sleep, flinging an arm over me. I nestled closer to him, feeling as if everything in my life had led to this moment, all the pain, all the struggle, every mistake. This was what I'd always wanted – this intensity and equality, creative partners as well as lovers. He had not been to see Marie-Thérèse since we began, and I held that close to me. It was a thought I tried to push away when he was awake, afraid that I would somehow raise her up in his memory. I knew it wouldn't be forever, but for this incredible time, he was all mine.

The next morning, we lingered in bed and got to work late. As usual, we began by reviewing my photographs from the day before. Pablo pored over a shot of the whole painting and said, 'Your pictures help so much. It's like having a fresh set of eyes. Look here.' He pointed with his finger. 'The women should rather be—'

An urgent pounding on the door cut him off.

Pablo raised his brows. 'Who could it be?' Sabartés had been tasked with making sure visitors stayed away till *Guernica* was finished. I followed Pablo to the door and saw Marie-Thérèse standing on the threshold. My stomach lurched and there was white noise in my ears, like a vast number of drawing pins rolling around. I could not believe she had turned up like this. I wasn't prepared for how beautiful she was, nor how young. She was tall and statuesque, with blonde hair cut into a bob, a Grecian profile and a complexion that glowed with good health.

At the sight of me, her eyes widened in shock. 'I came to find out why you've been neglecting us. Now it's clear!' she said to Pablo, through gritted teeth. I could feel waves of fear and fury coming off her. Pablo didn't answer, and so she strode into the studio, crying: 'Get her out! She must leave! She has no right to be here!'

A look passed between them and Pablo shrugged. Then he turned his back on us and began to mix colours, as though he were not implicated.

A breath went out of Marie-Thérèse and her shoulders sagged. 'I have his child. It's my place to be with him. Get out of here,' she said to me.

I straightened my spine, trying to rise above the humiliation of my childlessness. 'I've as much right as you to be here,' I said, as calmly as I could. 'I haven't borne him a child but I don't see what difference that makes.'

'You will never have his child; you don't belong here.' She spoke clearly and with emphasis; trying to hurt me. I bit my lip, determined not to give her the satisfaction of seeing me cry. Then she turned to Pablo. 'Make up your mind. Which one goes?'

He stopped working. 'I don't know,' he said, looking each of us up and down. 'I like you both, I'm happy with things as they are. You'll have to fight it out yourselves.'

'How disappointing that the only love you can be faithful to is your art!' I said bitterly. Marie-Thérèse shoved me hard, catching me off balance. I stumbled and nearly fell. Furious, I shoved her back, and then she yanked my hair. Pablo watched us pinching, scratching and tussling. His eyes shone – the sight seemed to energise him. A chilling realisation struck me: that conflict and destruction brought out the best in him. Happiness was not useful to his art. Finally he said, 'This is the finest moment of my life – two women fighting in front of *Guernica*, over me!' And he smiled; he *smiled*!

We stared at him aghast. We were both out of breath but Marie-Thérèse kicked out at me again. Pablo took her arm and pulled her away; she struggled in his grip.

'Do you mind going out for a bit?' he said to me. Marie-Thérèse was strong and he was having a hard time restraining her. 'Sorry, but it's the only way to sort this out, and we must get back to work.'

I obeyed, swallowing my pride, though I was trembling all over. 'Don't imagine you could ever take my place,' Marie-Thérèse hissed as I walked out.

115

I sat in a café within sight of Pablo's apartment and ordered coffee. It arrived quickly and I took a mouthful but it was too hot and burned my mouth. I hardly knew what I was doing. I had already seen the dark, almost sinister side of Pablo's nature but this was the first time I'd realised the depths of cruelty he was prepared to sink to. I was equally disturbed by Marie-Thérèse's sudden appearance. In her way, she seemed as unstable as Olga.

A butcher's van passed by. Marbled purple-and-white flanks poked out of its canvas covering. The butchers' aprons were crisp and clean. The van crept forward slowly in the sunlight, and I remembered Marie-Thérèse's words about me never bearing Pablo a child. How could she have known? Surely, he couldn't have discussed my fertility with her. But then I thought how callous he'd just been and understood that he was capable of anything. Whatever had prompted Marie-Thérèse's words, they filled me with foreboding because I was still not falling pregnant, and it gnawed at me continually.

Not long afterwards, I saw her leave Pablo's building, walking quickly, her head down. I paid for my coffee and went back to him. He kissed me lightly on the lips. 'There you are. Shall we start work?' he said, as if nothing had happened.

I squared my shoulders, determined to outlast Marie-Thérèse. I picked up my camera and willed myself to sink into the photography, to lose myself in it. I knew it was the only way to move on from what had happened. And as I became absorbed, I decided that Marie-Thérèse could boast all she wanted to about bearing his child. I was bearing something far greater – his work.

# Two

PABLO FINISHED *GUERNICA* IN less than a month. Preparations for the pavilion were equally intense – the building work was severely behind schedule, but somehow it was completed in time. I went to see it a few days after it opened. It was a modern metal-and-glass structure, with sculptures by Pablo, Julio González, and Alberto Sánchez along the exterior, and an enormous photo-mural of republican soldiers by Josep Renau at the entrance. Heat beat down from a clear sky, shimmering in waves, and the air smelled of scorched asphalt as I walked inside amongst crowds of people.

*Guernica* was the first image I saw. I knew it so well, yet its impact gave me a visceral shock, as if I'd tumbled onto hard ground. It was flanked by a fountain by Alexander Calder, flowing with Spanish mercury, and opposite hung an enormous photo of the poet Federico García Lorca, who'd been assassinated by Franco's forces a year earlier. Many of Spain's avant-garde artists, like Joan Miró and José Gutiérrez Solana, were also exhibiting. Mingling with the crowds, I listened to conversations, and it was clear that some people found *Guernica* baffling and contrary to the spirit of an exhibition dedicated to the pacifying role of art and technology in society. But I also heard a well-dressed woman say to her daughter, 'I don't understand what it means, but it does something to me – as if I'm being hacked to pieces.' And taking the girl by the hand she went off, uncertain, into the crowd.

Critics were divided about the painting. Some hailed it as power-ful and uncompromising. *La Flèche de Paris* wrote: 'This masterpiece addresses everyone who does not hide his face from it with the horrible language of truth.' But the Basque artist, Ucelay, dismissed it as '7 x 3 metres of pornography, shitting on Guernica, on the Basque country, on everything'.

'He can think what he likes,' Pablo said when he read this. 'I've worked for years to obtain this result. I can't use an ordinary style just to have the satisfaction of being understood!' And he crumpled up the review and stuffed it into the rubbish bin.

'Of course you can't,' I said.

He nodded, and I could see that although he was frustrated, nothing could make him deviate from his path. He knew that his work was right and true.

When the exhibition was dismantled, *Guernica* toured Europe and North America to raise awareness of the fascist threat. Pablo continued making brutal drawings of weeping women and animals in their death agony, and I carried on feeling involved in his work. I offered to photograph it, saying, to mirror his previous sentiment, 'I think my pictures let you see the work with new eyes.'

'Thank you,' he said, but his face closed down as if I'd said something ugly. He added, 'The thing is, these sketches aren't *Guernica*. I can see them without your help.'

I felt a painful void open up in me and went quickly to the window, so he wouldn't see my face. It was getting dark outside. Electric signs were coming on and streetlamps turned the trees' leaves silver. He had only needed me to see the direction in which *Guernica* was heading. The creative process that I thought had united us forever was finished. It was like walking a path, and exactly where I was planning to take another step, suddenly there was nothing. I should have heeded the message of *Guernica*: that all we love will be lost.

Life went on, nonetheless. I continued to take photographs; Pablo alternated between Marie-Thérèse and me. Sabartés returned with Elft, but Pablo had an inexplicable change of heart towards the dog, veering between indifference and impatience. The shorter his fuse grew, the more anxious Elft became, until he slunk around the apartment looking broken. Finally, he was banished to Le Tremblay to live with Marie-Thérèse and Maya. I knew how loyal he was to his master, and I worried that the move would break his spirit. I missed him, too. We were comrades of a sort, we understood each other. We both had to live at the mercy of Pablo's whims.

A month after the Fair, Pablo exhibited twenty oils and eight gouaches at Paul Rosenberg's gallery, next door to his apartment. We arrived to find a huge crowd of people already gathered. Rosenberg, a slim, dark-haired man with an angular face, was moving from group to group, shaking hands, listening to questions, and giving instructions to his assistants. He hurried up to us, smiling, but Pablo frowned at him.

'Why did you twist my arm to do this?' he asked gloomily. 'You know I hate shows. They interfere with my work.'

Rosenberg patted his arm, as he would a child's. 'I know, I know. But shows are necessary,' he said.

Pablo bit his lip. 'You make me exhibit and strip myself naked. But really, you've no idea how much courage it takes. People who own my pictures don't know what they have. Each one is a phial with my blood. That's what goes into it.'

Rosenberg looked at me for help.

'We understand. Exhibiting is hard. Perhaps an artist never gets used to people staring at his work,' I said, with a flash of irritation, because of my own desire to have a show.

'That's right!' said Rosenberg, shooting me a grateful look. He turned back to Pablo. 'The public needs your art. So please be sociable. Come and talk to the Garniers and the Rocheforts.' And grasping Pablo by the arm, he led him away.

I took a glass of champagne from a waiter carrying a tray of drinks, and stood to one side, sipping at it, and looking around. Many of the big canvases were in iridescent colours, arranged in precise, broad blocks. Together they imparted such an impression of light that they were like stained glass irradiated by the sun. At first, I didn't see anyone I knew. Then the door opened, and Olga walked in, dressed in her usual furs. I felt my heart constrict.

I watched her move around the room. Rosenberg had supplied a generous amount of champagne and she was drinking steadily. Everyone avoided her. I think that people were afraid to stop and speak to her because they knew what they'd be letting themselves in for.

'Dora!' cried a familiar voice. I saw Lise hastening towards me and smiled with relief. She kissed me on both cheeks and picked up my hand to look at the ruby ring.

'It suits you perfectly!' she exclaimed.

'Thank you for giving it up.'

'It was no hardship,' she said, shrugging. 'Pablo gave me a gem of a painting in return. You should come over and see it sometime.'

'I would love to,' I said, then cupped my hand to my cheek and added, 'I'm sorry I've been so bad at staying in touch.'

'I understand,' she said quietly. 'You've been taken over by that extraordinary man. He's at the top of his game. You must be good for him.'

For a moment, I contemplated confiding in her about our difficulties, but my pride held me back.

Lise was examining my face. 'How are you, my dear? Are you working these days?'

I grimaced. 'Work's going through a lacklustre phase. Being with Pablo is a full-time occupation.' As I said it, I realised that I hadn't stretched myself or grown as an artist since we'd met. My photographs were still selling, but they were my earlier ones. In the beginning, I had hoped that being with Pablo would improve my work, but the opposite had happened. Its dark alchemy was gone, and I felt a stab of grief.

Lise shook her head. 'You're too talented to let it go. In fact, you have a duty to yourself not to. A woman needs something that's just hers, no matter how deeply in love she is.'

Pablo came over before I could answer, and she said to him, 'What a marvellous show. I'll be happy all week after seeing it.'

'I'm glad you like it.' He smiled broadly. 'I'm exhausted. When I talk to this many people, it's like translating one thing into several languages. It's hard to find myself again afterwards.'

I could sense how curious Lise was becoming about our relationship. While Pablo spoke, she gave me sidelong glances. Beneath the surface of conversation, unspoken questions gathered. Then I felt a tug on my arm – it was Olga. I looked at her desperate, goaded expression and realised that she was truly mad. The hairs on the back of my neck stood on end. Pablo carried on talking, ignoring her. I saw how it enraged her even more, like a matador's red cape being flapped at a bull. It wasn't long before she burst out, 'Shut

120

up!' We all turned to look at her, and she said to Pablo, 'You're a phoney and a hypocrite! I'm sick of you shitting on me.'

Pablo closed his eyes briefly, then said, 'No one's shitting on you, Olga. We're just trying to get on with our lives.'

Her eyes flitted back and forth, coming to rest on mine, and pain moved across her face. 'You've bewitched him,' she hissed. 'If it weren't for you, my son would have a father.'

'That's not true! Pablo left you for Marie-Thérèse before I met him,' I retorted, but my cheeks burned with shame.

A strangled sound escaped Olga's lips and I realised it was a sob. I stared at her reddened eyes and crumpled face, sick with horror and with pity. Pablo gave her a look of fury and took a step towards her. 'For the love of God will you leave us alone?'

'I can't,' she said, and she made a motion with her hands, either to shove him away from her or to draw him closer. Just then Rosenberg and one of his assistants appeared on either side of her.

'It's time for you to leave, Olga,' Rosenberg said pleasantly.

She shook her head, an ugly flush creeping up her neck. The assistant took her arm and began to lead her away. She didn't resist but gazed straight ahead, her mouth working as she struggled not to cry.

'Don't think of coming back!' Rosenberg called after her. 'You won't be admitted.'

'Thanks, Paul. That was neatly done,' Pablo said, when the door had shut on her. He seemed untroubled by her hysterics.

'It's my job,' said Rosenberg, touching Pablo's arm. He smiled and raised his glass to the other guests, who had stopped talking to stare. They resumed their conversations – no doubt they were gossiping about us. Pablo went off to speak to another dealer. Lise took my hand and held it tightly but I couldn't stop shaking from shock, fear and guilt.

After that night, Olga began following us in the street again. Ten days after the exhibition ended, we were walking home from the Catalan, and she came up behind us and started pulling on Pablo's arm to make him turn around. He tried to ignore her but she wouldn't stop and he grew so exasperated that he wheeled around and slapped her across the face. The retorts rang out like gunshots.

She put her hand to her cheek and began to scream.

'Stop it, Olga. I had no choice. Stop it now,' Pablo said, but she only screamed louder.

The noise got inside my head: that was how it felt, waves of pain and vertigo filling my brain. A man in a dark suit and tie approached us. 'Is everything all right?' he asked, his eyes on Olga.

Pablo gritted his teeth. 'Fine, thank you. We had a little misunderstanding.'

The man looked at each of us in turn, and I shrugged and gave him the most charming smile I could raise. After a long moment, he nodded and carried on his way. Olga was still screaming. Pablo glared at her. '*God*, you're embarrassing. Shut up or I'm going for the police.'

At that she stopped screaming as suddenly as she'd begun. Relief washed through me, and the familiar sounds of traffic soothed my ears. Olga fumbled in her bag for a handkerchief and passed it over her sweating face.

'You aren't what you used to be,' she said hoarsely. 'Your son is worthless too, and he's going from bad to worse. Like you.'

I wondered what new trouble Paulo had got into. 'What do you want, Olga? What do you want Pablo to *do*?' I asked.

She shook her head slowly. Her eyes were bewildered.

Pablo took my arm, and we moved away. And then I heard Olga's footfalls behind us again. I tried to ignore her, concentrating on the solid feel of Pablo's hand in the crook of my elbow, but I was disturbed. Her failure to provoke the reaction she wanted was driving her off balance, and I understood exactly how that felt.

Back at the rue des Grands-Augustins, I stood at the window and watched Olga looking at our building. After several minutes, she turned and began walking slowly back the way we had come, her head bowed. She seemed a different person to the radiant dancer Pablo had shown me pictures of, and I felt a surge of compassion for her.

'I pity her,' I said, turning to him. And then with fervour, 'but she's scary, Pablo. She scares me.'

He sat down on the sofa and pulled me towards him. 'Let's forget about my wife,' he said into my hair. 'That's how life is. Adapt or die.'

His coldness made me shudder. And I realised that, despite everything, he would always regard Olga as his wife. In a strange way he needed her to be obsessed with him, however unhealthy that obsession might be. He fed on the energy of every person who loved him, and it made him feel stronger and more alive.

He began to kiss and caress me, sending ripples of feeling through me, and I gave myself up to passion. But I couldn't shake the feeling that our life was a powder keg that could detonate at any moment.

# Three

T HAT SUMMER, WE LEFT with Paul and Nusch for another holiday at the Vaste Horizon in Mougins. 'We're a happy family again,' said Pablo contentedly as we were shown to our room by the owner, Mme Lavigne, a plump woman with high colour and black hair parted in the centre. She threw open the door, saying, 'It's the same room as last year. I know you were happy here.'

Walking in felt like a homecoming. The luminous light of the south penetrated every corner. The doors to the balcony were open, bringing the scent of pine and eucalyptus from the garden. I noticed a few streaks of paint on the wall.

'Oh, look!' I said. 'They've kept the traces of our last stay!'

'We guard them religiously as a souvenir of your visit,' said Mme Lavigne, dimpling, and she left, urging us to call her if we needed anything.

Pablo was trying to settle Kazbek, his new Afghan hound, named after the mountains in his country. Kazbek was a skinny creature with a snout pointing towards the ground and large ears covered in drooping hair that looked like wings. He and Pablo were very close, as Pablo and Elft had been in the beginning. While I unpacked, Pablo persuaded Kazbek to lie down in his basket, and then he came over to kiss me. The dog let out a soft growl, low in his throat, but I ignored him and leaned into Pablo, my heart filling. We had left Olga behind in Paris, Marie-Thérèse was in Le Tremblay, and Pablo was mine – at least until the holiday ended. I hoped we might recapture some of the magic of last summer.

We went to join the others for lunch under the grapevine-sheltered pergola. The familiar smells of geranium and grapevine

124

flowers were heady, intoxicating. Man Ray and his lover, Adrienne Fidelin, were already at table. Man had brown, wavy hair, and seemed to be built of nerves and muscle, without an ounce of spare flesh. He clapped Pablo on the back and took my hands in his. 'It's good to see you again, Dora. I'm looking forward to more talks about photography,' he said.

'Oh, me too,' I said, feeling Pablo tense beside me.

Man had photographed me before I met Pablo, my face framed in black velvet so that my features looked feline and mysterious. I admired his inventiveness and we had similar aims, both striving to portray the uncanny beneath the surface of life, using experimental techniques like photomontage and rayographs.

'You must meet Ady,' he said. 'Ady, this is Dora.' We shook hands. She was slender and attractive, with almond-shaped eyes and short dark hair.

'She's a talented dancer and model, but you want to watch her,' said Pablo. 'She's cheeky. The first time we met, she threw her arms around me and said, "I hear you're quite a good painter."'

Ady punched him playfully on the arm and he grinned at her. She turned to me with an enchanting smile, and said, 'What a beautiful bracelet!'

'Thank you,' I said, smiling back. The bracelet was my latest gift from Pablo, made of chunky silver and engraved with a tiny portrait of me.

Then the Éluards appeared with Roland Penrose and his new girlfriend, Lee Miller. She was a blonde, blue-eyed American, and there was a composure to her that I'd often noticed in women from her country. Roland's marriage to Valentine had ended when she'd persuaded him to travel to India with her in search of enlightenment. Once there, he had found himself resenting her spiritual pilgrimage and had finally told her that although he understood what she was looking for, he needed the stimulation of city life. He had returned to France, while Valentine stayed on. I was sad – I liked Valentine very much.

In the midst of greetings, Man's gaze met Lee's and I detected tension, a small electric crackle. Pablo pounced on it, saying, 'I see you two know one another.' Silence fell. Everyone knew that Lee had been Man's lover – it was her lips that floated in the sky in his classic surrealist painting, *Les Amoureux*.

'Let's eat,' said Nusch to cover up the awkwardness and we began our meal: cold meats, cheese, pâté, salad, and bread still warm from the oven.

The same red-headed waitress as last year brought a pyramid of figs on a plate, and we hailed her like an old friend. The fruit was so ripe that seeds were oozing through cracks in their purple-black skin. My urge to take photographs began to stir. I wanted to capture their fleshiness, the varied colours, the fact that each leaf had its own singular design.

Pablo bit into a fig, juice trickling down his chin, and said, 'As a child, I used to eat these straight off the tree. That was before I knew they could ever cost money.'

Nusch said, 'They must have tasted far better.'

Pablo said, 'They tasted like reality. Assuming everything else – buildings, money, art – is unreal and mostly a distraction from figs.'

A ripple of laughter went around the table and then we were quiet, savouring the food. Eventually, I asked Lee and Roland how they met.

'I fell madly in love with her at a costume party,' Roland said. 'Max Ernst and I went as bandits. Lee was Carmen from Bizet's opera.'

Pablo looked at Lee and his eyes became penetrating. 'You're a living Carmen,' he said. 'I hear that you're a photographer. What brought you to Paris from America? Do you like it here? Tell us everything!'

'I started off as an art student in New York,' she said. 'My first winter there, I accidentally stepped into oncoming traffic. A stranger pulled me back just in time.' She looked steadily at Pablo over the rim of her wine glass. 'I thanked him and he took me out for coffee. Turned out he was the publisher, Condé Montrose Nast. He got me a job modelling for *Vogue*.'

'She was on the covers of American *and* British *Vogue*,' said Roland draping an arm around her shoulders. 'And you should see the photographs she takes. They're really something.'

'Sweet of you to blow my trumpet,' she said, kissing his cheek. Kazbek, who had been begging for scraps from our plates, lay down beside Pablo's chair, stretching out his gaunt frame and putting his paws in front of him so he seemed like a sculpture.

'See the way he's lying?' Pablo said, his eyes glinting. 'He doesn't look like a dog. More like a giant ray.'

'No, he's a giant shrimp,' I said, and everyone laughed. The sun and wine were drugging me into warm, sleepy contentment.

'You still haven't told us how you got to Paris,' Pablo said to Lee.

'I decided to go after I saw Man's photographs,' she said lightly. 'I wanted to find him and work in his style. I tracked him down and announced that I was his new student.'

'I told her I didn't take students and was leaving the next day for a holiday in Biarritz,' said Man, smiling wryly. 'And she said, "So am I."'

Their eyes locked and again I detected that small charge. I glanced at Ady to see how she was taking it. There was an enigmatic smile on her lips, and I wished I could be as free of jealousy as she was.

'After we broke up, I married an Egyptian called Aziz. We lived in Cairo,' Lee continued. 'He was kind and generous, but I didn't fit in there. It was all duck-shooting men, and ladies dressed in black satin and pearls. I came back to Paris and fell in love with Roland.'

'What have you got there, Pablo?' asked Paul.

Pablo had been carving a thin slice of tongue, he held it out to us. It's a portrait of Ambroise Vollard,' he said.

Nusch threw her head back and laughed. 'It's true,' she said. 'The fleshy part of the tongue looks like Vollard's head. It's the same domed shape.'

'And the squashed bit underneath is just like his features,' I said, and Nusch laughed some more.

'Mealtimes bring out the improviser in you,' added Lee in a sleepy drawl, and Pablo proceeded to cannibalise Vollard with relish.

But the easy, languorous atmosphere I felt at that first lunch did not last. After breakfast the next morning, Mme Lavigne handed me and Pablo each a letter. My envelope bore Jacqui's handwriting and I opened it as soon as we reached our room.

I hope you are happy, my dear, and that the holiday is everything you want it to be. I am waving gaily at you from across the sea – I'm in Ajaccio! Are you surprised? It's charming and intriguing, with statues of Napoleon everywhere. Annette Courbin invited me to stay, and we're painting and spending our free time on the beach.

André and Aube are in Paris. André is unhappy with me and I feel terrible about leaving them but I was suffocating and couldn't stand it any longer. When I get home, I'll try harder to be a good wife.

I miss you.

Jacqui

I folded up the letter. My heart was full of trepidation. 'Jacqui walked out on André. I'm worried about their marriage,' I said to Pablo.

'She isn't cut out for marriage,' he said. Then he frowned and added, 'My letter was from Olga.' He waved it in front of me and I saw that it was a long tirade, mostly in Spanish mixed with French and Russian. She had written in all directions: horizontally, diagonally, up and down the margins, and it was unintelligible. But she had enclosed a photograph of Beethoven conducting an orchestra on which she had clearly printed, 'If you were like him, you would be a real artist,' and this gave me the gist of the rest. I felt a flare of anger with her for disturbing our holiday, and understood that I would have to set my feelings aside to tend to Pablo's.

As the day wore on, he recovered from his agitation but our peace was short-lived, as the following morning brought another letter from Olga. He read it to me and was most perturbed by it, because it threatened divorce and splitting up his assets.

'I doubt she'll do anything,' I said. 'She just wants to spoil your holiday. Why don't you stop reading her letters?'

He shrugged. 'I can't. She's my wife. I have to know what she says.'

The letters seemed to feed something in him. The rest of us quickly settled into the same routine as last year – mornings on the Garoupe beach were followed by lunch under the cane arbours. In the white heat of the afternoon, we retired to our respective rooms for a siesta, or dozed in the sun. But Pablo was in the grip of a tremendous creative urge. While the rest of us relaxed after lunch, Pablo would say, 'to work, to work', and would shut himself in our room until dinnertime. There, he would paint the buildings of Mougins grouped against the sky, or pigeons tumbling through the air with the sea as their background. More often, though, he painted portraits. Most were of me, but he also painted Nusch.

The rest of us worked too, although not at the same fever pitch. On our third night, we sat on the terrace listening to the crickets chirping. There were big moths circling the lamp, and the smoke of our cigarettes made ghostly whorls that drifted upwards and vanished into darkness. Paul read us his latest poems, Pablo displayed a starry-eyed portrait of me, and Man presented a series of lavish drawings, to appear later in a book illustrated by the poems Paul was writing – *Les Mains Libres*. I spent more time thinking about Pablo than working, but I showed a few photographs I had taken of Paul and Nusch embracing, in love, my favourite models.

'What a talented lot you are,' said Ady. As she spoke, a moth fell onto the table, fatally intoxicated by the burning lamp. 'How I wish I could be a part of it.'

'I know, let's take photographs of each other!' Roland said, sitting forwards. 'We'll set this summer on record.'

So the following day, while we were at la Garoupe, he borrowed my Rolleiflex and began to take pictures of Ady in the sea. During the last day or two, I had noticed his eyes lingering on her. Ady swam like an angel, naked, and her body was sleek and supple. Then Lee took the camera and Roland waded into the waves to pose with Ady, his arms around her, drops of water shining on her rich skin. At one point, he laid his hand on her nude sex and I held my breath, but Lee carried on taking photos with a cool smile on her face. Man had gone for a walk with his camera. Pablo was sitting beside me, watching everything, his eyes glittering like coal.

At lunch, Roland asked me to photograph everyone beneath the cane arbour, and I couldn't refuse without seeming rude. But it heightened the already feverish atmosphere as I'd feared it would. Everything was distorted by the stark black shadows cast by the canes, and so it was awkward work. As I framed and took the shots, Lee began to tell us about setting sail from America to Paris, and about how her lovers had tossed a coin to decide who got to see her off.

'The loser flew beside the boat in a small plane and sprayed me with roses,' she said.

Nusch raised her brows. 'It's really something, isn't it? What you do to men,' she said, and there was an edge to her voice I hadn't heard before.

Lee gave her an amused glance and began another story. While she spoke, it wasn't her words that we listened to. Her body seemed to speak a language of its own. She was vibrantly alive – from her toes, sheathed in diamante sandals, to her smooth blonde bob. Pablo was gazing at her exactly as he used to look at me, his eyes like black fire. I detected a responsive quiver in Lee and jealousy shot through me. It was very hot – my head felt heavy. Soon my shoulders ached and my eyes became dazzled. I could hardly see straight. I set down the camera and my smile at the others was a grimace of pain.

After the meal, Pablo decided to photograph me and Lee on our bed. I went upstairs with them reluctantly. I refused to undress, but Lee unselfconsciously stripped to her underwear and lay down beside me, tanned and very beautiful. I heard Pablo's intake of breath. He began to photograph his eternal theme – two women, a blonde and a brunette. I knew that my pained, angry face was ruining his picture and I was not sorry. Then Lee took off her brassiere and lay on her side, so that her hair fell over her face and the sun coming through the shutters lay in streaks on her body.

'Look at her! She knows how to be seductive. You could learn a thing or two from her,' said Pablo, and she gave him a slow, sweet smile.

At that moment, I hated them both. I opened my mouth to reply, but he had already begun to shoot her, his eyes devouring her. A sensation of not being myself, of having lost control came over me. It was like moving under water. I took the camera from Pablo and photographed him in a strong contrast of light and shade. It was how I had come to see him.

After Lee had gone, I said quietly, 'How could you flirt so blatantly and then humiliate me? It was monstrous of you.'

Pablo looked at the ceiling briefly and said, 'It didn't mean anything. You should know that.' He let out a sigh. 'When I behave badly, it's to make *you* react. I want to see you get angry and upset, like you used to. But you just close up on me.'

My eyes swam with tears. I glanced at him and recognised the look on his face – he was gone. He shook his head and walked out.

I curled up on the bed, in blank, speechless pain. This had happened too many times – Pablo leaving me alone to deal with the suffering he had inflicted. Gradually, the room turned into a cavern of golden light and shadows as the sun sank lower in the sky. I lay watching the patterns, feeling pangs of loss for the person I was before this turmoil started.

I knew that the only way to reclaim my old self was through a disciplined return to my art. The best, truest version of me that existed was in my photographs. But the camera was tainted by memory now; every time I picked it up, I would see Pablo looking at Lee through its lens. Despair arrived, a sick feeling in my body. I watched a fly crawling up the wall. The pipes gurgled loudly – someone in the building must have switched on a tap. I wondered where Pablo was, if he was with Lee, and felt my breath come shorter. But then an idea appeared and something at the core of me steadied.

Pablo had been encouraging me to take up painting for some time, and not, I think, to crush me. He meant to steer me towards becoming what he considered a real artist. 'You have a gift and you don't use it fully,' he would say. And there were times I had considered painting, not only because of Pablo, but because ideas sometimes came to me that demanded more flexibility of expression than the camera could provide. For one thing, I missed being able to create textures. I had addressed this as best I could by using coarse grain, partial reversal of the negative and other technical variations. I had pushed photography to the limits of my inventive capacities, and it was no longer enough.

I got out of bed, drew back the shutters and opened the window to get some air. Then I put on a deep red kaftan, brushed my hair and splashed water on my face. I leaned my forehead against the mirror's cool surface and resolved to hang up my Rolleiflex for good and dedicate myself to painting.

From then on, I spent every afternoon with my brushes. It was invigorating to have a change after all the years of focusing solely on photography. I loved the smooth, buttery texture of the paint, and the variations I could achieve with colour and texture.

The first works I produced were portraits of Pablo in broad swathes of colour, separated by thick black outlines. These pictures reflected his influence on me but how could I avoid it? I was on a journey to finding my voice and the challenges were huge. I had to take off the training wheels and start again, shaking off the weight of my lover and master. But I was stubborn and determined to conquer painting, despite knowing I would never be as good at it as Pablo.

A week after I started, he and I went out into the blinding sunshine to find the others gathered at breakfast. They were smoking and looking solemn.

'Have you seen the news?' Nusch asked, reaching for the coffee pot and pouring us cups.

'Thank you,' said Pablo, touching her hand. 'What happened?'

Paul leaned forwards. 'Hitler purified Germany's art museums,' he said. 'You've been labelled a degenerate artist.'

My scalp erupted into goosebumps. I could feel them crawl across my skin. Pablo's face was blank – he was stunned. He pushed his cup away and reached for his cigarettes.

'Van Gogh is condemned to posthumous death for artistic heresy by the Nazis' "new order",' said Man, and a look of fear passed over his face. 'I'm surprised the Nazis haven't labelled me degenerate. If they found out I was born Emmanuel Radnitzky – well, it's pretty obvious my parents are Russian-Jewish immigrants.'

Ady took his hand. 'Be thankful you're under their radar,' she said, and he nodded. 'For now.'

'It's the beginning of the end,' said Pablo, looking at Paul.

Paul folded his arms across his chest. 'It seems we'll be among the first victims of French Hitlerism. He hasn't underestimated us.'

We fell silent, trying to take it in. The air smelled of smoke, with a waft of sweat.

At last Pablo said, 'I've always felt an affinity for Van Gogh.'

'Really, I find that surprising. Why?' asked Lee.

Pablo inhaled and held smoke in his lungs before blowing it to the sky. 'It's his suffering and tumultuous energy. Most people don't realise that painting isn't a question of sensibility. It's about seizing power, taking over from nature. Van Gogh was the first to understand that.' He looked at us, then looked out at the sea, adding, 'These mad proclamations have only made me love him more. I think I'll paint a set of variations on his *L'Arlésienne*.'

The others agreed it was a perfect theme, and they began to discuss the direction it might take.

My heart was so heavy. I ground out my cigarette – the nicotine had cleared my head – and many thoughts started running through it. I guessed that the others were as scared as I was, and that they were concealing their feelings behind cheerful facades, while Pablo felt driven to embark on some sort of heroic project. But I longed for the comfort of sharing my fear, and it made me feel acutely lonely.

Pablo began his series after breakfast, working feverishly for several days. I guessed that he was struggling against his own dread, because what emerged was a series of portraits filled with humour and fantasy. They were incredibly vital: the paint was applied with energy, the colours were bold, the light glowed deeply. At times, he distorted his subjects with demonically playful inventions. Nusch's eyes became vivid Mediterranean fish. Lee's lips were enormous and bright green, and her large, liquid eyes were allowed to run with wet paint.

Pablo started painting more portraits of Lee than of anyone else. His pictures were a nod to Bizet's opera because she had been Carmen when she met Roland, and because she embodied the femme fatale for all the men. Not one of them was immune to her charms.

# Four

ABLO TOOK A BREAK from the 'Arlésienne' paintings and
began work on a nude portrait of Nusch in tones of pearl
grey, with all the grace and sensitivity he was capable of. The
delicate neck, the wild hair, the thick, downcast eyelashes, appeared
on the canvas as though the brush had been dipped in light and was
throwing out a soft glow. It pleased him so well that the next day he
painted a naked portrait of me in the same tones, though mine was
less beautiful.

On the night they were finished, Pablo made a gift to each model
of her portrait. Nusch's face opened, and she said, 'Thank you, my
dear. I'll always treasure it.'

Everyone looked at me but I couldn't bring myself to thank Pablo.
I wasn't sure if he was being staggeringly insensitive or if he was
deliberately trying to mock and insult me. We were in the salon – a
whitewashed room with rugs covering the wooden floorboards, and
blue and yellow chairs. Lee put on a record – 'Parlez-moi d'amour'
– and began to dance by herself, eyes closed, her movements loose
and alluring.

Pablo was staring at her, his eyes so black that they seemed
to burn with the reflected lamplight. When the song ended, she
replaced it with 'When You're Smiling', and gestured for us to join
her. At first we danced together, but Lee soon ended up in Pablo's
arms, and the rest of us stopped to watch. Lee said something to
him and they both laughed, a comfortable, intimate laugh, as if
they had been a couple for years. Next thing they were kissing,
open-mouthed, his hand squeezing her backside. I closed my eyes.
*This can't be happening under my nose,* I thought. *It can't be.*

Nusch hugged me, holding me tight for a few seconds. 'We're going to our room. Would you like to come?' she said.

'No, thanks. I'm fine here,' I said, trying to smile. I was feeling so many things – gratitude, a lessening of resentment towards Nusch, and a terrible compulsion to stay near Pablo. But I couldn't articulate any of it to her.

The Éluards left and Roland began to dance with Ady, holding her close. Man tried to take me in his arms. 'I've always had a soft spot for you, Dora. We might as well balance things out,' he said.

'I can't,' I said, pulling away from him.

He looked at me and I thought I saw pity on his face. 'You know where to find me if you change your mind,' he said, touching my cheek, and he left.

I sat down on the window seat, smoking and downing glass after glass of cognac as I watched the couples on the dance floor. I thought: *Pablo, who are you?* My cigarette holder scattered ash, while drops of cognac spilled from my glass. Moths blundered around the lamps. At last the song ended and Lee came to sit beside me.

'I'm sorry if this is uncomfortable for you,' she said, a foot still tapping in time to the music, and I could see that she was drunk. 'I came to tell you it doesn't mean anything. Flirting is very different than love and Pablo loves you.'

'How can you be so hard?' I asked bitterly.

Lee's foot went still. 'It's not a nice story, but it is the truth and it shapes who I am,' she said quietly. 'When I was a child, I was molested by a family friend. It took years to recover.'

I was so shocked, I didn't know what to say. I held my cool glass to my cheek and whispered, 'I'm sorry.'

'Yes, well … My parents took me to a psychiatrist, who explained that love and sex were two separate entities.' She opened her hands and turned them palms up. 'The philosophy has worked for me ever since.'

This was taking me to a place I didn't want to go to. I supposed that the distancing of mind and body she practised had helped her attain her magnetic aloofness. And perhaps, underneath it, was a woman terrified of intimacy. But I mistrusted her even as she opened up. She was so beautiful, so liberated, so dangerous. She changed the mood and filled everything with menace.

Pablo came over – it was time for bed. I swayed slightly as I stood up and Pablo held my arm. I said, 'Why do you let me drink so much, darling? I should give it up, start drinking Evian like you. Dedicate myself to my art. Oh, Pablo, sometimes I feel so alone.'

He was leading me to our room. 'Of course you're not alone,' he said. 'You have all of us right here. What you need is rest. You'll feel better tomorrow.'

The air was thick with things that couldn't be said. He opened the door and kissed me lightly on the lips, saying, 'I'm not tired yet. I think I'll stay up and do some drawing. Go to sleep, darling.'

Kazbek had been dozing in his basket and got up to greet his master. Pablo caressed him lovingly, and I wished that he would show me a fraction of the care and compassion he lavished on that animal. Then he left, closing the door behind him and Kazbek started scratching at it, wanting to follow. I let him out and then stood still, looking at the door. I heard Lee laugh in the salon and the tears welled up.

It was a night of unpleasant dreams, arriving one after the other, and leaving me exhausted. In the morning, my mouth was sour with stale alcohol. The light coming in at the edges of the shutters hurt my eyes. Pablo was sitting up in bed, watching me. He said, 'You were sobbing in your sleep.'

I said, 'Really? How peculiar,' and his eyes were thoughtful as they met mine.

He was warm and attentive after that. At the beach, we lay a little apart from the others, and they did not bother us. The sea was calm, with lace-edged shallows, and the sky was deep and blue. Pablo caressed me and called me his true love, and I felt my heart begin to unfold. And then I realised that I hadn't confronted him about what had happened when he left me to go to Lee. I had taken whatever scraps came my way without making him answerable. I was stupid and weak and pathetic. And I hated myself.

'Darling, what's wrong?' he asked. I opened my mouth, then shut it. I felt my face grow hot. He held out his arms and, after a moment's hesitation, I went into them. I was still furious with myself, but I buried my face in his neck and he wrapped his arms around me, and his body felt warm and dense against mine. And I only wanted him to go on holding me.

At lunch he fed me the tastiest morsels from his plate. We drank several glasses of wine and giggled like children and my heart kept unfolding. Afterwards we went to work but Pablo came to find me during his break. I was in the garden painting the mountains rising beyond it, everything bathed in late afternoon sunlight.

'What, are you doing that view again?' he asked, surprised.

'Yes,' I said, not taking my eyes from the canvas. 'The light is better than it was yesterday.'

'You are just like me. We keep going back to the same subject, but try and do it better,' he said, and I felt he was present in a way he hadn't been since the holiday began.

I put down my brush and looked at him. 'The goal is always perfection,' I said.

'Exactly,' he said. 'And to me, perfection means going further, further, from one canvas to the next. Remember that.' He kissed me and went back to work.

I wanted to show Pablo what I could do in the medium he respected, but I was a long way from achieving perfection. My painting was improving but it lacked the personal gaze I had in photography; the slippage between reality and surreality that was my trademark. I resolved to work harder.

That evening, the others asked to see my work, and I showed them a few portraits. I was shy about it, but Paul said, 'Your paintings give off the same impression of grandeur and purity that you do,' and then I felt glad.

Pablo said, 'She works very hard. I admire her dedication. Plus, her fingers smell adorably of turpentine.' For a moment, I cupped his cheek in my hand, and he made a pantomime of sniffing it.

Man tilted his head as if he was considering my new incarnation. 'You will have hard moments, but you must carry on no matter what, because otherwise you'll have to start all over again,' he said kindly. 'Every time I pick up a brush, it feels like I'm painting with my blood.'

'That's true of Pablo too,' said Roland.

'Don't you think Pablo paints with other people's blood?' I asked, making everyone laugh, especially Pablo.

The conversation moved on and I sat quietly, letting it wash over me. The others' encouragement had awoken my old ambition. I thought about how I'd allowed Pablo to come between me and photography, and I vowed that nothing and no one would stop me painting.

Two days later, we lingered at lunch with the Éluards. The air smelled of freshly cut grass, bees hummed in drowsy circles, our wine glowed amber in the light. I longed to go to the bedroom and lie with Pablo. We rose to leave; my skin tingled with anticipation. Then Paul took Nusch's hand and put it in Pablo's.

'Would you like to spend the siesta with my wife?' he asked. 'Consider it a gesture of friendship.'

The ground slid from under me. My vision blurred. This was more than a shock – it was betrayal. Paul and Pablo exchanged a look, and the air between them changed. I glanced at Nusch, wondering how she felt about being passed around, but she didn't seem surprised. And I understood that she and Paul had already discussed it, and this made me feel even worse.

Pablo said, 'It would be churlish to refuse such a generous offer. It won't change anything, will it?' He looked at me uncertainly.

'Of course not!' said Paul, before I could reply. 'In fact, I'd be offended if you refused.'

I felt a great sense of unreality and my mind struggled to absorb their words. I think they mistook my shock for agreement, because Nusch squeezed Pablo's arm and looked up into his eyes. 'Shall we go?' she asked. He took her hand, smiling at her, and they went inside without glancing back.

I could not believe that Pablo could do that, just walk off with Nusch. I couldn't believe any of it. I turned to Paul and said, 'How could you do that? How *could* you? What about my feelings?' My throat was so raw, it hurt to speak.

Paul didn't answer, just stood with his arms by his sides. Then he said, 'Oh, Dora. I'm sorry. The thing is, I love Pablo. I want to make him happy.' I stared at him, aghast. I hadn't realised what a masochist he was. He added, 'Look, you already share him with Marie-Thérèse. At least we're keeping it in the family.'

Shame and rage poured through me. I couldn't look at him and, after a few moments, fled to the bedroom, flinging myself down on the bed. Stripes of sunlight shifted and lengthened over the walls, and the scents of the garden came through the open windows. I tried not to think about Pablo and Nusch together, but images appeared in my mind, clear as photographs.

Surely there was no worse way to live than in pain and uncertainty. I didn't know whether to be jealous of Nusch or Lee, and it made me crazy. To keep a hold of myself, I tried to focus on something extrinsic. I counted how many noises I could hear – the pipes clanking, the scream of a gull overhead, Ady and Roland talking in low voices outside. And in a moment of clarity, I saw that not only would there always be Marie-Thérèse, but countless other women at his whim, just as constant as she was.

I began to dream of escaping from Pablo. What if I came home one day to find out that he'd abandoned me for someone else? I vowed to be the one in control of the break-up. Just then, I was distracted by a piece of paper sticking out of his underwear drawer.

I got up to look and saw that it was a letter from Olga. I took it out and began to read, my pulse hammering in my throat.

> I beg you, what should I do? I do not know how Paulo spends his days. Do you realise we are talking about your son? I'm telling you again that you have no idea what's going on with him. And you haven't answered me. I can't believe that you can have changed that much.
>
> Don't interpret this letter badly, I beg you. It's not about me any more, but about our son. And it's not his fault. The change is too big for him, and you must realise how terribly, terribly sad he is to be separated from you, and he is also nervous when he comes back from your house. Don't leave him to his own devices any more, we have to do something.

I replaced the letter in the drawer and slid it shut. I was in great distress. Olga didn't sound unhinged at all, she sounded like a scared, loving mother. Perhaps I had been wrong all along to dismiss her as

139

crazy. Perhaps she was simply under more strain than one person could bear. I wondered why Pablo hadn't shown the letter to me, as he had her others, and hoped he hadn't ignored her concerns. There had been no word from Paulo for weeks. I had written to him but he hadn't answered and I was scared for him.

By the time Pablo returned, the air was cooling, and the early evening shadows had started creeping over the floor. He smoothed his hair down, looking very pleased with himself.

Having resolved to be strong and indifferent, just one look at him flipped the switch. I sprang off the bed and said, 'How can you fuck Nusch and Lee at the same time? Flesh and blood can't stand it!' My voice rose.

'It doesn't mean anything,' Pablo said, with a slight shrug. 'I am sorry if it caused you pain. It's just a good time among friends.'

'By the same logic, I mean nothing to you either!'

His face broke into real surprise, and he said, 'Why, that's absurd, *mia Dorrra*! You are the only one who matters.' I was weeping now – great, breathless sobs, like a child. He wiped my eyes with his handkerchief and said, 'It was a gesture of friendship on my part too. I did it to make Paul happy. I don't want him to think that I dislike his wife.'

I kept on weeping, but from anger and frustration now. Pablo held me limply – I felt that he'd had enough – and his arms were the loneliest place on earth. Soon, he kissed the top of my head and said, 'I must get to work, if that's all right?'

I was aware that I'd shown too much neediness, and so I said, 'Of course. Off you go.' He gathered up his equipment and left.

By evening, the weather had changed, with grey and purple clouds banking over the mountains. Pablo and Nusch paid little attention to one another, and I was sure that the others had no idea what had happened.

'How are you feeling?' Paul asked me when we were briefly alone. I shrugged, and he said, 'Everything is the same as it was before. There's nothing to worry about.' And then Nusch came up and said, 'I'm sorry we hurt you, Dora, truly I am, but it's over now. My life is with Paul, Pablo's is with you.'

I forgave her a little when she said that, and some of my affection for her returned. I said, 'I'm trying to understand, Nusch, I really am.' I think she realised that I meant it, because we embraced and she thanked me with tears in her eyes, adding, 'I'd be devastated if it spoiled our friendship.'

At that moment, rain came rushing and swishing over Mougins. We watched water pour off the edge of the roof in sheets, gushing and gurgling, our voices competing with the sound of rain. Pablo showed us the painting he'd just finished, the last work in his 'Arlésienne' series: a portrait of Paul as a peasant woman suckling a cat. I guessed it meant that he despised Paul's gesture of friendship much more than he valued it. When Paul saw it, his eyebrows shot up, but then he controlled himself and said, laughing a bit, 'It's genius.' And I hoped he realised that he deserved it.

The rain stopped at dinnertime, but heavy masses of cloud still rolled overhead, and the air was close and humid. We ate indoors and the meal seemed endless. Several bottles of wine were drunk, the conversation stopped and started. Lee got up from table before dessert and said languidly, 'It's so hot. I think I'll go take a bubble bath.'

'Can we come?' Man asked playfully. Lee gave him a long look from under her lashes, then left. There was silence, apart from the loud ticking of the clock on the mantelpiece.

At last Roland said, 'She didn't say no.'

'Then what are we waiting for?' said Pablo, and all the men rose and followed her.

Ady looked at me and Nusch, and said, 'Should we go too?'

And Nusch shrugged, saying, 'Yes, let's keep an eye on them.'

Lee had placed candles around the bathtub and they smelled like crushed rose petals. In the flickering light, her knees, chest and shoulders rose majestically from sculptural mounds of bubbles that served only to emphasise what they were supposed to hide. The men were staring. I thought I heard Pablo's breath catch.

'Let's join you,' Man suggested, and his voice was thick and slurred. He began to unbutton his shirt, with Pablo and Roland giving every sign of wanting to follow. Only Paul hung back.

'There's not enough room for you all,' Ady said drily, and Man's fingers halted. The bubbles covering Lee were beginning to subside.

'Time to go,' said Nusch, and we steered the men out of the bathroom before the bubbles vanished completely. Lee was smiling inscrutably.

Back in the salon everyone looked gloomy and out of sorts. Thunder growled in the mountains, like a waking beast. Someone suggested a game of cards, and we played a few rounds of gin rummy, but no one's heart was in it. Lee came back in a white silky robe, looking young and innocent. Pablo stared at her and a new light kindled in his eyes.

'Do you have the feeling of unfinished business? I know I do,' he said. We all looked at him and he paused, then added, 'But there's a solution! Why don't we swap first names and partners?' A frisson went around the room.

'How would that work?' Man asked carefully.

Pablo's eyes were huge, with hardly any difference between the jet-black irises and pupils. 'Let's rechristen you Roland Ray. I'll be Don Juan Picasso,' he said. 'There's a fine of two francs for anyone who forgets. Lee, will you be Dora Miller?' She nodded, looking amused.

There was something feverish about all of them. Lee wrote the men's names down, and Ady scrunched up the pieces of paper and threw them into a blue ceramic bowl. The women plucked names out of the bowl, one by one, but when my turn came, I pushed it away.

'Come on, Dora, be a sport!' Man said, and I shook my head.

Lee shrugged slightly and said, 'Well if Dora doesn't want hers I guess that leaves me with two.'

'Look who I drew!' exclaimed Ady, holding up Pablo's name. He smiled broadly and led her out of the room. On the threshold, she caught my eye and shrugged. It made me sad because I liked Ady. In different circumstances, we could have been friends. Nusch drew Roland, and Lee disappeared with Man and Paul.

Alone in the salon, I watched lightning streak from one mountain to another, while thunder rolled overhead. I told myself that if Pablo was sleeping with everyone, there was no need to be jealous of anyone. But I was horribly jealous of them all.

After the rain, the weather turned hot and humid. The garden was lush and deep green, and the lawn was full of puddles. Mixing up the couples became their favourite game. They photographed, filmed, and carried on with one another. Allegiances changed from one day to the next, the swap constantly evolving. It was impossible to keep track of who was with who. Everyone slept with everyone else, sometimes in pairs, sometimes in larger groups, and once, I saw Paul kiss Pablo on the lips as they went off with Ady. They were lost to surreal, debauched, almost satanic obsession. I was the only one who refused to join in. I was too possessed to be shared, even if Pablo had wanted to share me. I never put him to the test.

A week before the holiday ended, we sat at lunch, and the table was all cigarette butts and empty bottles and wilting flowers. Nusch fetched the blue bowl. I looked at their avid faces and sweat ran down my back. They seemed mad, completely mad, and I was a hostage in their lunatic world. The feeling of my childhood came down around me – the horror and the sense of entrapment. Just then, Lee drew Pablo's name. 'I am glad,' she said softly. 'My room or yours?'

'I don't care so long as we're together,' said Pablo. They exchanged a long, long look – they weren't with us any more – and jealousy took hold of me, like madness.

'You're killing me!' I shouted. 'I can't take it any longer!' I went on like this; I hardly knew what I was saying. The others were smiling, and this upset me even more. Neither my moods nor the looming war could spoil this 'happy family' holiday. Or was their desperate gaiety, all the carryings-on, because they knew war was coming? Everyone felt the fear and tension.

'Stop it. For God's sake, Dora. Stop it now!' Pablo said. There was a familiar gleam in his eyes, and I wondered where I'd seen it before. Then I remembered – it was during Marie-Thérèse's visit to the studio during the painting of *Guernica* – and I realised that what excited him most was the tension between the women in his life. All the fury drained out of me and I felt scared. Pushing back my chair, I stood up and half-ran to our room.

The next day, while Pablo was shopping with the others in Cannes, I packed a small bag and left. I would hitchhike to Nice and take a train from there to Paris.

I walked to the main road. Tall yellow gentians bloomed by the wayside and the heat had leached all the colour from the sky. I had a scarf covering my hair, and I was half walking, half jogging. Every now and then, I made myself slow down so as not to attract suspicion, but I soon started half walking, half jogging again. I grew thirsty. Drops of sweat ran down my back and thighs, under my dress. And then I heard a car slow down and stop behind me, and I thought, *Thank goodness*! But when I turned around, I saw that the car was the Hispano with Marcel at the wheel and Pablo in the front seat, and I was very frightened. Pablo sprang out, slamming the door.

'You must be out of your mind!' he shouted, his face dark red, flecks of saliva shooting from his lips. I had never seen him so angry. He paused, taking deep breaths, and I said despairingly: 'Why can't you leave me alone?'

'Because although you're not happy with me now, we share something extraordinary,' he said, mopping his face with his hand-kerchief. 'Don't you think so? When we met, I was on the point of killing myself, but you made me laugh. Laugh – do you understand? You're the first woman who's ever made me happy. There's no one I can talk to about the things that interest me, the way I can with you.' By now he had taken my hand and was pulling me towards the car.

I didn't resist. The heat was so cloying it was difficult to think. My head felt heavy and it hurt to move my eyes. Marcel opened the door and smiled at me but the smile I gave him back was lopsided. As the car pulled away, a breeze started flowing through the open windows, and relief washed through me. Now I didn't have to plan the rest of my life. Pablo would do it for me.

He and I alternated between quick glances and long silences. At last he said, 'Please don't throw our chance away. I'll be better, I promise.' Marcel turned off the main road. 'In love, you must listen to your heart, not your head,' Pablo continued, and Marcel nodded approvingly. Pablo said, 'You'll talk yourself out of the profoundest

144

things. What you need is a child. You don't know what being a woman is till you've had one.' He drew me close.

I leaned into him, feeling sweetness move through me. My longing for a baby had not abated – and he now wanted one too! With a child there would always be a part of Pablo I'd have access to, something we would always share. I would never feel lonely. I'd have purpose, direction, something to be proud of. The other women were simply diversions. I was the one Pablo had chosen to have a family with.

I held these feelings close, and they got me through the last few days of the holiday.

# Five

O N OUR RETURN TO Paris, the skies were deep and clear, and the days were warm but the air in the mornings and evenings held a chill edge, signalling the approach of winter. A portrait of Ady, taken by Man in Mougins, appeared in *Vogue*. She became the first Black woman to appear on the pages of a major fashion magazine, and I became the 'Weeping Woman' in Pablo's art.

He showed me the first work in the series, still on its easel, the paint scarcely dry. He was looking at me expectantly, but I was dumbstruck by the small, dazzling canvas. He had depicted me with one eye in front and one in profile, dressed for a fête, yet looking as if I'd just been struck by tragedy. The use of reds, blues, greens and yellows to portray deep sorrow was jarring. But most disturbing of all was the jagged black hole between my eyes, where the bridge of my nose should have been. I was shocked that he'd inflicted a gaping wound in such a vulnerable spot.

'What do you think?' he asked.

I found myself saying, 'I know I'm tortured, but really. You want to kill me?'

The portraits that followed were devastating in their violence, full of wailing and howling that seemed to explode onto the canvas. I scarcely looked human in them. My head was thrown back or biting on a handkerchief, tears of blood ran down my cheeks, my hands were claws.

In *Guernica*, Pablo had contorted and deconstructed my face to reflect the suffering of the times, and I'd been filled with pride. But these paintings were different. They made me feel raw all over, my nerves exposed and shrinking. Pablo was getting inside me and recreating me; worse still, he seemed to be doing it with hatred. It was confusing to be portrayed in so many states of disintegration. The portraits were like negative affirmations, prophecies of what I wasn't yet but would soon become.

I asked him how he could paint me with such savagery, and his eyes grew arrogant and defensive. He said, 'Painting is stronger than I am. It makes me do what it wants.' The lovebirds started laughing.

I said, 'I don't believe you. It's a vision you've foisted on me.'

Pablo tore off a piece of croissant, pushed it through the jam on his plate, and put it in his mouth. Then he looked me in the eye and said, 'That's not the way it works. Reality is more than the thing itself. I always look for its deeper reality. How can I explain it?' He chewed and swallowed, looking thoughtful. 'Every time you read about the violence in Europe, you get so angry and despairing. Your face is like a mirror through which I experience those feelings. Do you see? You are you *and* you're the essence of suffering.'

He held out the croissant to me. Our fingers touched as I took it, sending shivers racing through me. I thought that at least Pablo was obsessed with my image, even if it was my darkness and volatility that held him. I was his focus and, apart from increasingly infrequent visits to Marie-Thérèse, there weren't any other affairs. Even Olga was less present. I wondered why – her world seemed to revolve endlessly around her husband – and guessed that her hands were full with Paulo. I was anxious about the boy but there was also relief in not having to deal with him, with her.

There were no visitors that morning, so we started work straight after breakfast. I mixed up a glorious brown, dipped my brush into it, and was straightaway pulled into the world of my work. I had given myself over to painting completely and it was a great release. Hours passed without me noticing; even Pablo's hold loosened. I didn't have time to be his muse because I was too busy learning to be an artist.

Later in the day, he came to look at my work. I had painted a self-portrait in which I looked sad but whole. Perhaps deep inside I was still hoping for symbiosis or artistic dialogue with him. He puffed on a cigarette and wrinkled his eyes while I waited, hardly daring to breathe.

At last he said, 'Very nice, my dear. Carry on. Have fun!'

I turned away quickly, so he couldn't see my face. I remembered how flattering he had been about my photographs when we'd first met and realised that his sole motive had been to get me into bed. He didn't care about my work. He cared just as little for the work of the artists who came so hopefully to the studio to show it to him. He would feign interest, and not one of them guessed how little he cared. Or else he observed their paintings like a predator, ready to steal details and ideas that he would render so much better that everyone else would think *they* had taken it from *him*. But I was too determined, too preoccupied to let Pablo's attitude stop me. He would see – one day, I would become a great painter.

Once I'd finished work, I went to the Dingo to meet Jacqui and Huguette for a drink. We ordered a bottle of wine and I was about to tell them about Pablo's 'Weeping Woman' portraits, but Jacqui's eyes filled with tears. I put an arm around her and squeezed her shoulders. She leaned into me for a second, then sat upright, wiping her eyes with her shirtsleeve.

'I hate André,' she said.

'I understand, darling. I'd feel the same way in your shoes,' said Huguette.

'What's been happening?' I asked.

'I came back from Ajaccio determined to make the marriage work.' Jacqui's eyes welled up again. 'But he is impossible. He said to me, "I'm not interested in your painting. I want you to be properly present for Aube." I couldn't believe it. I just could not believe it.'

'Oh, Jacqui, oh, sweetheart,' I said.

Huguette took a handkerchief out of her bag and handed it to her sister. She said, 'Dora, I'm going to take care of her while she's having these difficulties.'

'You are?'

'Yes. She always looked after me. I was bullied at school, you know – taunts and name-calling. It was horrible. Once she heard a

148

girl saying I was smelly and she rushed at her, even though she was much smaller, and punched her so hard it winded her. That was it, there was no more bullying.' Huguette sat up straighter. 'And now it's time for me to be there for her. André is a bully, though I'm obviously not going to punch him.'

I was impressed, and although I had been longing to tell them about how awful Pablo's portraits made me feel, I understood that my problems would have to wait. After a time, to make Jacqui feel less alone, I told her about Pablo saying I should have fun with my painting.

'It's outrageous!' said Huguette, who was finishing her second glass of wine. 'You're both so talented. Why can't your men support you?' She waved a hand. 'You know what? You should have your own shows.'

Jacqui smiled. 'It's my dream to have a show.'

'Mine too,' I said, and an emotion that was like sunlight filled me.

Jacqui looked at her watch. 'Is that the time? I must go, André will be livid.' Huguette gave a tiny shake of her head and gestured to the waiter for our bill.

On the pavement, we hugged and said 'I love you,' and even though I hadn't had much chance to talk, I felt fortified.

Soon after I got home, the phone rang. It was Maman, and she was crying so hard she couldn't speak. I felt my heart lose its rhythm.

'Has something happened to Papito?' I asked hoarsely.

'No, it's Sophie,' said Maman, and I heard her blow her nose. 'We were out walking at lunchtime, and she slipped her lead and ran into the path of a truck. She's dead, Dora. I killed her.' She started crying again, steadily and loudly.

I was devastated too, but I had to stay strong. Maman had no inner resources, no will, nothing to make her resilient. 'It was an accident. It could have happened to anyone. Don't blame yourself,' I said. But I felt the crush of grief set in, and couldn't help blaming her a little.

Pablo consoled me by bringing Sophie back to life at mealtimes, making a series of small white dogs out of paper napkins or cardboard, sometimes with cork or wire. The nose, the eyes and the mouth were sometimes just holes in the paper, but more often they were scorch marks made with the end of a match or a cigarette.

When I looked at them, I no longer saw the creased paper of the napkin, just the wavy, silky coat of the dog, her soft, inquisitive eyes watching through her fringe. And Pablo was particularly tender with me, so that my grief became mingled with the sweetness of being loved by him.

It was the start of a restored compatibility between us. Dreams of escaping from him were replaced by a growing sense of comfort in his company. But the future was uncertain. My periods kept coming. Europe kept sliding closer to war. I was in turmoil about both. Work was the only thing I felt sure of, and so I threw myself into it, resolving to make more of my art and build its future.

1940–1944

# One

## 1940

THE FIRST THING PABLO and I saw was the round steel helmets of the Nazi scouts marching into Royan. Behind them came an endless procession of tanks, guns and lorries. Everything was the same dismal grey-green, as though the whole army had been sent to a paint shop to get sprayed. For a moment, a feeling of unreality came over me, but this was no fantasy. Nausea moved in my stomach and my skin pimpled, despite the warmth of the day. I moved closer to Pablo, and he put his arm around me. The column made a low, menacing rumble that turned into a roar as it neared, making the terrace of the Hôtel du Tigre vibrate beneath our feet.

We had moved to Royan with Sabartés and Kazbek, shortly after the declaration of war. It had been safer than Paris, a haven in which to recover from the last brutal eighteen months. In January 1939, we had received news that Pablo's mother was dead. Although old, she had still been active, running a household full of children and grandchildren. On the morning of her death she was getting dressed at dawn behind the door of the armoire, because the grandchildren slept in her bedroom, when she'd lost her balance and fallen. Her nephews had carried her to hospital in an armchair, but her spine was broken, and she had died a few hours later.

Pablo had been bedridden by a painful attack of sciatica and was not fit to go to Barcelona for the funeral. And even if he had been well enough, the war made travel hazardous. I suspected that he'd been relieved to miss it – it was his nature to run away from those kinds of situations. He rarely spoke about his grief, but I had felt his heart congeal as he locked it in. Less than a fortnight after his mother's death, Barcelona, which had always meant so much to him, had fallen into Franco's hands. Madrid had surrendered two months later, and the Spanish Civil War ended in defeat. Pablo had lost his mother, his country and a past that he would never see again. All he was left with were ghosts and ruins – 300,000 dead soldiers, 400,000 dead civilians. And all the while Europe was moving closer to war and I'd felt that blackness was enveloping us both, and an ice-cold emptiness.

At first in Royan, I had felt sheltered from the conflict. Pablo had left Marie-Thérèse and Olga in Paris, and I savoured having him to myself, the closest thing to happy I had been for a long time. But in May of this year, the German blitzkrieg had punched through the Maginot Line, France had fallen and the Nazis were everywhere.

Pablo said, 'They're another race. They think they are very intelligent. They've certainly made a lot of progress. But if you look carefully, you will see that they are very stupid. So many troops and machines, so much power and din to get here! What nonsense it is!'

'How can you be so nonchalant?' I asked. A German plane roared overhead, startling me.

Pablo shrugged. 'I hope the fighting won't disturb my work.' And I thought how ironic it was that Pablo, who couldn't exist without strife, found peace indispensable to his art.

In the days that followed, the high command set up its headquarters in the Hôtel du Golfe, near Pablo's apartment, and German soldiers were stationed at the Tigre. During the day they sunbathed in their boxer shorts on the beach; fat and pink, they pillow-fought with the dead, green, putrescent jellyfish that covered the beaches. A sense of horror underpinned everything. I couldn't predict anything or understand anything. But I reminded myself that at least we had the sea, fresh air and good food, unlike our friends in Paris, who were living in a prison with blackouts, long queues for food and no cars.

A week after the Germans arrived, Pablo fetched me from the hotel for our morning stroll. In the beginning, we had stayed at the hotel together, but he'd soon rented his own apartment on the second floor of a seafront villa called Les Voiliers. I had begged him not to leave, but he insisted on having his own separate living quarters.

'Hola!' he said, kissing me on the lips, and I saw that Kazbek wasn't with him. These days, he mostly left the dog with Sabartés. He had lost interest in him, as he'd done with Elft. He added, 'You look pale, darling. Are you feeling sick? Any sign of you know what?' and he looked hopefully at my stomach.

I shook my head and said, 'If I am pale, it's because I'm not sleeping properly. Having all these soldiers around makes me nervous.' Pablo's face fell, and I felt such shame at my inability to fall pregnant.

He took my arm and we set off along the flower-lined boulevard, past the casino, heading down to the rue de la République. It was a dull day, with banks of cloud working across the sky, and a tepid breeze that stirred up dust in eddies. We passed the gare routière on our right, surrounded by wasteland and thickets.

Pablo said, 'I had a letter from Olga this morning.'

'Oh, yes?'

'It's about Paulo. Things are going from bad to worse. He's keeping company with thieves, drug dealers and pimps. Of course, he admires them all totally.' He shook his head. 'It's only a matter of time before he gets into trouble.'

'You must do something,' I said.

Pablo was silent, his forehead puckered. At last he said, 'I'll phone my friends in Switzerland, the Geisers. Ask them to find a private clinic for him. We don't want any publicity in France.' Relief washed through me because Pablo was finally taking action. But I shuddered too, because it had come to this before he would do anything, and because he was paying for treatment instead of getting involved himself. It was another glimpse of his coldness and his willingness to discard people.

We had reached the marketplace, where we looked at the fruit and vegetable stands, and the stalls that sold rags or trinkets. Then Pablo said, 'Let's go to see the exhibition,' and he led the way down a narrow street to a tiny, cramped shop. Outside on the pavement were old, rusted irons, a rabbit skin stretched out in the sun, and a dilapidated parrot cage, twisted and dented. It was the cage's shadow, projected into fantastic shapes, that had first drawn his attention, and we came back to see it again and again. He looked at it intently for some moments, then we went inside and browsed through old books, the grate from a kitchen range, a broken kerosene lamp and a few scratched keys. Pablo exclaimed over each item and chattered to a small, toothless monkey as if they were old friends.

'I should buy you, *mi bonito*,' he said gently, and the monkey cavorted in his cage, seeming to understand. Pablo turned to me, his eyes flashing. 'Isn't he magnificent?'

'I'm in love with him,' I said. 'Let's take him home.'

But I knew from previous visits that Pablo had no intention of buying the monkey. His performance was a way of escaping and I joined him in it. It was an embrace of life in its simplest forms, a return to an instinctive, childish self that kept us alive and generated a kind of magic vital to our art.

In the afternoon, we shut ourselves up in our respective living quarters to work. Le Tigre was a grand old building with high ceilings and generously proportioned rooms. Mine was fitted out with heavy mahogany furniture and a four-poster bed, and I had set up a makeshift studio by the window. The light was excellent, and I refused to let the shortage of artists' materials hinder me. Pablo had made two trips to Paris in search of paints, brushes, canvas and paper, but there was never enough. Squatting on the floor for lack of an easel, I painted on planks or hardboard when canvas was lacking, using wooden chair seats that had been removed from their frames as palettes. I depicted the coming and going of the ferry boat, the reflections on the water, and the long, curving sweep of the bay with its hotels and villas touched by the sun. I marvelled at how the natural world seemed immune to the tension of war.

When I had finished painting, I cleared away my things and walked to Pablo's villa. He opened the door and kissed me, and we went upstairs to his studio. At this hour it was full of a murky, greenish light from the trees outside that put an end to his work. The space had been a dining room until recently, and there was a sturdy oak table and chairs in the middle of it. Pablo had covered every surface with his clutter, leaving little room for his canvases and colours, which were piled on top of the furniture or on the floor. It was difficult to move about. As he led me to look at his afternoon's work, I tried to avoid damaging anything – especially myself.

On his easel was a portrait of a young girl. She had a long, auburn plait, and was staring pensively at the bay. I asked if it was a painting of someone he knew, and he said, 'No. Her image just came to me.'

'It's a gem,' I said, and Pablo breathed out in relief. A lovely glow filled me because my opinion still mattered to him. We cleaned and tidied away his materials, and then went out into the warm, salt-laced air.

The wind had dropped, and the evening was clear and pleasant. From time to time, we lingered to watch the views we'd painted earlier in different light. We passed a tall, gaunt man pulling his dog away from a lamp post, a group of soldiers walking quickly, a couple holding their daughter's hands. Pablo halted and a look of terror crossed his features.

'What's wrong? The soldiers?' I asked.

Pablo's face was pale and clammy. 'No, no! Didn't you see? That child is the image of the one I just painted.'

I looked behind and saw that he was right, even down to the blue ribbon securing her plait. The hairs on the back of my neck stood on end but I straightened my spine, refusing to give way to fear. I had to snap Pablo out of it if I didn't want the evening ruined. So I touched his arm and said brightly, 'What a coincidence! Odd, but it doesn't mean anything.'

His brow lowered. 'I hate things that can't be accounted for.'

'You've probably seen the girl before and absorbed her image without realising.'

'I know it's a bad omen.'

We began to walk again, my nerves straining. We ended up at Café Le Régent, which was on the little square in front of the port. Pablo ordered an Evian, and I had white wine. We liked sitting in the square with its still-good restaurants and old houses, watching low sunlight paint them pink or caramel. There was an old man in a striped jersey mending fishing nets on the quay and groups of sailors walking about. A radio played the news – it was all war, hate and political dissent, and I was tired of it. I finished my wine and looked at Pablo from under my lashes.

'Will you stay with me tonight?' I asked huskily.

Pablo smiled, then frowned. 'I would love to, but I promised Sabartés I'd meet him for a drink.'

I felt a sharp twinge of disappointment. The air was growing chilly, so I drew my cardigan more securely round my shoulders and said, 'Why don't you walk me home, then.'

The sun had set and dusk was beginning to thicken as we started off. I loved this light that was not quite day but not yet night. The streets were quiet; most people had gone home. A hundred yards from the Tigre, I saw Sabartés and Marie-Thérèse deep in conversation on the other side of the boulevard, and pain took my breath away.

'What's she doing here? I thought she was in Paris,' I said, trying to keep my voice steady.

Pablo's eyes went small and he said, 'Sharing my life, just like you are. You agreed, remember?'

I felt utterly lost. Then came fury with myself for my own stupidity. We had lived like this in Paris, so why had I expected it to be different in Royan? And I realised that Marie-Thérèse was the real reason Pablo spent so few nights with me. He was organising his time around his painting and his women. Either Marie-Thérèse hadn't seen us, or she was pretending not to. I had no idea if she was aware of my presence in Royan or not. She towered over Sabartés, and as he looked up at her, smiling, I saw his capacity for tenderness and friendship, and my eyes watered from the sting of it. But there was relief too, in knowing there was nothing I could have done to make him like me.

I turned to Pablo. 'How long has she been here?'

'A month.' He was looking everywhere but at me.

'Where's she staying?'

'In a villa near mine.'

We had reached the entrance of the Tigre. He kissed me and wished me goodnight, then turned away and started walking down the boulevard in the direction Marie-Thérèse and Sabartés had taken. I walked into the hotel, knowing that another evening of turmoil lay ahead of me.

I didn't want to dwell too much on Marie-Thérèse's presence in Royan, because Pablo had simply transported his harem to his provincial exile. The pain I felt was nothing new, but there was no escaping it, as I couldn't break away from him. The surface of normal life went on. Pablo and I took our morning walks and ate lunch together. I visited his studio in the late afternoons and saw that he'd returned to confusing my and Marie-Thérèse's images in his painting, crowning me with her flowers or dressing her in a costume more fitting for me. He was as unrepentant as ever, and I gave up trying to argue with him.

After a fortnight of this, he began to absent himself even more. The waiting returned, the longing and the grief, because the terms of our relationship meant that I was at the mercy of his calls. Apart from painting, there was nothing to distract me except the war and my inability to conceive. Once or twice a week, he came to the Tigre and we spent terrible, sleepless nights, hardly touching or speaking. Sometimes he took me with joyless efficiency. Afterwards I would lie beside him, wondering if he felt the conflict of wills. When I closed my eyes, sparks flew inside my head.

During the day, we mostly talked about Jacqui. In early July, she had written to tell me that André had been drafted into the medical corps (he had originally trained as a physician), and she was struggling on her own with Aube. After some discussion, Pablo and I invited her to join us, and she accepted by return. I looked forward to giving her shelter, and to assuaging my growing sense of powerlessness. Once, I had felt like I could take on the world. Now, I needed a long-standing friend to help me come to terms with what my life had become.

# Two

THE FRONT DOORS OF the Tigre were open but not a breath of wind stirred. It was late July, and as Pablo and I waited in the lobby, sweat collected into drips down my back, gluing my dress to my skin. Pablo was watching the sky, which was obscured by high cloud, with sultry shafts of sun breaking through. Then Jacqui and Aube appeared, accompanied by a porter carrying their luggage. Jacqui looked fresh and cool in a yellow dress, her legs and arms deeply tanned. We embraced and she said, 'It's wonderful to be here. I can't thank you enough,' and I said, 'It's wonderful to have you.'

Aube stood by her mother's side, looking up at us with clear, tobacco-coloured eyes framed by curls of the same shade. Now four years old, she was chunky and perfect – a little lioness. I kissed her cheeks and Pablo swept her into his arms exclaiming, '*Ma petite poupée!*' while she giggled happily.

The porter came up to show them to their room – it was next to mine – and Pablo went to his studio to work. I gave Jacqui and Aube time to get settled, then knocked on their door, and the three of us went to the beach. Thick clouds had gathered, and the sea was a hard glimmer of slate. The wind had picked up, but it was still pleasant to sit on the sand, while Aube gathered shells and stones on the shoreline. These days, there were no soldiers on the beach. They were patrolling the streets, rifles pointed at the sky. I asked Jacqui how she was.

'I'm barely managing. You know how we live – no cash, surrounded by priceless art,' she said, chewing on her bottom lip. André earned little but was a compulsive collector. Then she said, 'Remember how I used to long for my freedom?' I nodded and she added, 'Well, being on my own with Aube is scary. I've always considered myself a strong person, but it's different when there are soldiers everywhere, and you don't know what's going to happen.'

'You're safe now,' I said, taking her hand, and we watched gulls flying overhead. 'Are you working?'

'A little, when Aube's asleep, but it's hard,' she said. 'It's not like André helps with anything in the house, but somehow, there's less time to paint when he's away. Aube is unsettled, for one thing.' For several moments she said nothing, looking ahead at the grey sea. Then, 'I get depressed when I'm not painting.'

'Me too,' I said.

Jacqui tucked her hair behind her ear. 'I'm so glad to be here. We'll spend lots of time together.' She took a closer look at me and asked, 'How are things with Pablo?'

'The same, except I'm not getting pregnant. I am devastated,' I said, relieved that I could finally unburden myself. At that moment, Aube hurried over, her cheeks whipped pink by the wind. 'Look what I found! Look!' she cried, and Jacqui raised her eyebrows at me and shrugged. 'There'll be other times to talk,' she said quietly.

We exclaimed over Aube's collection of small stones, shells and bits of sea glass. Then we laid out the pieces on the sand and began to make patterns with them. The clouds parted over the sea, and a slash of sunlight fell on the beach, dazzling against the purple sky. At six o'clock, we brushed the sand off ourselves and made our way back. I bought Aube a strawberry ice cream from the kiosk opposite the hotel, and she threw her arms around me.

That night, Pablo joined me at the hotel for dinner. The dining room was one of my favourite spaces, with bronze velvet curtains, wooden floors polished to a rich sheen, and a chandelier of clear and amber crystal droplets. Vases of lily-of-the-valley sat on tables, their sweet scent mingling with the smells of food and smoke from the Germans' cigarettes. There were more soldiers and fewer civilians every time I ate here. Pablo was sitting at a corner table. So far, the soldiers had left him alone, despite his 'degenerate' status.

'Hola! Good evening!' he said, getting to his feet and taking my hands in his.

'Good evening, Pablo.' I kept my eyes lowered.

Pablo scanned my face. 'Are you all right?'

'I'm fine, thank you.'

We sat down. I didn't feel like telling him that my period had just started, and that I was sure there was something wrong with me. We'd been trying for a baby for over three years now, and obviously Pablo wasn't the problem. I glanced at him and saw a deep worry line between his eyebrows.

'What's the matter?' I asked.

'Le Tremblay has been requisitioned by the Germans.' He looked so scared and defeated that I forgot my own problems. I reached for his hand, and he said, 'Delarue, the caretaker, phoned to tell me.'

'So sorry,' I said, shaking my head.

'What's going to happen to my paintings and sculptures?' he asked. I stroked his hand, and we said nothing for many moments. And then he took his hand away and sat upright, staring. I followed his gaze and saw Jacqui in the doorway, wearing a filmy silver dress and a necklace of tiger claws, with flowers and sea glass in her hair. She looked beautiful and dangerous, and all the air punched out of me. A table of Nazi officers leered at her as she made her way to us but she ignored them. Pablo rose and kissed her hand. His mood had changed; he was smiling.

'I hope you don't mind me joining you. One of the chambermaids offered to feed Aube supper in her room.'

We sat down and I started talking about the weather (rain was predicted). We ordered claret and roasted guinea fowl, which ran wild in the area. The wine arrived, and we clinked glasses and spoke of our friends. We spoke of Paul Éluard, who had departed with his regiment, leaving Nusch bereft. We told Jacqui about Paul Rosenberg, who for years had quietly been distributing his collection outside of mainland Europe. He had taken off for Bordeaux days before the Feldpolizei had looted his home and gallery.

Pablo's face had fallen into sad lines. He said, 'It's too much loss and destruction. For God's sake tell me something cheerful.' And so we talked about Aube, and about everything she had done on the beach.

'She's a prodigy! Adorable!' said Pablo, as our food arrived. 'My friend has a daughter the same age. I think you'd enjoy meeting them.' He cut up his guinea fowl and pushed a forkful into his mouth.

'I would love to,' Jacqui said, smiling.

Jealousy seized me – he could only mean Marie-Thérèse and Maya. I made my face expressionless and folded my hands over each other to hide their trembling. I knew that Pablo couldn't resist pulling all the strings to set his women off against each other but Jacqui's disloyalty cut even deeper. A memory came spilling back of Nusch in Mougins, squeezing Pablo's arm, and looking up into his eyes. As the conversation flowed, I pushed food around my plate, waiting for the evening to end. Jacqui was talking about her plans with André. They wanted to flee France and go to America by way of the unoccupied south.

'The thought of going into exile with him frightens me,' she said, flipping back her hair.

'Why?' asked Pablo, leaning towards her.

She waved a hand. 'He sees in me what he wants to see. He doesn't really *see* me. He wants me to be a muse and mother of his child, not the painter I'm trying to be.'

Pablo looked at her sympathetically. 'You're so much more than a mother and a muse.'

Jacqui nodded. 'I'm like a dog going round and round for him,' she said, and I felt a pang of recognition.

When dinner was over, Pablo wished us goodnight and left. He was probably going to see Marie-Thérèse and, once again, I had the disorientating sensation of not knowing who to be jealous of. Jacqui and I went slowly upstairs. She put her hand on my arm and said, 'You were very quiet, Dora. Is something wrong?'

I shook her off and said, 'How could you agree to meet Pablo's friend? How *could* you! Don't you know he meant Marie-Thérèse?'

Jacqui stopped and put her hands on her hips. With a flare of the temper that had earned her the student nickname 'Bastille Day', she said, 'Well, what do you expect me to do? I don't want him to think me ungracious.'

'What does it matter what Pablo thinks?'

She lifted her brows. 'He is my host. Men rule because they are men, women have to survive. What's more, there's a war going on. I'm doing what I've done all my life, I am simply carrying on.'

I bit my lip, feeling so betrayed by her that I nearly couldn't walk straight. We reached our rooms, said a perfunctory goodnight, and I went in and lay down on my bed, fully clothed. The rain started. I listened to large drops slapping against the windows and thought about the death of Jacqui's mother, and how determined Jacqui had been to carry on painting afterwards, even though some of the jobs she had been forced to take were demeaning. Thunder detonated overhead, making me jump, followed by a quiver of lightning. And I saw that nothing would stop her getting what she wanted, and that her needs would always come before anything else.

In the days that followed, Pablo deliberately encouraged the friendship between Jacqui and Marie-Thérèse, bringing them together for meals and walks by the sea. I knew this was also visually exciting for him, as the two women looked so much alike. Often when I looked out of my window, I would see them on the boulevard with Aube and Maya, blonde heads bent together in conversation. I wondered what they talked about – my irrepressible, clever Jacqueline and the less accomplished Marie-Thérèse. Surely it could only have been about their daughters. But I would have given anything to stroll by the sea with a friend, chatting about our children.

I reacted by withdrawing completely. Sometimes I had meals with Pablo and Jacqui, and I hated every one of them. Jacqui continued to enchant, flipping back her hair, and talking about art, literature and politics. Sometimes, she shot me reproachful looks, and once, on our way back to our rooms, she said, 'I don't think it's right to sulk and feel jealous. Pablo loves you, but he and Marie-Thérèse have a child together. It's a powerful tie.'

I was too choked up to answer and let myself into my room without a word, slamming the door behind me. I steadied myself against the wall, looking at my reflection in the mirror opposite, and my features seemed distorted, red around the eyes and nose. I began to feel the whole weight of Pablo's unfairness to me. *I'm so much younger*, I thought, *and this should be my season. But instead I'm being diminished and trodden underfoot.* This brought a host of bitter thoughts and feelings that I had to wade through. It seemed as if our relationship mirrored the dark times we were living through, and it was unravelling in parallel with Europe. I wondered what falling in love during peaceful times would have been like. Perhaps we would have been better together. Perhaps I would have flourished more easily as an artist.

Then one morning I woke up and the sun was sparkling on the waves, and for the first time in months, I felt joy bubble up in me. The world seemed to be saying *Look how glorious I am. Come, dance with me.* I threw on my robe, opened the doors and stepped out onto the balcony, soaking up the warmth, the flawless blue sky, the ribbons of sandy beaches hugging the coast. A column of Nazi soldiers marched past, their heavy boots thudding out the rhythm as they sang German songs. It brought home that we were sitting targets, utterly at their mercy, and a stab of fear went through me. Suddenly life seemed very fragile. I felt a longing to experience it as fully as possible, and a surge of resentment towards Pablo for stopping me. The feelings grew until I was all seething emotion, unable to see the beauty in front of me. I went inside and washed my face, changed into a blue silk dress, and hurried to Pablo's villa. On the way, I noticed that there were more soldiers on the streets. They seemed to have come out of nowhere, silently, to infest the town.

I hammered on Pablo's door, not caring if Marie-Thérèse was there or if I was disturbing his work. He opened it in shorts and an old striped top, looking astonished to see me. 'Dora, what brings you at this hour? Is something wrong?'

'Yes, you are ruining my life!' I said firmly, watching his eyes widen.

'What are you talking about?'

'Isn't it enough that I put up with Marie-Thérèse? Do you have to take Jacqui away from me too?'

Pablo shut his eyes and pressed his fist to his forehead. He said, 'Of course I'm not taking her away. I don't know what you mean.'

A deep and terrible anger rose in me, and tears came to my eyes. 'Liar!' I shouted. 'It's obvious you want them both. Or are you already sleeping with Jacqui?'

His lips tightened and he said, 'Don't be ridiculous! Look, I give you shelter and security. We spend time together. Why do you always find fault?' He folded his arms, slotting his hands into his armpits. 'Once you've calmed down, we will talk. But for now, I must get back to work,' and he shut the door in my face.

I was so shocked, I just stood there, breathing hard. It took several minutes to collect myself sufficiently to walk back to the hotel.

I took the beachfront route, waiting for my heart to stop thumping. The sun beat down on me, and the shadows lay dense and thick. I began to wonder if I should go back to Paris. At least I had friends and support there. The more I thought about it, the more clearly I saw that I needed to leave Pablo. Then a poster stuck to the side of a food kiosk caught my eye. It bore a picture of Nazi soldiers with savage-looking dogs and the words:

CAPITAL PUNISHMENT FOR THE TRAITORS
CUTTING OUR ELECTRIC CABLES!
HOSTAGES WILL BE TAKEN TO GUARANTEE THE
CESSATION OF SABOTAGE.

My skin prickled. We had heard that an unknown person or people had repeatedly cut the main cables outside Royan, but nobody knew if it was a lone wolf or organised resistance. As I stood and looked at the poster, life seemed so gloomy that I started to cry. After a couple of minutes, I noticed two Nazi officers coming towards me, tall in their high, polished boots, black peaked caps and uniforms with swastikas on the armbands. I began to walk again, looking at the ground, trying to stifle my tears.

'You!' a harsh voice yelled. I raised my eyes and saw the dark-haired officer pointing at me. A strange feeling swept over me. I struggled to breathe.

'You in the blue dress! Has the devil got your tongue?'

'No, sir,' I muttered as they reached me. 'I'm sorry, sir.'

'Give me your papers.'

I fumbled for them with fingers that trembled so badly, I could hardly get them out of my bag. He took them and looked at them, his face darkening.

'Your name is Markovitch? You're a Jew?' he barked. My stomach twinged and nausea spread through me, like a stain. Although I had shortened my name to Maar, Markovitch was on my papers; it had always been my legal name. Legally, I was one person; artistically, I was someone else.

'No, no. It's a Croatian name,' I stammered.

His porcelain-blue eyes bored into mine. 'Are you sure?'

I forced myself to hold his gaze. 'Yes, sir. My father was born in Croatia.'

They conferred quietly in German, while my heart pounded in my chest. Finally, the other officer threw my papers back at me. 'We'll be keeping an eye on you,' he growled, and I was flooded with panic. Not only could I be taken for a Jew, but I had also been an extreme leftist, and I'd photographed *Guernica*, which had been denounced in the German press (Pablo kept every one of the articles, like badges of pride).

When they had gone, I leaned against the sea wall, taking deep breaths. Was it an idle threat to keep an eye on me, or was it real? Black spots danced in front of my eyes, and I thought I might pass out. But I couldn't afford to draw more attention to myself, and so I straightened my back and forced myself to keep walking.

As my legs moved, my head cleared and my thoughts began to flow. I thought about how frightened Jacqui had been, alone with Aube in Paris. I reflected on the horrors experienced by women and children in the Spanish Civil War. And I saw that being on my own was too dangerous, especially with my undesirable name and background. What on earth had made me think I could travel back to Paris alone? Even if I wanted to leave Pablo, there was no choice but to stay and take whatever protection he could give me. I was more trapped than ever. As soon as I reached my room,

I splashed cold water on my face, lit a cigarette and sat down to write to him:

> My dearest,
>
> I'm writing to tell you that I am sorry for being such a fool and wicked this morning. It's just that jealousy made me mad and stupid with pain. Please be patient and I will correct myself.
>
> Your friend,
>
> Dora

Then I sat back and waited for him to come. I waited until long after midnight, but he did not come. The next morning, a hastily scrawled note arrived:

> The caretaker at Le Tremblay phoned to say that the Germans have gone on army manoeuvres. I am going there now with Marie-Thérèse and Maya. Try to stay calm while I'm gone. We will talk on my return.

# Three

J ACQUI AND I SPENT the week of Pablo's absence in an uneasy state of truce. She was careful not to defend Marie-Thérèse's position any more, and we mostly painted in our separate rooms. I was thankful for the diversion of work, because since the encounter with the officers, fear ebbed and flowed in me like a tide. While Jacqui painted, she left Aube with the chambermaid, a good-natured girl with hazel eyes and freckles. I watched them playing on the beach. Aube looked happy, and I was relieved that Maya was far away.

And then Pablo came back and sought me out at once. I had noticed that long periods of time with Marie-Thérèse seemed to bore him – he was generally pleased to see me afterwards. We embraced and I studied his face, noting how drawn it was.

I put my hand on his back and said, 'Come with me. We can have coffee on my balcony.' We went to my room and sat sipping at our drinks, with the bay spread out beneath us and the wind moving through our hair. After many minutes, I asked about Le Tremblay.

'It's a mess,' he said, gesturing helplessly. 'Furniture is damaged. They tore our clothes and sheets to strips to make cleaning cloths. As for the art, we managed to salvage some of the smaller works, but oh, the stupid destruction! It broke my heart!'

I shook my head. 'Awful for you.'

He took my hand. 'I can't bear thinking about it. You know the wax medieval sculpture of Christ I'm so fond of?' I nodded. 'They burned it like a candle.' There was terrible pain on his face.

'I'm sorry. I'm so sorry,' I said, returning the pressure of his hand. 'But it shows there's no future here. Why don't we leave France, like the Bretons?'

169

Pablo seemed to consider it. Then he said, 'I'm not looking to take risks but I don't like yielding to force. So I am staying here. The only force that could make me leave would be the desire to go.'

I took my hand away. 'What about what I want?' And I told him about being questioned by the Nazis, and about their threats.

He listened, the crease between his eyebrows deepening. 'Have they bothered you since?' he asked.

'No,' I said, 'but I'd feel safer if we left.'

He pushed the hair off his forehead, and I noticed how sparse it had become. 'My mind's made up,' he said, looking me in the eye. 'Staying on isn't an act of bravery. It's a form of inertia. I just prefer being here.'

I dropped my gaze, cut to the quick that my security mattered so little to him. 'But you're a "degenerate" and a foreigner!' I said quietly. 'Anything could happen! You could be interned, deported, held hostage.'

He waited a long time before he spoke, and then said firmly, 'I'll stay, whatever the risk. But I'm not too worried. It will be a global scandal if the Nazis touch me.'

'Your name won't make us invincible,' I said uneasily. Of course I was more scared for myself. I couldn't trust in being protected by personalities or intermediaries as Pablo was. But he wouldn't answer and, after a pause, asked me what I'd been doing while he was away.

'Painting, mostly, and spending time with Jacqui,' I said. 'Oh, and I made a doctor's appointment for tomorrow.'

Pablo narrowed his eyes. 'Why? You're not sick, are you?' He had a horror of illness. I suppose it reminded him of his own mortality.

'I want to find out why I'm not falling pregnant.' My stomach knotted up as I said it.

His face was blank – he seemed surprised. 'I am sure it will happen in its own time,' he said, and I shrugged.

He didn't stay that night, and I heard gunfire in the distance. I couldn't tell where it was coming from, and my heart started beating very fast. It was impossible to sleep. And then, hours later, I dropped into a fitful doze and dreamed that two minotaurs were tearing out each other's throats on my roof.

Dr Blanchet's hair was fair and he was clean-shaven, with blunt, even features. He held out his hand, his grip warm. 'It's good to meet you,' he said, showing me to the chair opposite his desk. The room was spacious and smelled of his cologne, with a whiff of disinfectant underneath. There were bookshelves stuffed with fat medical volumes, a sink, a weighing scale and a bed.

He took my pulse, and felt behind my ears and along my jawline. His touch was gentle. He weighed me, then went to his desk to make notes while I watched. Without looking up, he asked if I had trouble with my periods.

'Well, I have irregular bleeding and sometimes there's pain here,' I said, touching my lower abdomen.

The doctor's pen paused and he raised his eyes to meet mine. 'Let's take a look,' he said.

Minutes later I was lying on the couch with my knees wide open and my heels tucked up against my behind. I felt cool air on my intimate parts and humiliation rolled through me. He felt my stomach gently – he had nice hands, I noticed, with square fingers and a golden wedding ring. Then his fingers were inside me and I shut my eyes, trying to disengage from what was happening down below. With his other hand, he began to press down hard on my stomach, and I couldn't help crying out.

'I'm sorry. I have to be firm,' he said sympathetically.

I was so relieved when it ended. Dr Blanchet sent me to have an X-ray and asked me to come back tomorrow, so that we could discuss the results.

I spent the rest of the day alone. I wasn't strong enough to seek out Jacqui, and Pablo didn't come. At suppertime, I ordered a bowl of soup in my room and spooned it into my mouth, thinking that I'd never envisaged my life like this. I began to feel as though I was falling from a high building. I pushed the soup away and my mind cried, *Help me help me help me.* To relieve my feelings, I drank red wine until the walls began to turn and I passed out.

The next morning, Dr Blanchet shook my hand and asked me to sit down, and I was again aware of his gentleness. But although he spoke in a low, soft voice, nothing could hide the sting of his words.

'The X-ray confirmed what I suspected when I examined you. There's a build-up of abnormal tissue in your uterus.'

A sick, clammy feeling came over me. 'What does it mean?'

He was silent for several moments, looking at his hands. Then he said, 'The extra tissue creates less space inside your uterus. Think of the walls of a room getting thicker, so that the space in the middle of the room shrinks. When this happens, the sperm can't reach the egg for fertilisation.'

'Can it be treated?' I was gripping the arms of my chair.

He shook his head. 'I'm afraid not. I'm so sorry.'

My mind struggled to take it in. I was infertile. I was not a woman, I was some kind of freak. What I had feared was certain – I would never have children. I thought of Aube and Maya, frolicking outside my windows, and such a weight of grief and horror fell on me. Sobs rose in my throat and I tried to choke them down.

Dr Blanchet was looking at me with great kindness. He pulled a bottle of brandy from a drawer in his desk, poured me a glass and said, 'Drink this. It will help.' I downed it in one gulp.

The brandy numbed me just enough to get back to the hotel. As I walked, I mused about the girl with the auburn plait, and about Pablo's belief that it was a sign of malicious forces at work. And it seemed that these forces had singled me out, and that I was cursed, marked out for misfortune.

I had sent Pablo a note, asking him to meet me, and he was waiting in the lobby. He came towards me with outstretched hands. I took them in mine and said, 'Come upstairs. We can't talk here.'

My room was a mess, the bed unmade, cups and dishes every-where. Pablo perched on the edge of the bed. 'What did the doctor say?'

I didn't want to tell him. The words were locked in my mouth, hardened to stone. I was afraid of what they might do if I let them out.

Pablo was studying my face. 'You're so pale. What's wrong?'

I took a breath and it all came spilling out. 'The doctor said I'm infertile. Do you see? I'm infertile, I'll never get pregnant.'

His face changed as he took this in. His eyes met mine for half a second, then roved around the room, as though he needed to look away from me.

He said, 'Is it treatable?' and I said, 'No.' The shame I felt was bone-deep.

Silence stretched out, empty and dangerous. I wiped the back of my hand across my mouth and nose, willing myself not to cry. Then he asked if I wanted a second opinion, and I said, 'What's the point?' He lit a cigarette and went out onto the balcony to smoke it, standing with his back to me, gazing at the view.

At last, he turned to face me. 'You've lost so much weight recently, you're almost angular. I am sure it doesn't help.' He was probably thinking of Marie-Thérèse's generous curves and her fecundity. I sensed he couldn't stand having an infertile lover by his side, he felt the whiff of death in it, and it repelled him. The sensation of falling came over me again.

When he left, I drew the curtains and went to bed for three days, moving only to fetch a glass of water or use the bathroom. I no longer knew myself. How would I learn to live and work again with this horror, this atrocious lack? The pain was so keen, so raw, grief haemorrhaged out of me. At times it made me writhe in bed, tearing at the pillow with my teeth, and sounds I did not recognise came from my mouth. I could feel my mind slipping away. I tried to keep hold of it by calling up the old me, the photographer striding through the streets of foreign cities, but people and places mashed into each other and disintegrated. There were brief periods of respite when my thoughts shut down and I lay watching spears of sunlight fall through the curtains. But then the pain started up again.

Every now and then, Jacqui came to my door and pleaded with me to talk to her. The hotel staff left useless offerings of soup or fresh fruit outside my room. I could hear Maya and Aube playing, and imagined their mothers watching them fondly. I waited for Pablo to visit or at least write to me, but he was silent. I wished for him so hard, my breath caught in my throat. But as time crept by, I saw that I'd been right about him not wanting a damaged woman by his side. He was gone.

173

On the third night, I heard an envelope being pushed under my door. By then my heart was too tattered for human contact, and so I left it lying there. I went to bed but couldn't sleep. I tried not to hope the note was from Pablo – I couldn't take any more disappointment – but every time I closed my eyes, an image of him smiling at me played and replayed in my head. Finally I fell into a restless doze.

I woke in the early hours, feeling lost. What was I doing here? Who even was I? I switched on the lamp and reached for my robe; then went to pick the envelope up, tearing it open with my thumb.

Adora,

I miss you. I know how sad you are, but please don't shut me out. Meet me for breakfast tomorrow at ten o'clock?

I am yours,

Pablo

I walked to the window to look out at the beach. It was all dappled moonlight and shadows, with dustings of stars between the clouds. I could not believe that Pablo had made me wait three days. I didn't have the strength to go on like this – the endless waiting, the longing. On the other hand, I felt a terrible desperation at not being able to go on. I made my way back to bed, tossing and turning, until daylight began to filter through the curtains.

I thought I might as well get up. I was in a strange, trance-like state, my mind scarcely aware of what my body was doing. I bathed and put on my blue silk dress, then made my way to the dining room. After three days in bed, my legs had grown stiff and weak, and I put a hand on the wall to steady myself. Suddenly, I felt mortal. One day, they would put me in a box and bury me in the ground; all the little lights and impulses that made up my conscious-ness extinguished.

The dining-room windows were open and the breeze flowing through them smelled of the sea. I saw that Pablo was already seated and my heart gave a small jolt. He kissed me and asked how I was. We made small talk, carefully avoiding the subject of my childlessness, while doves called throatily to each other outside. He asked if I was painting and I said I couldn't.

He tore off the end of a croissant and folded it into his mouth. 'You must paint, Dora. Paint despite your sadness,' he said, chewing. 'I'm sad too, but painting keeps my dark feelings at bay.'

There was a lump in my throat and my eyes were stinging. My grief was too deep and black to be assuaged by painting. It was getting stronger, changing shape so the sharpness of the pain was never blunted.

'If we weren't unhappy, we wouldn't be painting,' Pablo said. 'We paint because we're not happy,' and this felt right to me. In a moment he added, 'I can't talk like this to anyone but you. Please don't withdraw from me.'

He looked at me beseechingly and took my hand. And tears that had been locked inside me for days began to run down my cheeks. I was weeping for us, for the baby I would never have, and for what had broken inside me forever when I'd learned that I was barren. Pablo put his arms around me and his cheeks were wet too.

# Four

THERE FOLLOWED A PERIOD of dull misery. Not the scorching pain of earlier, but a head that felt like it was stuffed with cloth, and the feeling that at the core of me, something was slowly rotting. It was impossible to work, I couldn't concentrate on anything. My thoughts shuttled between my childlessness and the fear of what the war might bring. Pablo was gentle with me and careful to pay less attention to Jacqui. We never talked about my infertility, but it was in the air around us all the same.

And then, on a windless, overcast morning in the middle of August, Jacqui announced that André had been discharged from the medical corps. The two of us were eating breakfast at the hotel. Not a leaf moved, even the birds didn't sing.

'He's in Salon-de-Provence. He wants us to join him,' she said. Salon-de-Provence, near Marseilles, was the only seaport in the unoccupied zone.

'You're on your way out of France,' I said, with a mixture of envy and relief.

'Yes,' she said, 'although we're still waiting for our visas.'

'How do you feel about leaving?' I asked, forking a segment of orange into my mouth.

She pushed her coffee away. 'At first I was nervous and didn't know if I'd be able to carry on painting. But everything's so tense now, I can't wait.'

I wasn't sure if she meant the Nazis or our domestic situation but before I could say anything, Diane, the chambermaid who looked after Aube, hurried up to us, pulling the child by the hand.

'Have you heard the news? she said breathlessly. 'A German sentinel guarding the *Kommandatur* was shot and killed last night!'

176

Aube began to cry, picking up the tension. Jacqui lifted her onto her lap and stroked her hair, saying, 'Who could have done such a thing?'

Diane shrugged. 'I saw it on a poster. The Germans are hunting down the assassin. There are soldiers everywhere.'

A worry line appeared between Jacqui's eyebrows. 'Safer not to leave the hotel,' she said. 'Let's camp in my room. Make a game of it for Aube.'

'Good idea,' I said, looking towards the seafront, which seemed subtly changed. Familiar markers, like the ice-cream kiosk, appeared to have moved slightly. I felt rudderless, disorientated, afraid.

We went upstairs and watched a swastika-emblazoned plane doing acrobatic stunts above the bay, flying upside down, rolling, looping the loop. It would have been thrilling if we hadn't known that the pilot was training to kill, but at least Aube was entertained. Then a bellboy knocked on our door and said, 'Monsieur Picasso is in the lobby.' I went downstairs to meet him.

'It's a bad situation,' he said, hugging me tightly. 'I am glad you're safe.' He released me, and I saw how pale he was under his tan.

We sat down in the corner. 'Is there any news?' I asked.

'Well, the town's plastered in notices forbidding dogs, Jews and French natives to use the beach. And another bullet's been fired.' He lit a cigarette and drew on it deeply.

'Where?'

'At my villa.' My stomach clenched and a wave of blood rushed up to my head. He added, 'It whizzed through an open window on the floor below mine, bounced off a wall and fell on the floor.'

'Christ, Pablo! You're lucky you weren't hit,' I said.

He tapped out his ash, frowning. 'The military police came and decided it was an act of resistance. They insisted on searching the house and were very careless with my paintings. Of course they didn't find anything.' He spoke with quiet contempt.

'I hope you stayed out of their way,' I said.

'I was too angry,' he said. 'I told them the bullet could only have come from the stunt plane because it was fired from above and at close range.'

My heart sank. 'Why did you do that?'

He looked at me as though I'd lost my mind. 'Because it was true.'

I touched his shoulder. 'You can't afford the truth.'

'They didn't believe me,' he said, shrugging.

He went home soon afterwards but stormed back an hour later to accuse everyone in the hotel of stealing his pocket torch that he'd put on the table while we were talking. He said, 'I left it right here and it's not here any more! You'd better find it immediately.' His face was like thunder.

We were in the lobby and no one said a word. They were too scared. Only Jacqui leaned towards me and whispered, 'He did it himself. He must have put it somewhere, and then forgotten where. I know him.'

'You're right,' I said, and sighed. I had had enough. I thought, *There must be a way of shutting off from Pablo, so I'm not hurt by every explosion, every fluctuation.*

After a tense half hour of searching for the torch, Pablo remembered that he had left it in the bathroom and went off to fetch it. He came back with it in his hand – at least he had the decency to look shamefaced. He said, 'It was by the sink, where I left it.'

He apologised to me and Jacqui, and to the staff. Sincere, pleasant apologies that did not diminish my resolve to take a step back from him. I knew I had to, for my own survival. Of all the cruelty, infidelity, mind games and manipulation, it was an outburst about a torch that finally tipped me over.

From then on, despite our efforts to continue with life as usual, everything around us became increasingly warlike. Those weeks were full of uncertainty and fear. Troops kept arriving, and the roads were filled with military vehicles. Schools, the town hall and most of the other big buildings were requisitioned. Tourists left the hotels, which immediately filled up with officers. Jacqui and I were lucky not to get kicked out of the *Tigre*. I went to bed late and slept badly or not at all.

Posters went up in public places announcing mobilisation, and then men started getting called up, including Pablo's neighbour. This was the final straw for Pablo. The next morning, he came to the hotel and said, 'Since the whole of France is occupied, we might as well go back to Paris.'

'I agree,' I said. 'At least some of our friends are still there.'

We set out for Paris on 25 August, after abrupt and apprehensive farewells to Jacqui and Aube, who were packing to go to Salon-de-Provence. Jacqui thrust a note into my hand and hugged me tightly, and then she gave Pablo a careful peck on each cheek. Marie-Thérèse and Maya were making their own way back to Paris with Sabartés and a driver. We left with Marcel, who had managed to get hold of enough petrol for the journey. As we set off, I opened Jacqui's note:

> I really do understand why I exasperated you so. I can't explain it to you here, it would take too long, but you were fully justified. I want you to be HAPPY! Please write to me. I'm going to miss you very much.

'What does she say?' Pablo asked, and I could hear how curious he was.

'Nothing much,' I said, thinking, *Well, at least she admits she did nothing to help me.* I slipped the note into my bag, enjoying the small power I had over him in that moment. The withholding of information, the half-truth, as he had done so many times to me.

Marcel avoided the obvious routes, which were crowded with German army trucks. Instead, we passed through gentle, sunlit fields, and villages where the church bells were ringing. Long processions of peasants leading their horses to the nearest mobilisation centre blocked the roads. These sights alarmed me, but I felt relief too. The fighting was coming, but at least I was freed from mothers and their young.

# Five

'PARIS LOOKS PROVINCIAL WITHOUT its traffic jams,' Pablo said.

'Oh, yes,' I said, with a touch of sarcasm. 'It would be charming if there weren't lists of hostages and executions all over the walls.'

It was dusk and we were walking to the Flore to meet the Éluards. Autumn had come early, and the wind was cold on my face. We'd got here a week before to find that the Paris we loved had become a city of grey-green uniforms, and giant swastikas floating over the hotels and public buildings, which had been requisitioned by the Nazis. Civilians were banned from driving. If you saw a car, it could only belong to the Gestapo or the French police. The rest of us went on foot or by bicycle or metro if there weren't any cut-offs, or on one of the infrequent, overcrowded buses. Pablo and I crossed the boulevard Saint-Germain, and a peremptory voice behind us said, 'Where's your mask?' My pulse started hammering in my throat and I whipped around to see a hefty French policeman with a worn face. Every schoolchild and French citizen had been given a mask to wear, but Pablo hated his and often left it at home.

Pablo said, 'I'm not entitled to one because I'm a foreigner.' His tone stopped just short of insolence, and I cursed him inwardly.

The policeman shot him a dagger stare. 'But you can buy a mask.'

'Yes, I'll do that,' said Pablo, conciliatory now.

The policeman nodded. 'Don't let me catch you without one again,' he said, and giving us another sharp look, he went on his way.

My hands were shaking. I hated my mask as much as Pablo did –
the grip of the rubber on my skin, its smell, the sound of my breath
rasping in my ears – but I would never have had the temerity to
leave it at home. It hung from my shoulder, where I'd once carried
my Rolleiflex. We reached the Flore with relief – it was a bright and
well-heated refuge. We had started coming here nearly every night.
The Germans never frequented it, though the other cafés were full
of them. The proprietors, M. and Mme Boubal, greeted us warmly.

The Éluards were sitting at the back and we embraced joyfully.
Paul looked tanned and lean, and it suited him. Nusch was still
magnificent, but she had lost so much weight, she was almost gaunt.
I didn't pick up anything but friendship between her and Pablo, but
perhaps I had started caring less. We took our seats and Pablo said,
'It's been so long! I don't want to lose touch with my friends!'

Nusch was looking from me to Pablo. 'You look well!' she said.
'All that sea air did you good.'

Pablo leaned towards her and said, 'Tell me the truth! I've
changed, haven't I? Look at this – look at my hair.' He swept a hand
over the thin strands covering his scalp. 'When I see an old snapshot
of myself, it scares me.'

'You've still got plenty of your old fire,' I said, covering my hand
with his, and he gave me a tender look.

M. Boubal came over with Pablo's Evian and a bottle of wine.
Glasses clinked and I drank thirstily, feeling the alcohol go straight
down into my stomach. Soon I felt completely at home. Better, in
fact, than I could have been at home because of the warmth, the
cheer, the distraction.

'Are you glad to be back?' Paul asked.

'Yes and no,' said Pablo, swallowing a mouthful of Evian. 'Paris
is home but it's changed. No taxis, no cigarettes, no sugar.'

'It's become a city of rhubarb, turnips and queues,' I said, and
the others smiled, but there was pain on their faces too.

Pablo said, 'I can't even get enough coal to heat my studio. I
dread to think what winter will be like. And I miss my Hispano.'

'Where is it?' Paul asked.

'Marcel took it to the outskirts of Paris and put it in a garage,'
Pablo said. 'He strapped an old mattress to the top so that if he

181

was stopped and asked why he was driving, he could say he was a returning refugee.'

'Clever,' said Nusch. 'And was he stopped?'

'Luckily not. He got there safely,' said Pablo. 'Before he left, he jacked up the car on blocks to ease the tyres and drain the battery. Then he caught the train back to Paris.' Pablo's foot started bouncing up and down. 'It's upsetting to think of it there. Marcel's been drafted into the army and that upsets me too.' The Éluards said they were sorry, and for many moments, Pablo sat with lowered eyes, lost in thought. Then he said, 'For God's sake let's talk about happier things!'

So we spoke about our friendship and about all the good times we had shared. We couldn't stay out late because of the curfew, and so we said goodbye at eight thirty, promising to meet again soon.

Pablo and I walked home through silent streets. Darkness had fallen, and the only lights visible were the ghostly blue streetlamps and the torches carried by pedestrians. Now and then a column of soldiers marched past, their boots pounding the pavement. The city seemed like an eerie warren, and I held Pablo's arm tightly, scared of being stopped again, or worse.

We rose late in the mornings and then I shopped for food. Most stores were closed, but a few opened at specified hours, and I queued up to buy what I could. Coffee was in short supply, and we were encouraged to mix it with chicory and take it with milk – a filthy drink. Oil and soap were also hard to find. Staples like bread, meat, cheese and milk were rationed, and the daily amount seemed to decrease by the day. To satisfy our hunger, we lunched at the Catalan and found it full. It was the only place in the district where a real steak could be had – M. Arnau had access to black-market supplies. 'Monsieur Picasso, Mademoiselle Maar,' he would say with a smile, taking our hands. 'Always a pleasure.' The Catalan was a respite from an increasingly grim reality.

After lunch we worked. I discovered that I could paint again, and it was better than before: a free-pouring current of expression that came from a place of deep instinct. I didn't think or plan, but simply followed the brush as fast as my hand could move it across the canvas. I was achieving a pleasing purity of line, with tight, almost photographic framing. I mostly painted still lifes of everyday objects: a jug, a clock, a piece of bread glistening with butter. I often painted food – all the missing foods I longed for. This plenitude in my art was a kind of compensation for my hunger, and also my barrenness. It didn't fill that void but I was grateful for it.

The news of Pablo's arrival spread, and visitors began to flock to his apartment. On a cold night in October when the wind blew in furious gusts, Lise came, stamping her feet and rubbing her hands together to get warm. Marie-Laure was there too, and she said, 'Lise, my dear, come and sit beside me and have a glass of Sancerre. I brought the last bottles from our cellar.'

She patted the empty couch space beside her, and Lise sank into it gratefully. 'You're an angel, Marie-Laure. I haven't had a decent glass of wine for months.'

Pablo poured the pale-yellow wine. I stuck my nose in my glass and inhaled the smell of apricots, with a waft of cut grass. Marie-Laure raised her glass and said, 'I'm glad you're back,' and we drank to friendship.

Charles had left for the southern zone, but Marie-Laure chose to stay in Paris. I admired her courage, especially given her Jewish ancestry. She would take the metro or cross the Seine by bicycle to meet me for lunch at the Flore or the Catalan, sometimes with Lise and sometimes just the two of us. She was also a frequent visitor to Pablo's apartment in the evenings.

Lise turned to me and Pablo, saying, 'You were brave to come back. It has really cheered us up.' She passed around a packet of cigarettes and we took them gratefully.

'It's a kind of passive resistance,' I said. 'Resisting through the act of remaining.'

Pablo's face was grave. 'This isn't the time for any of us creatives to shrink or stop working,' he said, and lit our cigarettes one by one, before blowing on the flame to extinguish it.

We fell silent, sipping at our wine and drawing in ambrosial breaths of smoke. At last Marie-Laure said, 'Are you still involved with the Prado?'

Pablo shrugged. 'I suppose I'm still the director since nobody's bothered to fire me. I get sent piles of reports. I'm bombarded with letters from my subordinates. They all want to express their devotion to me.'

'Wasn't the museum bombed?' Lise said.

'Yes, but we had already evacuated the collection to Valencia for safety. It was very stressful.' Pablo let out a sigh. 'You know, I never received a franc of my salary, not that it amounted to much. I guess it's not surprising, seeing as I'm the director of a phantom museum. A Prado with no paintings.'

Marie-Laure shook her head. 'Poor Spain. What a world we live in!' she said. Then she brightened, adding, 'I brought another bottle of wine. Let's open it.' Pablo did so, and we toasted each other again.

Lise's eye fell on my most recent painting leaning against the wall, a still life of a pitcher. She turned to me and said, 'It's very good. What's more, you've escaped Pablo's influence. It's not like any of his periods or his palettes.' She gave a warm smile, and I was suffused with happiness. I had escaped something. Not everything, but something. Staying with Pablo had become my own act of resistance through remaining.

Pablo said teasingly, 'I taught her everything she knows.' Blurred by the wine, I put my hands to my forehead in imitation of a bull and mock-charged him. He caught my wrists and kissed me full on the mouth, and the rest of the evening passed in a hazy glow, outside of time.

Two days later, I rang my parents' doorbell on place de Champerret. I had resolved to heal my rift with them because of the war, and because they weren't getting any younger. They had been happy to hear from me but had made it clear that they didn't want anything to do with Pablo. He didn't seem to mind. It was probably a relief to him.

Maman threw open the door, and we flung ourselves into each other's arms.

'Oh, Maman!'

'Dora! I'm glad to see you after all this time.'

She released me, holding me at arm's length to examine me. 'My God! You're so changed, you look like a different girl.'

I had been expecting this, aware that the stress and grief showed on my face. 'I'm fine, Maman,' I said gently.

My mother had changed too. Her face was thinner and her nose looked longer than ever. Deep lines fanned out beneath her heavy-lidded eyes, and there were creases between her nose and mouth. Seeing her like this gave me a pang. She took my arm and said, 'Come, Papito is waiting for you in the dining room.'

Papito rose and embraced me, and when he let go, I noticed that his hair had receded and his brown irises had faded to a watery blue around the edges. We sat down and I soon felt my old claustrophobia rise. There was homemade bread, with lard instead of butter on the table. Maman poured cups of coffee and began to cut the loaf.

'How are you, Dorita?' my father asked. 'I hope you're still managing to get assignments.'

'Oh, I've stopped taking photographs,' I said. 'I'm a painter now.'

Papito raised his eyebrows. 'Why? You have a gift for photography. You should be using it—'

'Have some bread,' interrupted Maman. She passed me a slice and I bit into it. It was made from cornmeal, as you couldn't buy wheat, and was coarse, crumbly and dry. But I was hungry and ate it quickly, and Maman cut me another piece.

'I wish I could have baked a cake. What have things come to?' she said, shaking her head as if to clear it. Then she added, 'What's happening to this country breaks my heart,' and something like a sob ran through her. Papito reached across the table and touched her hand. Maman squared her shoulders. 'But I wouldn't leave France again, even if I could.'

'Why not?' I asked. 'Don't you want to go somewhere safer? Doesn't having a Jewish name scare the hell out of you?' I felt a surge of my old anger but there was grief and pity mixed up with it. Tears rose and I struggled to blink them back. She was still my mother and the woman who had given me life.

She looked at me. 'Why don't you apply for Yugoslavian citizenship if you're scared?'

'I would love to but I don't know how!'

Papito said, 'I can help you,' and I felt a rush of gratitude. 'Your mother insists on keeping her French nationality. I wish she wouldn't.'

I looked at her in disbelief. 'Why, Maman? It's suicide!' But she only pursed her lips and shook her head, and we could not change her mind.

Since the Germans were occupying Le Tremblay, Marie-Thérèse had found an apartment on the boulevard Henri IV, a short walk across the river. Pablo would visit her and Maya there on Thursdays and Sundays. If he was being otherwise unfaithful, at least he was discreet about it.

Paulo was in Switzerland. He had been released from the Lindenhofspital into the care of Pablo's friends, the Geisers. He sent us a photograph of himself, tanned and smiling, his hair longer and falling over his forehead. It made me happy. Olga remained in Paris, despite Pablo's efforts to persuade her to move to Switzerland too. He visited her at least once a week. He always returned from these visits in a very bad mood, refusing to tell me what had happened.

I'd grown resigned to the presence of these women in his life. I was getting better at sealing Pablo off behind a sort of wall in my head, so that what he said or did no longer upset me as much. It made life easier, even if it meant killing off part of myself and of our relationship.

We took daily walks with Kazbek to Le Vert Galant, a small park at the tip of the Ile de la Cité, named for the equestrian statue of Henri IV in its centre. It was close to Pablo's apartment, and on the way we watched the river in all its different moods, flooded with sunlight, under blankets of cloud, and with the reflection of the city spread out over it. One breezy mid-November morning, Pablo looked at the opaque white sky and said, 'Do you know what scares me, what really scares me?' I shook my head and he said, 'Paris being bombed without warning, like Guernica was.'

'Me too,' I said, and panic shot through me. I took his arm.

He said, 'I've always loved the sky. Loved painting it. But now I dread it because it's the space of bombers.'

I willed my heart to stop racing. 'It's become sinister. One can hardly believe in a good God.'

Pablo looked at me and his eyes seemed even more penetrating than usual. He said, 'There is no God. Just evil spirits weaving a terrible destiny,' and I could not disagree.

We were walking down a gravel path, with trees and grass on either side. Kazbek went to sniff around the base of an old chestnut tree that had probably been there for hundreds of years. A gust stirred the sparse leaves clinging to its branches, sending a few drifting to the ground. I put one hand on the trunk and shut my eyes, wishing I could be transformed into a tree until peace came.

In the days that followed, Pablo did several drawings and paintings of this spot, wanting to commemorate it in case Paris was bombed. The same fear drove him to put a large number of paintings in the safe-deposit box of the Banque Nationale pour le Commerce et l'Industrie on the boulevard Haussmann, where Braque and Matisse also stored their work.

Eight days later we received a letter saying that the Germans were coming to inventory the bank vaults. Pablo was anxious about protecting his paintings. It should have been impossible for the Nazis to touch them because he was Spanish, but since he was *persona non grata* with the Franco regime, since he was a 'degenerate' artist, his position was uncertain. He decided to be present while they took the inventory, and he asked me to go with him.

It was a windless, overcast day. The gunmetal sky was like a lid pressing down. The building was massive and heavy, in an *Arts Décoratifs* style. A soldier accompanied us in the lift down to the depths. There were two circular levels, one below the other, with an interior gallery in the centre, so that the guards could see everything as they patrolled around it. It was chilly, but sweat began to pearl on my upper lip, and my collar felt tight around my neck.

Pablo had two large rooms full of Cézannes, Renoirs and Matisses, as well as his own work. There were two inspectors – fresh-faced German soldiers, none too bright. Pablo immediately started confusing them by hurrying from room to room, taking out canvases, looking at them, thrusting them back in again, leading the soldiers around corners, doubling back, so that in the end they were all bewildered. And since they didn't know his work, they had no idea what was in front of them.

'What are these things worth?' one of them asked.

'Oh, about 8,000 francs,' Pablo said nonchalantly.

They took his word for it. But then a more senior officer arrived, a heavyset man with crinkling hair and cold grey eyes. He greeted us brusquely, picked up a canvas and examined it at arm's length. He turned to Pablo, looking disgusted. 'It's you who have painted this?' Pablo nodded. 'And why do you paint like this?'

I was really frightened, but beyond a slight tightening of the eyebrows, Pablo showed no reaction. 'I don't know,' he admitted. He waited, watching the officer, but the man said nothing. At last Pablo said, 'I painted it because it amused me.'

Comprehension dawned in the officer's eyes. 'Ah!' he cried. 'It's a fantasy!' And delighted to have understood, he signed the paperwork and told the soldiers to replace the 'fantasies' in their vault. None of Pablo's things were confiscated. It must not have seemed worth the trouble. A new soldier took us up in the lift and showed us to the door. My knees were shaking with the reaction that had set in now that we were out of there.

It began to rain. Lightly at first and then it pounded down, a clammy wetness sinking through to my skin. The few vehicles on the road made slurring sounds as they passed. We stopped to cross, and I said with a shudder, 'I'm glad it's over.'

Pablo gave my arm a squeeze. 'Me too.'

But we soon learned that it wasn't over.

# Six

F ROM THEN ON, a group of uniformed soldiers came to the rue des Grands-Augustins every week and asked with an ominous air, 'This is where Lipchitz the sculptor lives, isn't it?'

'No,' Sabartés would say patiently, folding his arms. 'This is Monsieur Picasso's apartment.'

'Monsieur Picasso isn't a Jew by any chance?'

'Of course not,' said Sabartés.

'Hmm. Well, we will have to make sure Lipchitz isn't in there,' knowing full well that he was in America at that moment and that he had never lived there in the first place. 'We're coming in to search for papers.' And they would enter and rifle around the apartment, making a mess and harassing us. But at least they didn't damage anything.

On the third visit, a Nazi soldier remarked to Pablo, 'It's cold in here.'

'It doesn't bother me,' said Pablo. 'Nothing bothers me while I'm working.'

'What's your latest work?'

Pablo took a photograph of *Guernica* from a drawer and handed it to his guest, who looked at it closely. My gut churned.

Finally the German asked, 'Did you do this?'

'No,' said Pablo. 'You did it,' and the man gave him a baffled look.

After this, whenever we had an official visit, Pablo would hand out cards with an image of *Guernica* on them, insisting, 'Take them away. Souvenir! Souvenir!'

Despite Pablo's audacity, he said to me, 'I hate being watched all the time. Feels like I can't breathe.' I said I felt the same. The

189

Germans soon began trying to 'domesticate' him, offering him extra portions of food or fuel. He always refused, saying, 'A Spaniard is never cold.'

'What's the harm in taking a little coal?' I asked despairingly, after one of these visits.

Pablo crossed his arms. 'I prefer to freeze, like most Parisians. It reminds me of being a poor young man in Barcelona. I used to burn my drawings to keep warm.' He paused, then added musingly, 'But really, cold isn't a bad thing. It wakes you up and keeps you moving. You work to keep warm, and you keep warm by working.'

I turned away from him. The cold made me wretched. It seemed to scourge the skin from my face, to sink down into my bones. I had developed chilblains on my hands and feet, red, itchy patches that swelled and blistered. Even Kazbek went around shivering, his tail between his legs.

The cold and food were my two great obsessions. I fantasised about what I would eat and drink when the occupation ended, picturing and tasting each mouthful. Succulent steak oozing blood, juicy apples and oranges, strong coffee.

Then one icy day in late November, the postman brought my Yugoslavian passport, issued on behalf of His Majesty King Petar II. I opened it and under my photograph were the words

Markovitch, Henriette, artist painter photographer.
Personal characteristics: Catholic and Aryan.

Relief poured through me, making me feel so wobbly in the legs that I had to sit down. Henceforth, I always carried my passport with me. Thank God I could prove I wasn't Jewish! A huge fear had been lifted but others rushed in to take its place. I was afraid that if the Nazis became aware of my photographs, they would classify them as 'degenerate', especially the erotic ones. I felt limited as an artist, censored, fearful about what I could produce. I was scared for Pablo too. I felt strange, as though my body wasn't at home in my own city. At times it was like being in a tunnel, where everything was grey and depthless.

We stopped wanting to go to the Flore and Saint-Germain-des-Prés. The mood in Paris was oppressive. The sky always seemed to be stormy and icy, and the cold drove people into themselves. Except for bicycles and the Germans' big cars, the streets were empty. The Jewish Statute had been passed in October, which meant that all Jews had to register with the French police and have 'Jew' stamped in their identity documents. Certain cafés had begun to sprout ominous signs saying that they were for Aryans only.

There were more and more German soldiers on the streets. It was one thing to see them in predictable places – in front of major buildings or monuments – but quite another to encounter them on side streets or in the Flore, which they'd begun to frequent. Posters appeared on the walls, urging the population to regard the invaders as friends. There was a poster on rue des Grands-Augustins showing a Nazi carrying a child in his arms with a little boy following him, holding a piece of candy. The inscription said that the Germans loved children. A few days after it went up, someone scrawled across it in blue 'The French love children too'.

By the end of November, we had started avoiding any place where we might run into Germans, heeding André-Louis Dubois's advice to remain invisible. Dubois was former police chief and deputy director in charge of national security, and was now working undercover for the police force. He had always admired Pablo's work, and so he dropped in from time to time to check that everything was all right, always leaving with the words, 'For the slightest problem, call me.'

Mostly we stayed at home and painted. Without the luxuries of free movement, food, wine and parties, Pablo had no new temptations, and so we folded into each other. He must have realised how much he needed me, in the way I'd once needed him. Another small shift of power.

In the mornings he would make coffee for me while I huddled beneath the covers. He would bring the cups to the bedroom and, while I drank, he'd fetch the drawings and engravings he had done the previous day. He would spread them out on the red tiled floor, and I'd bend down to look at them.

'I love the way you've balanced the skull with the other lines of force,' I would say or, 'I'm not sure about this green.' And he would listen and appear to take my suggestions seriously.

Life flowed by quietly until, on the last day of November, I received a letter from Jacqui who was in Martigues:

> We are living in an impoverished but beautiful shack on the beach, heated by open fires and lit by candles. The nearest shack is two kilometres away. I am painting. Life is almost bearable but I miss you and the talks we used to have.
>
> In a few days, we're taking the boat from Marseilles to New York. Very sad at the idea of going so far away for such a long time. Please take care of Huguette – I'll be grateful to you forever. You know how fragile she is.

I wondered if I would ever see Jacqui again, and felt a pang. It had to be much worse for Huguette, and I resolved to see her at the earliest opportunity. But she was ill with the flu, and it wasn't until just before Christmas that I was able to take her to lunch at Les Vielles, in a passage off the rue Dauphine. Their food was still good, and their Chablis was superb.

Huguette looked girlish in a loose grey silk dress with a white collar, but her blonde hair was lank, and her smile didn't reach her eyes. We hugged each other and sat down.

'How are you?' I asked.

'Getting by, but I'm still tired from the flu. The apartment is freezing. I can't sleep with all the soldiers around.' She spoke readily, like someone who had stored up her thoughts for a long time and was relieved to get them out.

I touched her arm and said, 'I know it's hard, but please try to take care of yourself. Go for walks, rest during the day.' She gave a helpless shrug and I saw that the more assertive Huguette I had glimpsed at our last meeting was gone.

We turned our attention to the menu, noticing that it had become much smaller due to wartime shortages. Knowing that Huguette had a weakness for cheeses, I encouraged her to order the baked Camembert, one of the restaurant's specialities. When the food arrived, she took a mouthful and said dreamily, 'It's the best thing

I've eaten for months.' I had ordered turnips and sausage, which arrived in a coil, and we fell silent, enjoying the food.

Then Huguette dabbed at her lips with a serviette and said, 'I got a letter from Jacqui yesterday.'

I sat upright. 'Oh?'

'They're in New York. She says the only way to stand it is by working. It's awfully brash and she misses France. She cries a lot.' Huguette put the last piece of cheese in her mouth, half-closing her eyes, then neatly licked the fork clean, like a cat. 'They're in a fifth-floor walk-up in Greenwich Village. Jacqui won't buy anything for it, though there are artisans working nearby. She's worried it could mean they stay there.'

I took a mouthful of Beaujolais. 'Perhaps when she settles down, she'll see it as an opportunity. They could travel – say to Mexico City to visit Frida Kahlo? You know how Jacqui admires her. Anything's possible!'

Huguette sat back, cradling her glass. 'Actually, I think she'll do better than André, once she settles,' she said. 'He's just another surrealist now, not the leader of the pack. He refuses to learn English, while hers is excellent. She's painting better than ever. Says unhappiness feeds her art.' She rolled her eyes slightly. 'If she lands a show or two, their roles might even get reversed.'

'Yes!' I said, smiling. 'She could become the popular, important one.' I did not dare to believe that this would ever happen with Pablo and me, but I had built up a body of work, and the longing for my own exhibition was as strong as ever.

I had started writing to gallerists. Many had turned me down, but Jeanne Bucher had written back, 'Your work moves my heart,' though she hadn't committed to anything yet. Her gallery at boulevard du Montparnasse had exhibited all the big names of the avant-garde: Arp, Miró, De Chirico, Léger, Picasso ... I hadn't told Pablo because of the uncertainty, and anyhow, I was determined to pull it off without his help.

At the end of the meal, Huguette and I said goodbye, promising to meet again soon. I watched her walk away, hunched deep in her dark-brown coat, as if she didn't want to be seen.

# Seven

I GOT BACK TO MY apartment after lunch with Huguette and found a letter from Maman.

Your father has run away. He left in the middle of the
night, while I was sleeping. No goodbye, not even a note. I am
devastated.

The words punched through me like knives. I sat down heavily on the bed and everything in me cried out, *No! This can't be true!* I couldn't get my head around it. I tried to imagine Papito packing a case, then tiptoeing through the silent apartment. He must have put on his shoes at the door, so as not to wake Maman. And I wondered what could have been in his mind as he hurried away.

As soon as I'd collected myself, I went to place de Champerret, past never-ending queues of housewives waiting outside shops. Maman opened the door looking exhausted, her eyes raw from weeping. She clung to me and I could feel tremors running through her body.

'God,' I said. 'My *God*,' and Maman said, 'Yes.'

Papito hadn't taken much, but already it felt bereft. Looking around, I saw that a few books were missing from their shelves, and his slippers had vanished from their place in front of the hearth. His chair still bore the indentation of his head. 'God,' I breathed, again.

We sat side by side on the sofa and were quiet for a long time. It was so much harder for Maman. 'I feel betrayed,' she said at last.

'Of course you do.' I put my hand over hers. 'I'm so sorry.'

'Oh, Dora. How could he have done it?'

'I've no idea,' I said. 'Do you think it could have been what he was talking about last time I was here? Fear about his surname, or maybe he had some political issues we don't know about?'

She looked at me with blank-faced panic, not seeming to address the reasons I was offering. 'Things are getting worse and worse,' she said. 'There are no buses any more. Food's getting scarce – no eggs, nor rice, nor potatoes. Queues are longer than ever. How am I going to manage?'

'I'll help you. We'll do it together,' I said, giving her hand a squeeze.

She said, 'You're a great comfort to me, Dora. You know how I suffer.' She gave me a stricken look. 'Do you think he'll come back?'

I held her gaze. 'I don't know.' I didn't want to give her false hope.

'I never even saw it coming,' she said, and her lips trembled.

'How could you have? It was out of the blue.' I was suddenly consumed by the old feeling of not being able to give her what she wanted. I hugged her, adding, 'I am here for you. But I know it's not the same.'

'Thank you,' she said, and we fell silent again.

I stayed with Maman until the light began to fade. Through the windows, the city looked grey and sombre. When I rose to go, she wept, but I was worried about walking home alone in the dark, and so I tore myself away, promising to come back the next day. I went straight to Pablo's apartment and told him about my father's disappearance. He held me and said, 'My poor darling. Your poor mother. Christ, what a way to leave your lifetime companion. It's unthinkable.'

It was unthinkable, but hearing it from Pablo touched something deeper in me too. My father had also left me, his only daughter. He didn't love me enough to stay.

'Let's get some proper food and send it to her,' said Pablo. He had begun to access small amounts of black-market supplies.

I tightened my arms around him and said, 'We're lucky to have you.' I had been holding myself together for Maman's sake, but now tears began to seep from my eyes as the crush of abandonment set in. Pablo gently wiped them away. 'I'm the lucky one. I love you, Dora. I will never leave you.'

On Christmas Day, we went to the Éluards for lunch. There was thick snow everywhere and a biting north wind. Paris was covered in white, muffling the footfalls of Nazi soldiers marching past. We took the metro to the Éluards' apartment at 35 rue de la Chapelle – three rooms on the third floor of an unassuming building. It was small and painted beige and grey, with belle-époque moulding on the ceiling, a marble fireplace, and books and paintings everywhere. It wasn't much warmer inside than out.

We hugged joyfully and Pablo said, 'Thank you for inviting us. Christmas with you is doubly precious because we normally live in seclusion, like prisoners.'

'It's wonderful to have you,' said Nusch, beaming. 'I'll fetch a little something to keep out the chill. Please, sit down.'

We sat and Paul said, 'We spent a month without opening the shutters because of the cold.'

'I don't blame you. I've never known such a winter,' I said. Nusch came back with four glasses of brandy on a tray and passed them around. She raised hers and said, 'Merry Christmas!' and we drank. The liquor warmed my throat, my chest. 'So much for peace on earth,' she added wryly.

Paul turned to Pablo. 'You must take care, my friend. I hear Franco's thugs are active in Paris. They're taking wanted republicans back to Spain, for hard labour or death sentences,' and I felt chilled again.

'I've heard that too,' said Pablo, scowling.

'It frightens me,' I said. 'Have you seen the press's attacks on Pablo?'

'Yes. I just read John Hemming Fry's diatribe against his "degenerate" influence,' said Paul.

Nusch shivered. 'It's so worrying. Please lie low, both of you.' She looked at us uncertainly, adding, 'Did you know Paul's thinking of joining the Resistance?'

'What are you talking about?' said Pablo, sitting upright, and at the same time, I said, 'You are?'

'Yes.' Paul looked a little sheepish. 'We're planning something now, though I'm not supposed to talk about it.'

Nusch said, 'I'm scared. They're going to—' but Paul put up a hand to stop her. He said, 'I might have to go into hiding afterwards.'

'You'd better take me with you,' said Nusch, and Paul looked into her eyes. 'Of course I will.'

Nusch rose suddenly. 'Yes, but please, I can't think about it now. It's Christmas. Let's eat.' We followed her to the dining room, which had a large, bare-breasted portrait of her by Pablo hanging over the fireplace. She had managed to get hold of a chicken, which she'd roasted with potatoes and carrots. It was delicious, and we tamped down our anxiety and praised her cooking.

She smiled modestly, her eyes bright with tears. 'I'm so thankful to be spending Christmas with my favourite people. That's it, that's all I want to say. I love you,' she said.

For dessert, she had baked a *bûche de Noël*, a rolled cake which she'd stuffed with plums, and I thought what superb black-market contacts the Éluards must have. The dense, buttery sponge was perfectly paired with the tart, juicy fruit. Afterwards, we drank real coffee and stayed till it grew dark, reminiscing about old times. Saying goodbye was hard. We clung to one another, not knowing when we'd see each other again. Finally Paul touched my cheek. 'Don't cry, my dear.' Pablo raised a hand in farewell, and Nusch gave us each a last hug. 'Goodbye, you two. We love you.'

We walked down the boulevard, a welter of emotions running through me. I drew a packet of cigarettes from my pocket, but my hands were numb with cold, and I dropped it. We crouched down in the darkness, looking for it. Suddenly, the harsh glare of a flashlight blinded us.

'HANDS UP!'

Two German soldiers stood in front of us, pistols raised. We put our arms in the air. I was shaking all over, my mouth so dry that my lips stuck together. The other pedestrians began to cross the street, their eyes averted, looking petrified.

'GIVE US YOUR PAPERS!'

But how could we get the papers in our pockets with our hands up? I glanced at Pablo in his old windbreaker fastened by safety pins, his Basque beret and shabby scarf. For a moment, I saw him through the soldiers' eyes and fresh fear gripped me. We lowered our arms gingerly, hoping we wouldn't get shot. The soldiers looked at our identity cards, noted down our names and addresses, and searched us roughly. Finally, they let us go and we carried on walking. My legs threatened to give way under me. We didn't talk, but my thoughts raced. Had we been harshly treated because they recognised Pablo or because they had seen us coming from the Éluards' apartment? Were they watching Paul too? What would my mother do if something happened to me? I didn't know anything any more, especially not how to keep us safe.

For weeks afterwards I had dreams of being searched by faceless soldiers; dreams that pinned me to the bed, as though by blocks of earth. I continued to grieve for my father, and saw my mother at least once a day. She was leading a locked-in life, her only purpose finding food and waiting for my visits.

'I am glad to see you. It's been so lonely,' she said, hugging me as I came through the door. It was two o'clock on a mid-January afternoon and already getting dark. All day, the sky had looked like slate and I'd felt exhausted by the endless occupation. 'Sometimes, I cry like a girl,' Maman added, releasing me.

'I know how hard it is,' I said, touching her shoulder. 'Any word from Papito?'

'Nothing,' she said.

We went to the kitchen, and I started unpacking the cans of beef and vegetables Pablo had sent.

'You're very good to me. And so is he,' said Maman. She still refused to call Pablo by his name. Then she gave me a sideways look. 'But I know nothing about your life. I wish you'd tell me.' I didn't answer and she added, 'You always were secretive.'

I felt a flash of anger with Papito for leaving me to deal with her, and then I felt guilty and sorry for Maman, but I simply couldn't confide in her. I felt invaded. I found myself saying, 'I will always love and care for you, but I need to keep my private life private. I hope you understand.'

A sound came from her and tears started rolling down her cheeks. She wiped her eyes with the handkerchief I gave her and said, 'An old woman like me is no good to anyone.'

I hugged her. 'No, no, that's not true!' I felt terrible about hurting her, but also felt as if I were fighting for my life. For as long as I could remember, I had experienced her neediness as tentacles trying to wrap around me. And since Papito had deserted us, she was needier than ever.

But then we moved to the living room, and somehow I found the strength and courage to open up. I talked about my life with Pablo, though not so much that she would worry, and we spoke of the past.

'I struggled to get pregnant,' she said. 'I was scared I might be barren, and it just about destroyed me. But then it happened, after five years of trying. A miracle! I couldn't wait to meet you.' She touched my arm.

'You were a beautiful baby. You ate and slept and did all the things you were supposed to. But there's something I regret.' She looked out of the window, at the treetops moving back and forth in the wind. 'Your father and I were having problems. It made me a self-centred mother.'

*It's true!* I wanted to shout. *So how will you make it up to me?*

She closed her eyes, put a hand to her chest and said, 'I am so, so sorry.' And I realised how claustrophobic she must have felt, trapped in an unhappy marriage in a city she hated. My anger drained away, and I felt a great compassion for her.

'I know you did your best,' I said, looking her in the eye.

She held my gaze. 'Thank you, sweetheart. It haunted me for years.' She stretched out her slippered feet. 'We tried for another baby, so you'd have a brother or sister. But that wasn't God's plan.'

It dawned on me that my condition could be hereditary, but I didn't want to upset her by asking. It was not as if knowing would change anything. As we talked on, I mused about how much we had in common. We had both longed to be mothers, we had both been abandoned by a man, we were both survivors. I was glad that she had helped me understand our relationship, but the parent-child roles were reversed now.

Rain began to fall in grey sheets, hitting the windowpanes, and Maman said, 'Sorry I am so clingy. It's just that I miss Papito.' A single tear rolled down her cheek.

I moved closer and took her hand. 'I know. I do too,' I said, and again the feeling of not being able to believe things came over me. I could not believe that my father had left us like that. *Why?* I thought. It brought home how little I knew about anything.

'I've been getting headaches,' Maman said. 'I think it's stress. My whole head squeezes with pain, so I can hardly see straight.'

'Are you drinking enough water?' I asked.

'I drink plenty.' She didn't look at me while she spoke, she glanced all around the room, but I looked at her and noticed how much weight she had lost.

I made her a cup of tea and tucked a blanket around her legs, and she seemed calmer. But I was not calm. For the rest of the afternoon, anxiety pulsed through me.

Pablo and I continued to work side by side. I was his exclusive model.

'Each of your expressions inspires me. Serene, happy or distraught,' he said on the night of my visit to Maman, and an emotion ran through me that was almost peaceful. When I had all but given up on him, our changed circumstances had brought him back to my side. I looked at him: he was stockier. His eyes still held their magic but were surrounded by a network of wrinkles. Nothing remained of his forelock but a few strands of hair combed across his scalp. He was nearly sixty, and I wondered if his physical decline played a part in his mooring himself to me. He was no longer a young, handsome artist.

I said, 'Your hair doesn't look good like that. Why don't you shave it off? Who cares if you're bald? You are Picasso.' It wasn't the first time I had mentioned it, but Pablo waved it away. He never listened.

And then, at the end of January, another postcard arrived from Jacqui.

Huguette is pregnant. It's awful. Can you help her?

# Eight

## 1942

OVER A DREADFUL CUP of 'coffee' – sweetened barley water – Huguette confessed the whole story to me. We were sitting in her tiny kitchen – blue and white tiles, and shelves bearing almost-empty jars of jam, honey and spices.

The previous July, she had managed to get a pass to visit her aunt, who was recovering from appendicitis and had no one else to care for her. The aunt lived just outside Biarritz and there was a small dairy farm next door. Every day, half a dozen prisoners of war were bussed from their camp to work on the farm. It was brutally hot and Huguette fell into the habit of taking them pitchers of lemonade while they worked. 'My aunt loved my lemonade, and it was no problem to make an extra batch for the men,' she said. 'And then, one of them began to look at me in a way that made me feel … alive.' As she spoke, her face grew even paler.

'We started talking. He told me he was a Spanish republican. He was terribly homesick and worried about his country. Soon, we were meeting whenever we could get away. We had to be careful; the risks were high. Oh Dora, he was so kind and cultivated! We talked about poetry and philosophy and our families. It was the best month of my life.' Her expression was dreamy, remembering, but then her face hardened. 'My aunt got better, and I came back to Paris in September. That's when I found out I was pregnant.' She rubbed her hands over her thighs in hard, agitated movements until I took them in mine.

'I'm sorry, Huguette. I understand those feelings – and how it happened,' I said gently.

She looked me in the eye. 'Dear Dora, thank you for not judging me.' Then she withdrew her hands and added, 'I don't even know how to find him. He was about to be moved. I'll probably never see him again.' She started to cry silently, fumbling in her pocket for a handkerchief. 'Do you know something? When you invited me to lunch, I lied. I didn't have the flu. It was morning sickness.' She blew her nose, and I remembered her loose dress, and the way she had hunched into her overcoat. No wonder I hadn't noticed she was pregnant. Her bump was small and neat, even now.

A sob choked her, and she said, 'I'm an unmarried mother in an occupied city. It's an impossible position. What will become of me?' She turned towards me again and I saw she was trembling, as though she were about to fall apart.

'Don't talk like that,' I said, and smiled. 'We'll get through it together.'

She tried to smile too but said nothing. The tears had stopped, her eyes were red. We drank a second cup of the barley water and saccharin, and she said, 'You're the only one I can turn to.'

'I'm happy to help. When is the baby due?'

'The end of April.'

'We don't have much time. We must start planning.'

But as we talked, sharp pangs went through me. Huguette and I were the same age, but she was carrying the child of a man she scarcely knew, while I, who had been in love with Pablo for years, could never get pregnant.

The harsh weather continued. It froze and thawed and froze again. The wind howled all day and into the night, moaning in the chimney, making the windows tremble in their frames. I spent my time shivering despite wearing my coat indoors, my hands frozen despite keeping on the move. My chilblains itched and burned.

Pablo and I painted late into the night. I was refining my existing works and painting new ones, with the goal of having my own show always on my mind. I still hadn't received confirmation from Jeanne Bucher, but I told myself that someone would give me a chance eventually. In the mornings we couldn't bring ourselves to get out of bed, huddling together for warmth. It was as cold in the apartment as it was in the street, and in the street it was twelve degrees below freezing. One February morning, I tried to get a fire going by burning some logs that Marie-Laure had brought. It wouldn't light. Smoke filled the room. We coughed; we couldn't breathe. I had to open the window. And then we froze. It put us into a terrible mood.

Arrests, hunger, unpredictable regulations and suspicious neighbours added to the dismal atmosphere. Denunciations were common. Everyone in Paris knew somebody who had been arrested, deported or killed. No one talked – fear and suspicion were the watchwords. The Éluards had left Paris and there was no news of them. Everyday life had become a nightmare, the only escape in work and sleep. And then, on a sodden, late February afternoon, Maman opened the door of her apartment, and her eyes shone. 'Look what came! A letter from your father!' she cried, waving it in front of my face. And I felt incredulity, joy and a surge of resentment towards Papito.

We sat on the sofa so I could read it. Papito's handwriting was wild and shaky.

My dearest Julie,

I am sure my departure came as a terrible shock. I am sorry I hurt you. I had to leave and knew you would never come with me.

I am in Buenos Aires. I've rented a three-bedroomed flat that's almost empty. I live like an anchorite, and it doesn't bother me because I am used to it. You would like the flat, it's filled with light. But to be honest, things aren't going well. I am anxious and I've been drinking. I went to the doctor because of pain in my kidneys and he said that the level of my uric acid is too high because of the drinking. I'm trying to cut down but haven't succeeded. Regarding everything else, the future is uncertain. I am on the edge of the abyss but haven't fallen yet. I must set up something modest. I have enough money to live for a year.

I wired some money for you to the branch office of the Crédit Lyonnais. Go and collect it and buy yourself something nice, if there's anything nice left to buy in Paris. Write to me and tell me how you are, and how Dora is.

Lots of kisses for you both. May God guard you,

Josip.

I put the letter on the coffee table, concerned and disappointed. I said, 'It sounds like he wants you to join him.' It was the only positive remark I could think of.

Maman said, 'But he doesn't actually say that. And anyway, wild horses couldn't drag me back to Buenos Aires.' She put her face in her hands, which were shaking. 'He didn't say why he left, or if he'll ever come back. It's all about him.'

'It always was,' I said.

She lifted her face. 'How much more can I stand before it breaks me?'

I had no answer. I often wondered the same thing about me and Pablo. But at least I still had him in my life, and painting. Maman only had me and I vowed to be there for her. I thought about how much closer we had grown since Papito's departure. I had started to understand and forgive her.

'How are your headaches?' I asked.

'The same,' she said.

I reached for her hand, which looked papery and frail, and squeezed it gently. 'I'll take you to the doctor.'

Maman shook her head. 'The only thing wrong with me is grief, and there's no doctor on earth who can fix that.'

My mother wasn't the only person I was taking care of. As I had promised Jacqui, I looked after Huguette, making sure she had everything she needed. Thanks to the black market, Pablo had provisions delivered to her, and I visited regularly. I went to see her the day after Papito's letter came.

'How are you?' I asked, putting out two hands.

'Quite well, thank you. I'm glad to see you.' She took my hands, then stepped aside to let me into her apartment. It was untidy, with crusted plates in the sink and clothes scattered everywhere. The air smelled of decay.

She watched me take it in and said, 'Sorry about the mess. I've let everything slide.'

'What can I do to help?' I asked, removing a pair of stockings from the armchair, and sitting down.

Huguette cradled her swelling stomach. 'How can I keep my mind healthy with everything that's going on? The round-ups have given me nightmares.'

'I don't know,' I said, frowning. At the beginning of the month, several thousand Jewish men had been summoned to police stations across Paris and told to bring their identity documents with them. From there they were bussed to the Vélodrome d'Hiver and, after enduring days and nights in the open stadium, they were taken to the Gare d'Austerlitz and packed onto trains bound for internment camps.

Huguette said, 'Can you imagine being on one of those trains?'

I could, vividly, and it made me shudder. The air vents sealed with wooden planks and barbed wire, people crammed together like animals, so tightly there was only room to stand. My face jammed against the sweat-smelling back of a stranger, trying not to listen to the cries ...

'What kind of world am I bringing this baby into?' Huguette said in a low voice.

I shook my head, unable to think of anything reassuring to say. And then I collected myself. 'Look, I've been thinking. You don't have the resources to raise the baby alone. I think you should entrust him to an infant care home.'

Huguette's eyes widened. 'Why would I do that? I'm going to keep him here, I have to.'

And so I went through everything she would need for the baby, and what it would cost. I had done my research. I described the practicalities of queuing for food in the freezing cold with an infant strapped to her chest. And what if she or the babe fell ill?

Something in Huguette's face shifted and I knew I was starting to get through to her. But she wasn't won over yet. 'Let me think about it,' she said.

I rose to go, glad to escape the stuffy apartment. 'Take your time. It's a big decision.'

Winter finally gave way to a wet, grey spring, and I moved into a new apartment at 6 rue de Savoie, a small, peaceful street in the

7th arrondissement. It had honey-coloured stone buildings, and a couple of shops selling books and art supplies. The entrance to my apartment was through a pretty courtyard, which I intended to fill with potted plants. The apartment had two spacious bedrooms, a comfortable kitchen, and heating, which I was sure I would appreciate when I could get coal. I moved because my rent at rue d'Astorg had increased, but also because rue de Savoie was a minute's walk from Pablo, and I wanted to be closer to him. He still hadn't invited me to live with him, still insisted on seeing me by appointment, even though we spent practically all our time together. This gave me the occasional pang of frustration or yearning, but I was mostly resigned to it.

In the middle of April, after months of indecisiveness, Jeanne Bucher finally said yes to putting on my show. And oh, it was the most exquisite feeling, my painting career taking off. Joy vibrated through me. I imbibed it like champagne.

The show wasn't until next year, but I began preparing for it immediately, painting new work and deciding which of the old ones I would include. Pablo was nice about it when I told him. I was surprised, as he had rarely seemed to take my painting seriously. 'Congratulations, my dear. I knew you could do it,' he said, hugging me tightly. He even started telling his friends about it.

I was fortunate to have the show to keep me afloat because the unofficial news filtering through to us on the grapevine was frightful. Acquaintances were being deported because they had the misfortune to be Jews. Others were tortured or put to death because of their clandestine activities in the resistance movement. Paul and Nusch had gone into hiding at a psychiatric hospital in Lozère. They were being sheltered by their friend, Dr Lucien Bonnafé. I worried so much about the Éluards. We waited for more news, but none came.

Huguette's voice on the other end of the phone sounded proud and tired.

'My baby arrived! A girl! I've called her Brigitte.'

It was the end of April and my bedroom at the new apartment was bathed in sunlight. I watched leaf shadows dancing on the wall and said, 'Congratulations! I'm so happy for you!' But the pain of exclusion was sharp and I couldn't help adding, 'Why didn't you call me?'

'My waters broke at midnight. I didn't want to disturb you. I phoned for an ambulance and got on with it.' I felt that she was not sorry to have given birth alone, but she quickly added, 'I'd love it if you came now. Please come!'

I dressed and hurried to the hospital. The spring sunshine splashed down on me, its warmth delectable on my winter-pale skin. On reaching the building, I saw a woman in a navy-blue dressing gown leaning against the wall. Her dark hair was pinned into a bun, her lined face was still pretty. She was watching clouds travel across the sky, as tenderly as if they were a lover's features she was trying to memorise, and I realised that the world of the sick was a world apart, entirely consuming. Huguette had been assigned a private room off the ward, and I was given directions by the receptionist.

The room was stark and shabby, but I hardly saw the battered furniture or Huguette's wan, smiling face. I went straight to the crib and drank in every detail of Brigitte: the shape of her face, her full little lips, the soft tufts of dark hair. Her eyes were closed so I couldn't see their colour.

'May I hold her?' I asked, and Huguette said, 'Of course.'

Gingerly, I picked her up, and she nestled into my body. I dropped a kiss on top of her head. She smelled intoxicating – sweet and soapy, with a waft of milk. Huguette started telling me about her labour, but I was so absorbed, I scarcely heard her – *the most painful experience of my life ... thank God it was quick ... I hardly tore ...* And then Brigitte opened her eyes and looked at me. They were nearly violet, with dark rings circling the irises, and I felt myself gently fill with everything I'd been missing.

'Will you be her godmother?' Huguette asked shyly.

'I would love that,' I said, repositioning the baby so that her back lay against my forearms, her downy head cupped in my palms. For a long moment, Brigitte and I looked at one another. 'I think we'll get along very well,' I said.

# Nine

I took my mother to the doctor the next morning. He examined her, did blood tests, and assured us that there was nothing to worry about. Her headaches were caused by the stress of Papito leaving, he said, and he was sure she would recover.

'Well, that was a waste of time and money,' Maman said on the way home. It was a dull day; the sky was the colour of wet cement. 'What was the point? I told you there's nothing wrong with me.'

I clamped my lips shut to prevent an angry retort. Why couldn't she appreciate my care and concern? For days we were not happy with each other.

Huguette put Brigitte in the care home I had found, but it had strict regulations and she was only allowed to visit twice a week. I never missed one of those visits. Brigitte was in an infants' ward – a large, bare, high-windowed room smelling of carbolic acid and floor polish. Babies lay in rows of cots, for the most part quietly, as if they'd already learned that they wouldn't get their needs met by crying. There was something disturbing about their passivity.

The staff gave us the use of a small room near the entrance, so that we could enjoy some privacy with Brigitte. We spent hours together, taking it in turns to hold her. She slept a lot in the beginning. I was mesmerised by her peaceful face; one tiny fist flung above her head. But sometimes while I rocked her, I felt sad because of all the things I'd needed from my own mother but hadn't got. It was a deep and dreadful feeling – the sadness of a child. I thought about Paulo suffering the same deprivation, and resolved to give Brigitte everything he and I had missed.

From time to time, Huguette shot me sharp glances while I held Brigitte. She realised that I was experiencing motherhood vicariously. But I didn't care. I couldn't help imagining Brigitte was mine. And in a sense, she *was* mine. I decided everything, shopped for baby clothes, bought extra bottles and powdered milk. Huguette was so relieved, she mostly accepted sharing her, and the baby was happy to go to both of us. Yet the love I felt for her carried an underside of anxiety and fear. She was so small. As the weeks passed, she became more alert and hungrier, but she disliked the bottle. She would spit the teat out again and again. The staff were busy – the war meant more abandoned infants than ever – and there was nobody to help us.

'Do you think she's put off by the taste of rubber?' Huguette asked despairingly when Brigitte was a month old. She was holding her daughter, trying to get the teat into her mouth, but the baby kept turning her head from side to side to avoid it, her lips clamped shut. She said, 'I should have breastfed her.'

'That would hardly have been practical with twice-weekly visits,' I pointed out.

Brigitte started to wail again. I couldn't bear it when she cried. I ached to take her from Huguette and cover her little face with kisses. And then her crying turned to coughing, and she began to fight for breath, her skin purpling.

Huguette looked terrified. 'Oh, Dora. Jesus, Dora. Help me.'

I was in pieces. I ran out of the room to get someone, not stopping until I found a hard-eyed nurse in a starched cap measuring out pills in the dispensary.

'The baby's choking! Please come!' I cried.

The nurse's face was full of dramatic disbelief, eyebrows raised, lips compressed. But I kept on pleading until she followed me reluctantly back to the room. She took one look at Brigitte, seized her from Huguette, and banged her hard on the back till the baby's legs thrashed and her eyes bulged out. Huguette and I held our breath. Finally, Brigitte let out a whimper and subsided, limp as a boned fish.

'There now, that should settle her down,' said the nurse, and she walked out, without a single word of comfort or advice.

Huguette and I looked at each other, and I saw my fear reflected in her eyes. She said, 'I hope that never happens again.'

I was so worried about Brigitte and my mother that Pablo was no longer my focus. He was immersed in work and didn't seem to notice. The mood of his painting was angry and bitter, but he had found a way to balance it with a new medium: sculpture. The shortage of materials meant that he had to apply his inventiveness to whatever came to hand: pieces of wood, bones, bottle caps, newspapers, scrap metal, even the metal seats of abandoned bicycles. 'I am the king of the ragpickers,' he liked to say, but these odds and ends came to life as he reassembled them in different ways. Carpentry nails transformed into rays of light from a candle, clay jars, a goat's udders, and my favourite – the head of a bull made from the saddle and handlebars of a derelict bicycle. Bronze was in short supply, as most of it went into feeding the German war machine, and so Pablo did a great many pieces in plaster.

The bathroom became the sculpture studio. I would come back from seeing Brigitte to find the sink clogged with plaster and a dove stretching its wings in the bathtub. A skull grinned away in the soap dish and on top of the toilet stood a goddess whose face Pablo had been perfecting for weeks. There was something magical about his creations and, leaning against the door to watch him one hot night in July, I felt joy and gratitude that he could halt the general march towards destruction.

'It's marvellous,' I said, gesturing at his work.

'It's a marvellous mess,' said Pablo, washing and drying his hands. 'Might as well leave it like this. What's the point of tidying up?' And we went to the kitchen, arm in arm, to find something to eat for supper.

We had just finished our meal when Maman phoned.

'Why didn't you come this evening?' she asked plaintively.

'Oh Maman, I'm sorry. I am really tired.'

'I waited for you.'

'But I came this morning!' I said. Maman tutted and I felt a flare of exasperation. 'Nothing I do is ever good enough for you.'

'How can you think that? It's crazy.' I could hear her breath coming in short bursts and my irritation turned to concern.

'Do you have a headache?' I asked.

'Yes. A bad one,' she said, and I felt terrible. She continued, 'If only you would—' and fell silent. I heard the receiver fall – and nothing. How brutal the silence was!

'Maman!' I cried, as if I were a child, petrified of being abandoned in the night. 'Maman!' again, my voice rising. My throat grew sore from shouting. I started to run out, to get help, but Pablo put his hand on my arm. 'It's after the curfew. You can't go,' he said firmly.

Tears soaked down my cheeks – then I was on the floor, holding the phone, not daring to hang up. Listening to the endless silence, hoping for a sound, any sound, apologising over and over for what I had said. How I longed to take the angry words back! I began to shout 'Maman! Maman!' at the top of my lungs.

Pablo lost patience. 'Put the phone down. You'll go there tomorrow. I am sure she's fine.' But how could I wait till morning without knowing, without doing anything? In bed that night, I was filled with anguish. I felt such a weight pressing on my chest that I sobbed loudly on purpose, hoping Pablo would wake up. He didn't.

First thing the next morning, we hurried to place de Champerret. What greeted me was a vision from a nightmare. My mother on the floor, the telephone in her hand, stone cold. I ran towards the phone to call an ambulance but stopped. Maman was dead, there was no rush to get help. Soon, I would call a doctor, but for now I just wanted to sit with her. I lowered myself to the floor, pulverised by grief, and saw that when a person dies, the soul leaves the body instantly. Maman was not herself any more, she was a carcass.

Then Pablo came in and his eyes lit up. He walked round and round the body, examining it from every angle.

'Don't, whatever you do, make her into art,' I said through gritted teeth.

'Of course I won't,' he said. I longed for him to put his arms around me, but instead, he went off to fetch Sabartés.

'See the stiffness of the limbs. Rigor mortis is setting in,' he said, when they returned. 'And that strange sheen on the skin.' Sabartés turned his glasses towards my mother. Pablo wrinkled his nose. 'She's already starting to smell.'

'Stop it! Just stop! You're revolting,' I shouted, and his eyes went small. I knew that he was trying to make light of death, because he was so terrified of it. But it was always, always about him. He hadn't comforted me at all.

On the death certificate, Maman was declared dead at one o'clock in the morning. The cause of death was an embolism. She must have passed out while we were arguing, and my guilt was like a stone. I knew I would never get over it.

The doctor said, 'It's better this way. Trust me. If she had lived, she would have been paralysed.'

I held fast to the idea. 'Perhaps it's better this way,' I wrote to Papito in Argentina. 'Although if you had been there, it might not have happened.' I never admitted to him that Maman had died during our phone call.

There weren't many people present to see her laid to rest in the family vault in Clamart. It was a trek to get there, especially during the occupation. Pablo didn't come. I understood that he chose to live as if nothing came to an end, but his absence devastated me. Lise and Marie-Laure were there, and they stood on either side of me, holding my arms, as a cold wind shuddered through the trees, and I gazed unseeingly at my mother's coffin vanishing into the ground.

When I returned, Pablo said, 'Even the most terrible grief, like mine for Conchita, is helped by time. It never goes away but you get used to it.' His tone was the one he used when he wanted to be left alone to paint, and fresh pain moved through me. I went to my apartment and sat in my studio. As I looked at my paintings, it seemed that I was completely alone – worse off, actually, than if I were alone. Once, I'd had a strong sense of my presence in the world, but now the universe had tilted, and I was by myself at the edge of it. There was no meaning anywhere. I was fighting for survival, out of fear of being arrested, deported or left by Pablo.

A fortnight after my mother's funeral, Brigitte fell ill with bronchitis and was moved permanently to the small room by the entrance. Visiting hours were waived for Huguette and me, and we sat on either side of the cot, watching her breathe. Her body was a tiny hump under the covers, and the muslin cloth by her head fluttered slightly every time she exhaled. I wished Maman was here. In my head, she had turned into an infinitely warm, comforting presence, and I missed her horribly. I looked at the patch of blue sky outside the window, wondering if she was up there watching me.

Huguette said, 'I don't trust these nurses. We must get a proper doctor. Will you ask Pablo to help?' And I nodded. 'Of course.'

The baby began to cough – a horrifying rattle. Huguette leaned over the cot and rubbed her back, trying to relax the tightness of the muscles. 'We'll make you better soon,' she whispered.

But Paris was full of the sick and wounded, and medical men were in short supply. It was a full five days before a doctor knocked on the door and said, 'My name is Éduard Laurent. I've come to see the baby.' He was a serious-looking man with a fine head of silver hair, and I immediately felt safe with him.

'She's getting worse and worse. *Please* help her,' I begged. Huguette was looking at him with hungry desperation in her eyes.

'May I examine her?' he asked, and we nodded.

He washed his hands in the cracked basin in the corner, dried them, and went over to Brigitte, placing her on her back. She was sleepy and limp, her eyes glazed. Dr Laurent unbuttoned her gown and listened to her chest with a small stethoscope. Her ribs protruded – I was shocked by how much weight she'd lost. He dressed her again and took her pulse. He felt her forehead and her glands. And then he stared straight ahead, as though he was thinking hard.

I thought about the time that had been squandered waiting for him to come, and guilt tore me apart. I picked up Brigitte and held her close. Her breathing seemed easier. She was turning a bluish colour around her lips.

Dr Laurent shook his head and turned to me. 'I'm sorry to tell you, but the baby's dying. She will not make it through the night,' he said brusquely.

'Oh, God. *No!*' I cried. 'There must be something you can do!' My eyes filled with tears, but they did not fall.

He said more gently, 'I know it's terrible for you. You're her mother,' and I didn't have it in me to correct him. Huguette put her head in her hands and wept. He gave Brigitte a shot of morphine to keep her comfortable and left.

Huguette and I sat in a sombre, anxious mood, listening to Brigitte breathing. We did not talk. I felt that our grief magnified our suppressed resentment of each other, and it drove us apart. It was like being stranded on separate islands with a churning ocean between us. Brigitte's chest rose quickly and fell slowly, there was a whistling sound in her lungs. It went on and on, with no change. There were raised voices in the corridor, a bell rang shrilly. A door shut and cut off the sounds. After about an hour, one of the nurses put her head in the door and offered us a cup of tea. The doctor must have told her how bad things were – it was the only kindness we'd been shown in that place.

Towards nightfall, Brigitte's breathing began to rasp. We looked at each other in alarm. And just like that, it stopped. Huguette collapsed into hysterical weeping. I still couldn't cry, though I wanted to. I felt as if I were filling with cold cement that was hardening to stone.

The cemetery was strangely beautiful: grassy and peaceful, enclosed by high stone walls through which I could hear the occasional vehicle rumbling past. It was a dull day, with almost no wind. I'd drunk a large glass of red wine to get me through, and I was at the numb stage of drunk. I stood next to Huguette and hardly heard a word the priest said. I watched the neat, rectangular hole in the earth, fresh and moist around the edges; the tiny coffin being lowered in. Spadefuls of earth rained down on it; the sound was like a shower of small bones. A wave of blood rushed to my head and it seemed, for an instant, that I was going to pass out.

After the funeral, Huguette and I could hardly face each other. All our friends, including Lise and Marie-Laure, feared that Huguette would once again sink into depression. They surrounded her, comforted her, helped her.

I was hurting too but no one came to me. A few days after the funeral, Pablo put an arm around me, and there was something terrible about the way he held me, so loosely and coldly. He said, 'You shouldn't take it so much to heart. What kind of chance in life would the child have had?'

I pulled away and started crying. All I craved was some simple, human warmth. But I had begun to realise that human warmth was something he would never give me. It had taken years to see it because I couldn't get rid of the hopes I'd had for something more. And I loved him so very much.

Pablo tutted. 'Be more like me. No one really means anything to me.' He pointed to some specks of paint on the wall, adding, 'As far as I'm concerned, other people are like those marks. One wipe of the cloth and they're gone.'

'So I've seen,' I said. 'But in case you hadn't noticed, I am not a spot of paint. I don't need a cloth, I can leave by myself.' And I did, slamming the door behind me.

I ran down the rue des Grands-Augustins and turned into my peaceful street, but there was no peace for me. In my bedroom, I took out a tiny gown belonging to Brigitte and lay down with it under my head. It smelled of her. I closed my eyes, wishing I could wake up and discover that it had all been a nightmare – that Maman was still alive, that Brigitte was waiting for me at the home, reaching out her little arms as soon as she saw me. But the nightmare didn't end. I let the tears come. I cried till the pillowcase was sodden.

In the morning, I heaved myself off the bed and walked slowly to the kitchen. The sun fell in dazzling fluid strips on the counter. I knew I should eat but couldn't face food. I couldn't remember the last time I ate.

There was no word from Pablo. I pictured him at his easel, the look of concentration on his face. Nothing existed for him except work, and I knew I was far from his mind. His absence seemed like death. I wandered from room to room; time was empty. At one point I found myself at my easel, looking at my latest painting, a sunlit depiction of the Seine. But I couldn't work, although I should have been preparing for my show.

From then on, all my ghosts came together in my dreams: the mother I had killed, the lover whose heart I couldn't keep, the baby I should have cared for better. I had failed to protect what was most precious in my life, and it destroyed me.

# Ten

PABLO AND I BREAKFASTED on toasted cornbread, spread with lard. It was early spring, and I gazed at the tomato plants he was growing for their fruit. A few were beginning to ripen, their pale green deepening into orange. Pablo's studio was already filled with drawings of them. Ever since my bereavements, I had been clinging to the beauty in the everyday, to try and anchor myself and fend off the shadows in my mind. My other consolations were preparing for my show and Pablo's respect for how hard I was working. He treated me almost as an equal. An oblong patch of sunlight appeared on the wall, quivering in the breeze, and my eye was caught by it, held.

Pablo said, 'It's going to be a good day for painting. Just look at the light.'

A sudden hammering on the door. Terror flooded me, a cold, bowel-loosening sensation. Pablo sat up straight and his face became rigid. 'Sabartés will get it,' he said. Moments later, we heard the clatter of Nazi boots on the stairs. The kitchen door was flung open: two men in long green raincoats and peaked caps stood on the threshold. The Gestapo, with Sabartés behind them, white and trembling.

We stood up. Pablo tried his best to appear impassive, drawing on his cigarette. 'What can I do for you, gentlemen?' he asked.

'We've come to search your apartment,' said one with grizzled hair. He stood with his arms folded, his features hard or exhausted, a blue vein beating in his temple.

Pablo raised his arms in a sign of surrender. 'Be my guest.'

They began to make their way slowly through the apartment, looking around and behind everything, and I realised that Pablo's bric-a-brac was an invitation to them. They paused by the 'Weeping

216

Woman' portraits, examining each one. In them, my features were deformed and scattered about my face in every position. Bizarre hats gave me a crazy look, and hairs sprouted from anywhere Pablo wanted them to.

The grey-haired man turned to Pablo and his lips curled back, baring his teeth like an animal. 'You're sick,' he said.

'He's a Jew,' spat the other one, who was short and skinny, with a scattering of moles across his face, and he knocked the canvases over with a sweep of his arm. As they crashed to the floor, I saw that his eyes were bright – he was enjoying himself. A cold turbulence rose in me. The men began to kick in the paintings with a horrendous, calculated violence, and I experienced each assault as a physical pain, as if those heavy boots were landing on my flesh. Pablo clenched his jaw. I thought I heard Sabartés whimper. A smell of sweat had imprinted itself on the air. And then they stopped, just like that, and stared at us coldly. My stomach seemed to flip into my throat, choking me. I was sure they were about to attack us. But they simply brushed off their uniforms, and the older man said, 'That's all for now,' and the short one said, 'We'll be back.'

As soon as we heard the front door slam shut, I sank onto the sofa, shaking violently. I couldn't believe that they had gone without hurting us.

When I could speak again, I said, 'Oh, Pablo. Christ, Pablo. What was that all about?'

And Pablo buried his head in his hands, saying, 'I've no idea.'

Sabartés said, 'They're coming back.'

'Phone Dubois,' I said to Pablo. 'He said we should if we're in trouble.'

Pablo raised his head. 'Yes, but let's tidy up first. I can't stand looking at this carnage.'

He and Sabartés began to stack the fallen canvases, and we saw that many of them were ripped and roughed up. A terrible feeling of loss rolled through me. Pablo inhaled sharply; his face was white. He threw away his cigarette, his umpteenth of the morning, and lit another.

The Gestapo didn't come back, and this was even more puzzling.

'Do you think it's Breker's doing?' I asked Pablo, a week after their visit.

'Perhaps,' said Pablo, shrugging.

Arno Breker was the Führer's appointed sculptor, and his work celebrating the ideal figure of the Aryan man had received honours and praise from the Nazi regime. But Breker was also an admirer of Pablo's and had promised us, 'Picasso won't be touched.' The telephone began to ring and I hurried to answer it. It was Dubois on the other end of the line, phoning to check on us.

'Do you think the Gestapo will come back?' I asked him anxiously.

Dubois had a slow, low-pitched voice that I found reassuring. He said, 'The Germans have reached an agreement about Pablo. They will intimidate him to keep him in line. But short of some big transgression, he won't be harmed.'

Despite the agreement to leave Pablo alone, the Gestapo kept his apartment under close surveillance. A man in a green raincoat stood opposite it day and night. And there were politer visits. The publisher Gerhard Heller, in charge of censorship, came by Pablo's studio occasionally. He looked at the paintings as one would in a museum. On his second visit, he was particularly struck by a series of asymmetrical heads of me. By the look on his face, I could tell that he was repelled rather than admiring, and I felt a clutch of anxiety. 'There's some kind of alchemy in your work,' he said to Pablo.

Pablo considered this. 'There are chemists who spend their whole time searching for the hidden elements in a piece of sugar. Well, I'd prefer to know what colour it is,' he said cryptically.

Heller listened carefully to everything Pablo said, his intense dark eyes behind thick glasses never leaving his face.

The opening of my show came at last, a spark of brightness amid the insecurity and fear. On one side of Jeanne Bucher's gallery were my still lifes and portraits, and on the other side were landscapes. I had a few moments of being alone with my paintings before the guests arrived, and it was very strange. Suddenly, my work seemed separate from me. It had taken on a life of its own, and I wondered what other people would see in it.

At that moment, Jeanne came up and rested a hand on my shoulder. 'Are you happy with everything?' She wore a black trouser suit that showed off her dark eyes and milky complexion, and her hair was drawn into a low bun.

'Very happy. I can't thank you enough,' I said. 'You look so chic tonight.'

'So do you,' she said, and then people started arriving. A lot of people. Henri Michaux, the gallerists René Drouin and Louise Leiris, Valentine Hugo, Jean Cocteau, Pierre Reverdy, Georges Braque, Georges Hugnet, the Éluards, Marie-Laure, Lise and Pablo.

Jacqui once told me that on her wedding day, she had felt as though she were under water, and the whole thing had seemed unreal, as if it were happening to another person. It was exactly how I felt now, as waiters circulated with trays of champagne and people came up and shook my hand and said how much they loved my work. I watched Braque, who had once been Pablo's friend and partner in cubism, but was now his semi-estranged rival, looking intently at one of my still lifes, and I wondered what he thought of it. He left without speaking to me or Pablo. I missed Jacqui and wished that she were here.

Presently, Jeanne went to the front of the gallery and tapped the side of her glass with a spoon for silence. She beckoned me to join her, then said, 'I want to say a few words of congratulation to Dora.' There was applause and she said, 'I was magnetised by Dora's work from the first time I saw it. I love the way she paints landscape in reflection of a very personal mood. Vast, lonely, temperamental, sometimes savage – and at the same time, sumptuous and exhaustive.'

Jeanne went on like this for several more minutes, then she raised her glass and said, 'I think we all agree that Dora is remarkable artist. Please join me in a toast to her.'

'I encouraged her to take up painting!' Pablo called out. 'I couldn't be prouder!'

Everyone clapped again and lifted their glasses. The emotion running through me was deeper than contentment ... I was finally at peace. My achievement was worth something. Perhaps it would even change my relationship with Pablo. Perhaps it would get him to commit to me at last, as an equal creative and life partner.

By the end of the evening, most of the paintings had red sold stickers on them.

# Eleven

## 1943

THE AFTERGLOW FROM MY show faded and life went on. I missed the direction and fulfilment it had given me, particularly as it was impossible to think about the next stage of my career. The situation in Paris had become so dire that all my energy was focused on survival.

I continued to queue to buy food. France had the lowest rations in Europe, with a shortage of vegetables and only one meat ticket a week. In April, we heard that the Catalan had been closed down for a month for serving steak on a meatless day (three days a week had been declared meatless to save transportation for munitions). Deprived of the last place we could count on for a decent meal, the very leaves of the chestnut trees became appetising.

Electricity was rationed, thirty metro stations were closed and we walked everywhere. Buildings had taken on a dull look due to years of neglect. Gardens had been turned into car parks and vegetable plots, and it took away the joy of seeing another spring replace a harsh winter. The Germans were building more and more concrete barricades and bunkers, putting grilles and bars in the windows of the hotels they used as headquarters. Paris was turning into a fortress.

Callers continued to drop in, mostly old friends. But we mistrusted some of the visitors: an enigmatic curator and a photographer who came often, claiming they were admirers of Pablo's work. Pablo thought they were spies, but we had no proof and no reason not to admit them. He used to amuse himself by giving them postcards of *Guernica*, as he'd done with visiting German soldiers. 'Take it as a little memento,' he would say. But we were scared that one day they would plant incriminating papers, so that if the Gestapo returned, they would find something.

At last the month was over and we could eat at the Catalan again. We had lunch there with Marie-Laure, whom we hadn't seen for months. At the entrance, M. Arnau pressed our hands with tears in his eyes, saying, 'I'm so very glad to have you back. I saved some wonderful beef for you.'

He served us juicy, marbled steaks with frites and buttered carrots. The first rich taste of meat brought saliva to my mouth in a painful rush. I ate the whole plateful, scarcely chewing, swallowing it down, famished.

Marie-Laure was telling us that she had been in a car accident. 'It was two o'clock in the morning, and I was leaving a *boîte* with a German officer,' she said. I raised my brows and she added, 'Please don't ask. Our affair was a secret till this happened. His driver went into a bollard at speed. I guess he'd been drinking.'

'My God, Marie-Laure. Were you hurt?' I said. Beneath my concern, I was aghast that she would let herself get close to a Nazi, especially as she was part-Jewish. She would be judged harshly if the liaison became public knowledge. Perhaps she was trying to protect herself, but where was her sense of moral responsibility? For a moment, I wondered how well I knew her.

She sighed and said, 'The impact slammed my face into the back of the front seat. It broke my nose, which had to be remade. That's why you haven't seen me for so long. Do you like my new nose?' She turned her head from side to side so we could admire it.

It was so subtly done that I hadn't noticed the small bump on the bridge was gone. 'You look wonderful,' I said. Pablo wiped his mouth with his napkin and said, 'Thanks to the officer you have an Aryan nose.'

Marie-Laure grinned. Only Pablo could talk to her like this and get away with it. But he was distracted. He was looking at a young girl lunching with the actor, Alain Cuny, at the next table.

She was tall and slender, with long chestnut hair falling freely around her face, green eyes, very wide and asymmetric, and an adolescent, slim-waisted body. She gave an impression of freshness and restless vitality. As the meal went on, Pablo couldn't take his eyes off her. He kept twisting his neck to look at their table. Whenever he said something particularly amusing, he smiled at them rather than at me and Marie-Laure. I froze up, I couldn't say a word. Marie-Laure talked louder, trying to relaunch the conversation, but Pablo got up and went to the girl's table with a bowl of cherries, a rarity at the time. After a few pleasantries, he said, 'Well, Alain. I would like to be introduced to your friend.'

'Pablo Picasso, this is Françoise Gilot,' Alain said easily. 'Françoise, meet Picasso.'

'*Enchanté*,' said Pablo, lifting the young woman's hand to his lips and wrapping her in a warm, dark gaze. 'What do you do?'

She said, 'I'm a painter.'

He laughed. 'A girl who looks like you can't be a painter.'

She lifted her chin and said, 'I am very much a painter.'

He pretended to be surprised. 'Really? … I'm a painter too. You must come to my studio and see some of my work.'

'When?' she asked.

'Tomorrow. The day after. Whenever you like.'

Fear and darkness gripped me. I ground out my cigarette and sat like a statue, though my heart was beating so violently I thought it would rip my chest apart. I had done more than any other woman to inspire Pablo's work, and yet I could never turn up at his studio unannounced. I had to make an appointment, and here he was telling a stranger to visit whenever she wanted to! One of the things that had kept me going was the belief that with the war and Pablo getting older, the worst of his infidelities were behind us, and I had more power than I used to. And in an instant, I discovered that this was not true.

In the days that followed, he began to stay away more and more. Vacant, fearful days that had to be got through somehow. On the fifth day, he phoned and invited me to lunch at the Catalan, but I knew that the fleeting happiness of the invitation was only the prelude to future pain. When the time came, I arrived at the restaurant early, through sheer nerves. M. Arnau showed me to a table opposite the door, and I ordered a glass of Chablis to calm myself. Fifteen minutes later, I watched Pablo walk in, and an icy jolt passed through me. It was the beginning of the end.

Pablo's famous forelock that used to fall across his forehead, but had in later years been swept sideways over his scalp to cover his baldness, had been shaved off. Instantly, I knew why he had done it: because Françoise had asked him to. I had been asking him to take it off for years. But he hadn't listened to me, he had done it for her.

Terror rose in me like dark water. I stood up and ran out of the restaurant and Pablo ran after me. The streets seemed, surreal, off-kilter, muted. Even a passing military vehicle was muted, as if my ears were clogged with water. He caught up with me and I began to weep, clutching one of his fingers with the desperation of a lost child.

'You're in love with that schoolgirl,' I said, between sobs. 'How could you? She's young enough to be your daughter.'

His forehead puckered into soft furrows. 'What are you talking about? Françoise amuses me, but it doesn't change anything between us.'

How often had I had heard those words before, or versions of them. But this time everything was different. When I could speak again, I said, 'I don't have the courage to learn to live without you.' And I broke away and he did not follow. I went home and lay on my bed.

I was toppling. Until now, I had staggered, got back on my feet, grabbed at handholds. But now the ground had been torn away, and I fell and fell. I was consumed by all the anguish I had ever suffered: my parents and their unhappiness and arguing, Pablo's infidelities, my barrenness, Maman and Brigitte's deaths, and now the agony of losing Pablo for good.

I kept to my bed, wishing I could stop picturing certain things. Far from feeling compassion, Pablo resented my lapse.

'Whenever women are ill, it's their fault,' he announced when he came to visit a few days later. He thrust a bunch of lilies into a vase and perched on the end of the bed. He took out his cigarettes and offered me one. I shook my head. I was spent and listless.

'I don't like sick women,' he said, lighting his cigarette. He took a drag and blew thin jets of smoke through his nostrils, waiting for me to speak.

I heaved myself into a sitting position and said, 'Look, I'll make a deal with you. I'll get well again. I'll take up my place and do everything you want me to. But on one condition – that you see the schoolgirl in bed and not at table!'

Pablo looked at me warily, then glanced away at the sunlight falling against my drawn curtains, making it look like they were on fire.

In that moment, I understood certain things about him. He had needed me to understand his work, to admire his work and to love him, because that's where he got his energy from. At first, he had seemed to give so much, but really, he was like a vampire, taking what he wanted, sucking all the joy out of me. And after he'd bled me dry, he moved on to someone else. Briefly, I wondered how Marie-Thérèse was coping with the arrival of Françoise.

Pablo was still smoking and gazing at the irradiated curtains, indifferent to everything else, totally absorbed in what he saw. When the cigarette was finished, he rose to leave. 'Phone me when you feel better,' he said, kissing me on the forehead. I heard the front door close and sank back on my pillows. I was in frightful inner pain. I looked out at my courtyard, and it seemed as empty as I was.

On a July day so beautiful that Paris looked like a picture on which the paint still glistened, I phoned Pablo.

'This is torture! How can you expect me to live like this?' I said and drove my fist into the wall. It hurt and I started crying. 'Give her up. Please, darling. Let's go back to how we were before.'

Pablo exhaled roughly. He said, 'I'm working. Don't you realise you're destroying my concentration? We will talk later.' And he hung up.

This was the abyss. I wanted to die. I sat down and stared at the wall opposite. It was a cream wall with beautiful cornicing and, as I stared, I thought I could make out something lurking behind the paintwork. I looked more closely and saw a pair of eyes staring back at me. I felt scared and confused. I knew I had to get up and do something, or I'd go mad. Fetching notepaper and a pen, I wrote to Pablo.

Forgive me, I was crying again, getting out of control again.
Without you I am losing my grip on life, on painting, on

everything that I owe to being with you. Please come back. I promise to behave myself and stay calm. Please, darling.

I delivered it to his apartment, both wanting to catch sight of him and dreading seeing him with the schoolgirl. But the windows were shuttered, giving no clue as to the life within.

The next morning, Marie-Laure phoned. She said, 'I haven't seen you for weeks! Lise has gone to her villa in the south and I'm lonely. What are you up to?'

'Working, mostly,' I said.

'Hmm,' she said, 'I know what's going on. I've seen them out and about together. I am here if you want to talk.'

I gritted my teeth. 'Thank you, but I'm fine.'

'Well, just let me say this. When Pablo has a new woman, he takes his time ending with the last one. He thinks his women belong to him, even when he leaves them. If he could, he'd keep them locked away with all that clutter he can't throw out.' She gave a sigh. 'You must protect yourself. He's a genius but he's also a demon.'

'I appreciate your concern but I am dealing with it.' My voice was just a thread. I wanted to confide in her but I had my pride, my stubbornness. And since her affair with the German officer, I wasn't sure I trusted her. A rip of missing Jacqui went through me. She was the only person I could speak to about being a woman and an artist, and about the pain and pleasures of living with a gifted man.

We said goodbye. Again I felt the desperate need to *do* something, to stop thinking about my situation, and so I plunged back into work. Maybe unhappiness was driving me to be a better painter. But as I pushed myself to work later and later into the night, often forgetting to eat or drink, I sensed the danger of this path. Where was the line between creativity and madness? As always, I knew nothing, least of all myself.

I painted another self-portrait. In it, I was mourning what I knew was coming, sad but still magnificent, with amber eyes and symmetrical features, trying to get a hold of my chaotic life.

I stood back to examine it, and it dawned on me how much suffering I'd had to live through to paint like that.

# Twelve

WHEN I WASN'T PAINTING, time seemed vast and empty. I ate alone night after night. Afterwards I paced the living room. I counted the steps I took (there were ten) and I sensed a shadow walking behind me. If I stopped, the shadow stopped too. Truly there was no one, but fear clawed at my mind, reducing it to a wasteland. If only I could see Pablo again it would be less dreadful.

The sun sank below the rooftops. It was September and the room grew cold but I didn't feel the cold. I felt fatally sad. Fetching a piece of paper, I started to write a poem, the words pouring out of me like blood from an unstaunchable wound.

> I rested in the arms of my arms
> I slept no longer
> It was summer night winter day
> An eternal shiver of thoughts
> Fear love Fear love
> Close the window open the window

My writing looked strange, as if a big gust of wind had come along and blown all the letters awry. I tore the paper into pieces and lay down on the floor. Nothing lasted, nothing could be counted on. The world was tottering. Reality was coming unstuck. I only knew that I was alone and mendacious … I longed for death. I wanted everything to vanish, even the pain. Hours later, I heaved myself off the floor and rang Pablo again. His telephone number was a drumroll beating on my brain. ODEON 2844. ODEON 2844. It was so hard not to call.

'What are you doing? Can't you leave me alone? It's two o'clock in the morning!' he shouted. 'I passed all last night without sleep, without rest, because of your incessant calls.' And he slammed down the receiver.

From then on, I would dial and hear the telephone ring in a void. Pablo did not answer, and eventually, he took the receiver off the hook. I didn't care; he knew it was me. I was calling to ruin their idyll, to let out a shriek, to make sure he remembered I was in pain. After a long time I got tired and stopped. I don't know how long – the days and nights were starting to mash into each other. After that, it was Pablo who sometimes phoned, to make sure I hadn't forgotten him.

'The consolation for love is friendship,' he said cheerfully, on one of these calls. There was a pause, then he added, 'I never loved you. You're like a cup of faded memories I don't want to drink from any more. But I don't want to smash it. So what do I do?' His voice was pleasant, conversational, and it floored me. We said goodbye and I caught sight of my reflection in the mirror.

I looked unfamiliar. Repulsive. I wanted to claw at my face, to mutilate it. I pictured taking a knife to carve strips of skin from my cheeks, so that I would look like one of Pablo's portraits of me.

*No, don't turn away. You have to look. Look!*

I felt myself dropping into darkness. I knew this place, had always known it.

*I never loved you.*

At times, I was almost felled by a nostalgic love for Pablo that came from the depths of me. I remembered the extraordinary joy of our lovemaking, and desire surged through me. With all my strength I tamped it down, pushed it back, but I couldn't stop craving those mad, rapturous sensations.

*I never loved you.*

I awoke with a gasp to find Paul's face inches from mine. I didn't know he was back in Paris. He was speaking to me. 'Dora?' And then more insistently, '*Dora!*' His hand was on my bare arm, and I realised that I was naked. My cheeks were wet with tears. I was sitting on my bottom stairs, not knowing how I'd got there, and terror shrieked through me.

Paul chewed on his lip, still staring at me. 'I came to find out how you are,' he finally said. 'Your door was unlocked, and so I pushed it open and found you like this.' He frowned, adding, 'Look at you, you're shaking. Seems like you haven't slept for weeks. Come, let's get you into bed.'

He helped me to my room. My clothes were strewn about, closet doors were open, the bed was unmade. But he ignored this and put a nightgown on me, as if I were a child. I climbed into bed, and he heated some soup from a tin and brought it to me. I sipped at it – the warmth was comforting – and he sat down on the edge of the bed.

'I was worried,' he said. 'I know you're going through a dreadful time. Pablo told me what's been happening to you.'

'What are you talking about? How could he know? How could he know anything about my life?'

'You don't know?' he asked, and I shook my head, pushing the soup away. He looked at me briefly, then down at his hands, clenched in his lap. 'Well, last Monday a policeman found you by the Pont Neuf. You were agitated. Said you'd been attacked by a man who stole your bicycle, but it was found untouched at the spot where you'd left it. You were also turned out of a cinema for making a disturbance.'

I looked at him in panic, untethered. He said, 'Don't you remember?'

I shook my head sharply. 'Not a thing.' My head was filled with dust. All I knew was that somewhere along the way, I had been broken and cast aside. I began to have the odd, destabilising feeling that I had died.

On a crisp November morning, Pablo came to see me, bringing Paul with him. It had been a long time since Pablo's last visit and the sight of him upset me. I burst out, 'Your life is corrupt! Don't you see it? Just think about the afterlife!'

'I won't take that kind of talk from anyone!' he said angrily. And then his face changed and he began to laugh. But I didn't think it at all funny.

'You'd better repent while there's still time,' I said, clenching my fists. 'You might be a brilliant artist, but morally, you're useless.'

His brow knitted and he said, 'Conscience is a personal matter. It doesn't concern anyone else. Focus on your own salvation and leave me alone.' But I couldn't stop repeating what I'd said over and over.

Finally, Paul put a hand on my arm. 'Don't upset yourself, Dora. Let's talk about it another day.'

Just then, it came to me that Françoise was hiding somewhere in the apartment. 'Where is she?' I demanded, and began to search for her in my cupboards and behind all the doors. The men were looking at me strangely. There was a thin film of perspiration on Pablo's face.

'I know why you're so worried!' I heard myself say. 'I can see the future. You'll both meet a dreadful end if you go on like this.' And seizing their arms, I tried to bring them to their knees to pray.

They shook me off and led me to the sofa, where they sat on either side of me, holding me down. When I was quiet again, Pablo went off to make a phone call.

'I should have started worrying about her sooner,' he said to Paul when he returned. 'I thought she was only trying to get my attention, to spoil things with Françoise.' They behaved as though I wasn't there. I tried to say something, to make my presence felt, but I could not move my lips.

Paul looked Pablo in the eye and said, 'You're responsible. Surely you know that. You made her suffer so much that it broke her.'

'What do you mean?' Pablo asked, indignant. 'If I hadn't taken her up, she would have reached that state long ago. I left her out of fear. Fear of her madness. Dora was mad long before she actually went mad.' He tapped the side of his head with his finger.

Paul's face seemed grey. 'God,' he said. 'My *God*. If Dora scares you, it's surely because of your guilt. She gave her life for you.'

Pablo raised his hands and said, 'It's not my leaving that drove her mad, it's the surrealists' fault. All those speeches praising the irrational forces in the mind.' Paul looked sceptical, but he pressed on. 'Dora has always been crazy. Think of how we met, in the Deux Magots. She always had a sense of the occult and look what happened.'

229

A sound of protest came from my lips but they ignored me.

Paul was staring at him in disbelief. 'So you're not responsible?'

'Absolutely not!' said Pablo. 'In fact after she met me, she had a more fulfilled life. Photography didn't satisfy her. She started painting and she improved fast. I made her what she is.'

Paul sat forwards, rubbing his face. 'Pablo, you know I love you,' he said. 'But that is rubbish.'

There was a peremptory knock on the door, and a man in a suit walked in.

'Thanks for coming so quickly,' said Pablo, pressing his hand.

'You said it was an emergency,' the man said, and turned to me. 'Hello, Dora. My name is Jacques Lacan. I'm a doctor. We're going to a lovely place where you can rest and get better.' He took my arm and began to lead me out.

# Thirteen

I WOKE UP IN A room with a small, high window. Apart from my bed, there was a wardrobe, a table and chair, and a door which I later learned led to the bathroom.

Being awake was miserable. My head and body ached, the place reminded me of a hospital, and I thought I must have been in some kind of accident. A tall, well-built nurse with grey hair and narrow-set brown eyes was watching me.

I tried to ask her where I was and why I was there. She told me that her name was Nurse Bernard. I asked her more questions; she gave me evasive answers. I wondered how long I'd been unconscious.

'Where is Dr Lacan?' I asked.

'He has left.'

'Left?'

'Yes, for his house in the country.'

'Will he come back and take care of me?' I asked, and she shrugged.

I felt that I was becoming untethered as the conversation went on, drifting into strange and unfriendly territory. Nurse Bernard then said I was here for treatment and I wondered what she meant. I was wearing a blue hospital gown and there was a plain blue dressing gown hanging in the wardrobe. I got out of bed and put it on, and wanting to know what was outside, I went into the corridor, the nurse following close behind. She did not try to stop me, and so I walked along it till I came to a window that overlooked a court-yard and a garden. The windows were barred on the inside, and I thought: *Why have they locked me in?* I yanked at the bars and began to weep, refusing to listen to Nurse Bernard, until my hands were sore and sweat ran down my back. Finally, she called a burly young man in a nurse's uniform to prise my hands away.

'I only want fresh air. Give me air,' I pleaded, and eventually, Nurse Bernard agreed to escort me. We walked outside and I found myself on the edge of a great park. The hospital seemed to consist of two fine buildings, and there were gardens between them with flowerbeds, rose bushes, and benches to sit on.

We passed another patient with wrinkled cheeks and quiet blue eyes, sitting on a bench beside her nurse. She gave me a wide smile and held out a half-open pillbox containing a small piece of excrement. I recoiled in alarm. Nurse Bernard tutted loudly, and the woman's nurse snatched the pillbox away. Seeing her strange conduct made me feel that I was in another world, perhaps on another planet, and that I had lost all frame of reference.

My keeper wanted me to sit on a chair and behave myself but I refused, suddenly overcome by a terrible longing to see Pablo. I paced from one bench to another, Nurse Bernard following. I muttered, 'He must come. He can't have forgotten me,' convinced that if I said it enough times Pablo would materialise and take me away to the rue des Grands-Augustins, where I belonged.

In the daytime, I was watched by Nurse Bernard and at night by Mary, a thin slip of a girl with wide grey eyes set in a heart-shaped face. Mary washed me with a damp towel, and her hands were quick and competent. Then she brought my dinner and spoon-fed it to me – vegetables and raw eggs. I hadn't tasted an egg for years and opened my mouth eagerly, which made Mary smile. Other patients shuffled past my open door, and sometimes they peered in and greeted me. I turned my face away, I wasn't here to make friends. I heard someone say, in a high-pitched voice, 'He is always stressed after work, always very stressed, so I'm going to pour him a nice glass of wine.'

At bedtime, Mary gave me a cocktail of different-coloured pills in a small paper cup, saying, 'It will help you sleep.' She watched me swallow them, one by one with a glass of water, and when she had gone, I thought about the terrible thing Pablo had done, sending me away, locking me up so that I wouldn't cause trouble between him and the schoolgirl. I grew distressed and angry and desperate for oblivion. I lay there in torment until waves of drowsiness began to wash through me, each one stronger than the last, tugging me into a darkness that was like death. And I had appalling dreams about Pablo. His eyes were tearing me apart. I was shut in a long, blind tunnel of pain. The end of that tunnel was the destruction of my mind in agony, with no salvation. I struggled towards wakefulness. Opening my eyes, I saw sunshine coming through the high window, and thanked God it was daytime. I was dazed and thirsty. I don't know how long I lay there for. At last I heard doors slam in the hall, and Lacan appeared in the doorway.

'How are you feeling?' he asked, sitting in the chair by my bed.

I shook my head and croaked, 'Water.' He poured a glass from the jug by my bed and held it to my lips. I drank steadily, and when I could speak again, I said, 'Where am I?'

'Jeanne-d'Arc de Saint-Mandé,' he said and paused, making little grunts in the back of his nose. 'I thought it the best, most pleasant place for you. Don't you like it?'

I shrugged. Jeanne-d'Arc was a private mental hospital. I thought, *At least Pablo has locked me away in comfort.*

Lacan tried again. 'They told me you were agitated yesterday.' Sunlight glittered off his round glasses, so I couldn't see his eyes. He was wearing a pale blue silk shirt, bow tie and matching pocket handkerchief.

'It's this war,' I said. 'It's happening in my head too.' Lacan nodded and a great wave of drowsiness rolled through me. I closed my eyes and when I opened them again, he was gone.

My days fell into a routine: an early morning visit from Lacan, followed by hours in my room; then the garden in the afternoon before returning to my room for supper. I tried to cooperate with the nurses, to be 'a good girl', figuring it would get me out of here quicker. But on the inside, I was churning. I belonged to Pablo and needed to go home to him, but no one understood that, and it was getting harder and harder to contain my feelings. The only thing that helped was running in the garden until the pain began to ease and I stopped feeling like I might explode. Nurse Bernard would run after me, panting, 'I wish you'd behave.'

233

The worst thing about the hospital was the pills Mary gave me at bedtime – the nightmares and the groggy mornings when I could hardly lift my head from the pillow. I became adept at hiding the pills under my tongue and, when Mary had gone, I flushed them down the toilet. Sometimes I thought about hoarding them. Perhaps one day, I'd have enough to kill myself with. But I didn't do it because I needed to see Pablo, to be near him again. Without my pills, I couldn't sleep, and the madness flowed and ebbed. It was a private terror that visited me often.

One night, I fell into a kind of waking dream in which fat black insects crawled out of my eyes, as if I were a cadaver. And then I found myself alone in a forest because I'd lost the straight path. I couldn't tell what this forest was, this wild and black forest that frightened me so much. I wanted to run naked with my eyes shut and smear filth all over my body. Pain was boring into my head, and I had to conquer it. Then I woke up, but couldn't remember what I did in that room. I was in a frenzy. I wanted to hang myself. And when I was spent, I lay on the floor in a heap, and cried until there were no tears left.

Then I heard Lacan say 'You did this?' and there was disgust in his voice. At once, I was awake and alert. What I saw slowed my blood: the mattress half off the bed, ripped sheets, a puddle of urine on the floor. I hung my head, more ashamed than I had ever been.

'I had hoped to avoid this, but you've left me no choice,' Lacan said sorrowfully. 'I am sending you for treatment now.' Through his glasses his eyes looked magnified, terrifying, and I saw that he was possessed. I shrank away from him.

He called two male nurses who came in with a large sheet, which they threw over me, twisting and binding it tightly around me. A nurse picked up each end and carried me out in this hammock-like contrivance. I would have walked with them quietly, but they never asked.

I had no idea where we were going. I was shocked and dis-orientated, and the swinging motion made me dizzy. When they set me down, I found myself in a small, windowless room, with a high bed. In the corner was a large machine that had wires sticking out of it, and I began to tremble all over. They strapped me to the bed. In the distance, I could hear a woman shouting. Then one of them applied a smelly paste to my temples and put clamps over the paste, fastening them into place with a strap that cut into my forehead. I opened my mouth to scream and the other one quickly stuffed a wad of rancid-tasting cloth between my teeth. I tried to struggle but it was useless. Then the taller one flicked a switch on the machine and it made a high-pitched shriek. The air crackled with blue light. A jolt of current went through me and shook me till my teeth rattled and I thought my spine would snap. They did this several times and it was bad: rigidity, convulsions, hideous reality. Finally, my mind and body collapsed.

I don't know how long they left me there, lying in my own sweat and urine. Finally I was wrapped in the sheet again and taken to my room in a cataleptic state.

I must have slept for a long time, as when I awoke, my lunch had congealed on its tray. A stout, bald-headed man with a doctor's bag at his feet was watching me. He told me his name was Dr Martin. He spoke with courtesy. 'So you are feeling better, mademoiselle? You're no longer a wild animal, you're a lady.'

'Who are you? I've never seen you before,' I said, and he smiled at me and said, 'Ah, but I know *you*. Dr Lacan will be pleased when I tell him.'

After he left, there were long periods of blankness, interspersed with painful moments of lucidity. I didn't go to the garden that day but Nurse Bernard took me to a pretty sitting room with a piano. A patient sat at it, repeating the same three notes over and over again, but I hardly heard her. Like the other patients stuffed into chairs around me, I sat motionless and stared into space.

For days after the treatment, my whole body hurt. I shuffled down the corridor overlooking the garden, but I didn't know if I was still in the hospital or at home. Each time I tried to concentrate, my thoughts curved and doubled back on themselves. Disjointed glimpses of forgotten events and half-remembered faces passed through my head, before I lapsed into blankness. I was defeated with no hope of redemption. I was resigned to being a prisoner in this place, resigned to dying. It was all the same to me. I don't know how many times I went through what they called my 'cure'. I never asked. Presently, Lacan began to talk about 'improvements' in my condition and then, cautiously, about sending me home. 'But only on condition that we continue our talking therapy,' he added.

I think he expected me to be pleased. But I tried not to think about what would happen to me when I left this place. Sometimes I thought I'd go properly crazy in here and *never* leave, and sometimes I thought losing Pablo would drive me right back. But I did know that I'd rather kill myself than go through this again.

Not long afterwards, I looked out of the window and saw young, fresh, glossy leaves on the trees. I realised it was spring, and I had been here for many months.

The next morning I waited for Lacan impatiently, wanting to tell him that I'd become aware of the passage of time. But instead, a strange nurse came in and tossed a bundle of clothes on the bed. I recognised them as my own, and gladness and confusion spread through me.

'Get up and get dressed,' she said. 'This is your big day. You're being discharged at noon.'

'Who says so?'

'Dr Lacan.'

I was hoping that Pablo would come to collect me, but instead, they called a taxi to take me home. I sat in my apartment, dulled and weakened. I tried to think back to leaving the hospital – surely I must have signed paperwork, said goodbye – but I couldn't remember a thing. Someone – Pablo probably – had left bread, cold meat and tomatoes for me. I wasn't hungry.

He phoned in the afternoon. 'All's well that ends well. You've been treated and you are healed,' he said brightly.

I knew he wanted to get out from under the burden I'd become but I no longer had the strength to contradict him. So I said, 'It's true.' Something strange had happened to my voice. It sounded muffled in my ears.

After a hesitation, Pablo said, 'You must come and visit soon. Keep well in the meantime,' and we said goodbye.

I wondered if he was worried about my state of mind. He needn't have been. I had stopped crying, lost the urge to call him during the night. The current of my illness seemed to have pulled me away and deposited me on a distant shore. Nothing interested me any more but I felt lighter as well. If certain memories had been washed away, some of the torment had gone too.

I slept deeply and dreamlessly that night, and in the morning, I went to my appointment with Lacan. His building was a fifteen-minute walk along the Seine, and I drank in the trees along the quais, the Pont Neuf, the Pont Saint-Michel, the water reflecting purple-grey skies. Lacan showed me into his office, which was enormous and high-ceilinged, with a library on the mezzanine where a portrait of Freud had the place of honour. Lacan sat at his desk and I lay on a chaise longue with my back to him.

He said, 'I'm glad to see you out of hospital. Your cure was successful.'

I said, 'But my cure almost destroyed me!'

Lacan made the soft grunting sounds in the back of his nose. Then he said, 'Electroshock isn't perfect, but it's the best we have for now. Put it behind you, you'll recover.' He shifted in his seat. 'You'll come here and we'll talk. That's it. You don't need treatment or medication. The hard part is over.'

'But I don't want to talk about the hospital. I barely survived it.'

'You don't have to. *You* choose what to talk about.'

'All right,' I said, after a pause. 'Let's talk about why I ended up in hospital, why I'm with you now. Apparently I had psychotic episodes. Pablo thought I was going crazy and phoned you for help. But I doubt he was really bothered.'

'Why do you think that?'

'Because he had me committed to get rid of me.' I twisted around to look at Lacan.

He met my eyes but said nothing. A shaft of sun broke through the clouds, lighting up the portrait of Freud above the fireplace. The room smelled of books and cigars.

'Let's talk about my years with Pablo,' I said. 'I'd like to understand why I broke down.'

237

'Go on,' said Lacan.

And so, I told him about the meeting I'd engineered at the Deux Magots. It was hard to believe that I was once a young woman with the audacity and determination to seduce Picasso so boldly. I told him about our first magical months and he listened without taking notes. When I got to the part about finding out that Pablo was still seeing Marie-Thérèse, I fell silent.

Lacan prompted, 'And ...?' He often didn't finish his sentences, as if silence offered different paths than words could.

I began to talk, but tears came instead of speech. I cried silently, my mouth twisted. From time to time, I blew my nose with my handkerchief.

After several minutes, Lacan said, 'That's all we have time for today.'

Five days later, I opened my closet and took out a charcoal-grey Balenciaga dress that hugged my body in all the right places. I shook it out, thankful that it didn't have moth damage. I hadn't had a new dress for years; everything had been altered or mended. I put it on and found that it hung off me. I had become gaunt without realising, and a rip of grief for my beautiful figure went through me. I made up my face and carefully and painted the backs of my legs with a special product that came with a small brush to imitate the seams of stockings. Pablo had invited me over.

He opened the door and kissed me on both cheeks. 'Hola, Dora! You look well!' But I caught sight of my reflection in the mirror behind him and saw an exhausted woman who would have been better off in bed. Lise and Marie-Laure were there. They threw their arms around me, and Lise said, 'Dora! You're here at last.' I returned their embraces uncertainly, wondering what they thought of the alternate presence of Françoise and me in this room. Pablo handed me a glass of wine and I sat down, letting the conversation flow over me. In the distance, I could hear a fire engine's siren and the honking of horns.

After about ten minutes, Lise turned to Marie-Laure and said, 'I hope you've recovered from that unpleasant business with the Gestapo. I've been worried about you.'

I felt a twinge of alarm. 'What happened?'

Marie-Laure grimaced and said, 'They came pounding on the door in the middle of the night. Tried to arrest me for having Jewish blood.'

A wave of fear for Marie-Laure went through me, and I remembered my own terror of being arrested. I pressed the back of my hand over my mouth, and Pablo said, 'Is this too much for you?'

'No, no, I'll be fine. What happened?' I said.

'I showed them genealogical documents,' said Marie-Laure. 'I had been expecting their visit for some time. Everything was ready.' She shrugged. 'They looked through them and got frustrated at not finding what they wanted. Smashed up a few trinkets on their way out. But they left me alone.' She held out her glass for more wine.

'Isn't she indomitable? There's no one like her,' said Lise, going to fill it.

Pablo and I agreed. There was no one as entertaining, shocking, cultivated, resourceful and cunning as Marie-Laure, but I suddenly longed for the peace of my apartment.

I went home soon afterwards. On the way out, Pablo insisted on taking me to his studio, and showing his latest portrait of me. It was tender and compassionate, and I thought it was typical of him to paint such a picture after I'd been replaced by Françoise. He was looking at me expectantly, and I told him I loved it, but the truth was that I was more hurt than pleased. And I couldn't shake the feeling that it was the last painting of me he would ever do.

The next morning, Pablo showed up unannounced with Françoise. I hadn't slept well and the sight of them side by side on my doorstep squeezed the breath from me. Somehow, I managed to get a hold of myself. I let them in but couldn't think of anything to say.

After a hesitation, Pablo said, 'Why don't you show us some of your paintings?'

I took them into my studio and showed a couple of still lifes. 'You have a very original sensitivity,' the schoolgirl murmured.

'Isn't she marvellous?' Pablo exclaimed, putting an arm around her. 'What a mind!' but I ignored this and said, 'I take it you came for something else?'

'Exactly,' he said, leading the way to my living room. We sat down but I couldn't bring myself to offer them drinks. Pablo continued, 'We're here because I want you to tell Françoise. She won't move in with me because she thinks we're still together.' He waved a hand dismissively. 'I've told her we're finished. I want you to tell her too, so she knows it's true. She's worried about her part in our break-up.'

I felt my cheeks grow hot and turned to look at the girl. She was wearing flat-heeled shoes, a checked skirt and a baggy sweater, and her long hair was tied back. To her credit, she looked uncomfortable.

'He's right,' I told her, my mouth dry. 'Pablo and I finished a long time ago. You had nothing to do with it.' I turned to Pablo, adding, 'If you think you can live with that schoolgirl, you must be crazier than I thought.'

He glared at me and said, 'I love her.'

To get through this without weeping was all I asked. I managed to say calmly, 'You make me laugh, taking all this care to set up an affair that won't last. I give her six months. No more, since you can't form proper attachments. You don't know how to love.'

'You're hardly in a place to judge,' he said, and his eyes glinted dangerously.

I stood up and said, 'That's enough.'

'One more thing,' Pablo said at the door. 'Don't think people are interested in you for yourself. You might think they like you, but they're simply curious because you were once my lover. You'll be left with nothing.' He went, pulling the girl behind him.

I sat down on the sofa, awash with fear and bitterness. Why did Pablo feel compelled to knock me down each time I struggled to my feet? He made it impossible to heal. I felt that I was going under, that hatred was poisoning me like cancer in the blood. I'd become someone I didn't know, didn't think I could be.

# Fourteen

PABLO WAS RIGHT. PEOPLE who had been lavishly attentive when I was with him now stopped phoning, or crossed to the other side of the street to avoid me. Paul and Nusch remained faithful. They were living in hiding at the antiquarian bookseller Lucien Scheler's shop, and occasionally I had visits from them both, but more often Paul came alone because of the risk. He rarely spoke of it. He found me always sitting by myself with a cigarette in my hand and the curtains closed, Pablo's paintings keeping watch all around me.

A month after I got out of hospital, Paul knocked on the door and entered, drawing back the curtains and opening the windows to get some air. 'Do you mind?' he asked. My courtyard was shot with grains of sunlight, and the sky was deep and blue.

'Pablo couldn't bear that you got sick,' he said, coming to sit beside me. 'With him, a woman never has the right to give up.'

'Could I help it? It was more than anyone could stand!' I said, grinding out my cigarette. I took a handkerchief from my pocket and dabbed at my eyes. 'I'm beginning to think our whole relationship was a sham. There was never a time I truly had him.' I opened my handkerchief on my lap, then balled it up again. 'His portraits of me are lies too. They're only his perceptions. Not one of them is the real me.'

'But they live,' Paul said. 'They're in museums and art books all over the world. They're his finest works, and people say, "Look, it's Dora Maar." You are famous. You will never be forgotten.'

'So what?' I said bitterly. 'I'm an artist too. I want my own work to live on. And I have the advantage of faith over Pablo. He doubts. That's why he can never stop.'

'Religious faith?' asked Paul, his forehead creasing. 'I didn't think you were religious.'

'Well, I am. I've gone back to Catholicism,' I said, giving him a small smile. I was not happy with him. 'Feels like the natural thing to do.'

Paul said, 'But you're still young. You'll meet someone else.'

I knew this was impossible because I felt profoundly changed. I saw things differently; I lived in a different body and in a different world. I said, 'After Picasso, there can only be God. Why should I settle for second best?'

'What do you mean?'

I took a moment to rearrange Pablo's bird sculptures on the coffee table. Then I lifted my head and looked at Paul, saying, 'Lacan thinks that Pablo didn't drive me mad. We found each other.' Paul's eyes widened and I continued, 'When things were good, I felt this sort of ... well, *fusion* with Pablo. It made the rupture all the more devastating. So God has to replace him.'

'Lacan may be right,' said Paul, sitting forwards. 'But here's what I think – that Pablo had power over you not because you were free but because you were guilty. You were punishing yourself for a crime you couldn't remember.'

'Maybe that's true,' I said. 'But even so, I never stood a chance. Don't you see that every thing and every person exists only to be used by him for his art? I thought I could relate to him but he only exists for his art.' Feeling ready to cry, I added, 'That was our basic misunderstanding. There is no Pablo, there's only Picasso.'

'I know,' said Paul, touching my arm, and we sat in silence for many moments.

After he had gone, I thought about the difference between the yearnings of my heart and the reality of how things had turned out. My life had all that wreckage, all that blood, *and I had chosen it*. I pushed down the pain as hard as I could, determined not to let it drown me. I got up and fetched an unused notebook with a plain maroon cover from my desk drawer. Lacan was guiding me towards clarity but I didn't want to rely on him. I needed to do something for myself. Writing would help me pull myself together, it always had.

I sat at the desk, breathing in the crisp smell of new paper. The blank pages gave me pleasure but they terrified me too. I told myself to focus – that it was simply like preparing to stand behind the camera again. All I had to do was focus and look into – myself. But I could barely remember the desire to take photographs, let alone that feeling of freedom and control.

I picked up a pen and wrote:

Breaking up with you
Wasn't worth a tear and however
I still think. But at least if I cried
I knew I didn't have to laugh.
I looked as I could.

I had to learn how to live and work again. On my better days, I set aside afternoons to paint and took long walks through Paris with my sketchbook, absorbing every sight, sound and smell. Life moved on and on, and it brought a lighter feeling, a lessening of pain. But during bad times, I shut myself away for days on end. Tears, shame, wanting to die. I feared that strangers on the street would know me as a reject and an outcast. I had passed so far beyond the perimeters of ordinary life that I was shunned and feared by normal people, condemned to solitude.

Tired. No desire to paint. Worked anyway, without concentration … Infinitely sad, as a long time ago … Proof of my uselessness or simply a dry time? Difficult time in any case. It seems that this is a failure of analysis. At least I have God. Increasingly, I feel myself turning away from Lacan to Him. But my mood is so low …

I was disorientated in my sadness. Once, in a field in the south, with wild white narcissi and a sky as blue as the ocean, Pablo said, 'To have made all of this, God must be someone in my style.' His words were a blasphemy but living with him *was* like living at the centre of the universe. It was electrifying and humbling, sublime and destructive, all at the same time. And I had gone from that to total emptiness.

I found refuge in a small Roman Catholic church near my apartment, filled with icons and flowers. I often saw Olga there, which surprised me, as I would have expected her to go to the big Orthodox church. Once, I was crying, and she dropped a handkerchief in my lap as she passed. I thanked her and she smiled at me without saying a word. We never acknowledged each other again, but from that point onwards, I felt that we'd made amends. I finally understood her and what had made her mad.

The truth is that my love for Pablo never went away. Nobody who had ever fallen under his spell could quite free themselves from it. I told myself that at least I was a constant in his work. If there was a link between history and art, surely it was me. But I had paid with my blood for everything I'd got from him.

I withdrew more and more from life. People had sharp edges on which I bruised myself again and again, and solitude stopped me getting hurt. It also stopped me missing my parents, my old friends and Brigitte. I had the sense that they were all alive somewhere, the living and the dead.

One muggy August morning, the telephone rang, startling me. When I said hello nobody spoke, but I could sense a presence at the other end of the line and knew it was Pablo. Instead of saying hello over and over, I decided to exercise my will and wait; my silence was a matter of volition. I waited for ten minutes or more, and the person on the other end waited too.

Outside the window trees hung limp and parched, and sullen clouds gathered in a whitish sky. At last, he spoke: 'You win.' I smiled and hung up on him.

The next morning, I awoke to a room flooded with sunlight, and found that the longing and suffering were gone. There was a fullness and sweetness to my solitude, a kind of unfurling of my soul, followed by a flare of happiness I hadn't known I could feel again. Taking my rosary from the night table, I knelt and prayed, looking to the skyline of Paris – a view for which I thanked my Lord every day.

Afterwards I picked up my camera, feeling it settle into my hands like an extension of my body. Turning towards the window, I framed my beloved city through the lens and, once again, felt the urge to wander the streets and take pictures. It was so strong it made my fingertips tingle, and I knew that photography would take hold of me so that nothing else mattered. A story is never finished. My work was mine again, in all its dark magic.

# A Note on Sources

*The Paris Muse* is based on the biographical facts of Dora Maar's life but is a work of fiction. Liberties have been taken with facts, characterisations and particularly chronologies.

I found many books helpful, but most especially *A Look at My Life* by Eileen Agar, *Picasso: Life with Dora Maar* by Anne Baldassari, *Dora Maar* by Louise Baring, *Finding Dora Maar* by Brigitte Benkemoun, *Picasso & Co.* by Brassai, *Down Below* by Leonora Carrington, *Picasso's Weeping Woman: The Life and Art of Dora Maar* by Mary Ann Caws, *The Militant Muse* by Whitney Chadwick, *Dora Maar* by Victoria Combalia, *Dora and the Minotaur* by Slavenka Drakulić, *Life with Picasso* by Françoise Gilot and Carlton Lake, *Sunshine at Midnight* by Genevieve Laporte, *Picasso and Dora: a Memoir* by James Lord, *Pablo Picasso and Dora Maar* by Enrique Mallen, *A Life of Picasso* by John Richardson, *Picasso* by Jaime Sabartés, *Picasso: Creator and Destroyer* by Arianna Stassinopoulos Huffington. My book draws on all of them but any errors are my own.

# Acknowledgements

Firstly, a huge thank you to the team at Bloomsbury Publishing, to my publisher, Katy Follain, for her wise and inspirational input, to my editor, Sophie Wilson, who transformed the book, to my copy editor, Charlotte Norman, for her talent and sensitivity, and to my managing editor, Francisco Vilhena, for always being brilliant to work with. I would like to thank Amy Donegan, Cristiana Caserini, Helen Upton, Ben Chisnall and everyone at Bloomsbury who helped bring the book to life. Huge thanks to my agent, Sonia Land, for her faith, hard work and patience. Special thanks to Miranda Vaughan Jones for being my most longstanding and trusted reader, and for always lifting my work onto the next level.

To my friends for seeing me through the ups and downs of the writing life, especially Simone, George, Arnie, Susan, Becca, Suzanne and Steph. To my family, especially my sisters, Charlotte and Philippa. And most of all to my children, Adam, Imogen and Alexandra. You are my everything.

# A Note on the Author

Louisa Treger is the author of three novels, *The Lodger* (2014), *The Dragon Lady* (2019) and *Madwoman* (2022). She has written for *The Times*, the *Telegraph*, *Tatler*, *BBC History Magazine* and English Heritage. Radio appearances include BBC Radio 3's *Free Thinking Programme*, and BBC Radio 4's *Woman's Hour*. Treger has a First Class degree and a PhD in English Literature from UCL, and currently lives in London.